Call to Me

By the Author

Call to Me

Call to Me

by Helena Harte

2020

CALL TO ME

Cataloging information
ISBN: 978-1-8380668-2-6
CREDITS
Editors: Jan Stone & Nicci Robinson
Cover Design: Nicci Robinson, Global Wordsmiths
Production Design: Global Wordsmiths

Acknowledgements

Thank you to everyone at Global Wordsmiths involved in the production of this book. You've made my debut at self-publishing a breeze. Thanks to Gemma at Writing Gems for "making the words shine." And thank you to my beta-readers for their lovely comments and encouraging critiques. I hope I've done you all proud.

And to Mama. I wish you were still around to read this, but I know you're watching over me.

Dedication

For all the romantics out there who
believe in soul mates and true love.

Keep believing.

Chapter One

A sh looked at the dashboard clock for the fifth time since she'd pulled up and parked. *1:30 p.m.* Still another half hour before she could go into the Hound Hotel. The crunch of gravel drew her attention to a fancy Audi pulling into the car park. A new model TT RS Roadster. Wow. What she wouldn't give to own a car like that.

The car door swung open and two shapely legs in skinny jeans and block heels swung out, moving Ash's attention from the car to its owner. The lady eased out of the car ever so elegantly, pushed her door closed, and made her way to the main reception. Every inch of her screamed sophistication and intelligence. Ash wasn't sure exactly how that looked if anyone asked her to explain it, but that woman was the definition. Her hair was cut just below her chin in a sleek one length bob that added to her put-together look. She'd tucked one side behind her ear, giving a glimpse of her face, but from this distance, Ash couldn't make out any real detail other than she was late twenties, maybe early thirties. Ash shook her head. Older women had always floated her boat and this lady was no exception.

Ash lowered her window, but the cold rush of autumn air did little to cool her jets. Should she shout hello? She rested her arm on the door sill and was temporarily distracted by the small ball of fluffy moss growing on the ragged, rubber trim. No doubt Audi lady would be mortified by the state of her battered old Clio…unless she liked a bit of the rougher side of the tracks. Ash looked up to see she'd dithered in her decision too long, and the woman was already inside, no longer in range. Maybe she owned the kennels, and Ash would see her every time she visited.

Ash glanced at the clock again. It still wasn't time to see the little guy yet. God, she'd missed him, missed his soulful brown eyes and the way his whole body wagged when he was happy and excited. She *hadn't* missed the army of fleas he'd had trooping across his little pink belly or the bites she'd got as a result of sharing her bed with him.

Waiting two weeks while he settled into his new surroundings had been unexpected torture. She shook her head. How had she fallen in love so easily? She'd not managed it with a person for her whole life, and the all-inclusive holiday was supposed to have been a simple blow-out before she started her new job. Ending up with a little pup to be responsible for hadn't been part of her plan.

She picked up her phone and flicked to the video of her finding him, tied up at the end of an unfinished road, left to perish in the hot Spanish sun. His fluffy, fox-like tail looked broken, but he still wagged it frantically as she approached him. And he'd lapped up the Sprite Zero as if he'd not had a drink in…well, she couldn't imagine how long.

Her decision had been easy. She'd cut the rudimentary rope securing his chain link collar to a post in the dirt, and he'd claimed Ash as his own.

She thumbed through all of the videos she'd made in the two days she'd had with him before coming home. They'd kept her company these past two weeks as she'd shopped for all things puppy at her local pet store. Staring at his empty bed for ten days hadn't been especially healthy, especially since it was going to remain that way for another four months of quarantine, but it sealed in her mind that she'd done the right thing, even though she'd gone about it the wrong way.

Java was hers, and she was Java's. The dog she never knew she wanted was a part of her life now, and she was ready.

Chapter Two

E vie launched the ball as far as she could, but it was still only twenty-five seconds before Kirby retrieved it and plopped it at her feet again. They'd been at it for nearly thirty minutes, and sweat dripped down her back. She patted the big dog's head, scooped up the ball, and threw it again. When he returned this time, he ran right past her, daring her to catch him.

Evie turned and saw Sarah coming up the main path from the reception to the kennels. Evie's gaze settled on the young woman with her, and she sighed. Even from this distance, it was clear the woman was family. Which wasn't about stereotyping, although the woman did wear baggy jeans, had short, spiky hair, and barely any breasts—pecs, more like. No, this was about gaydar, the almost infallible, tried and tested, universal tool of divination for all people queer. This was the internal interpreter that picked up subtle codes being transmitted subconsciously to allow identification and connection. And Evie's was a finely tuned machine, honed from nearly twenty years of pining for intimate liaisons with other women exactly like the woman she was now staring at.

Both Sarah and her customer waved Evie's way. *Busted.* How long had she been gawking? Evie offered a weak wave in return and called for Kirby, as if he might've been the reason for her looking that way in the first place and her gawping could thus be excused. The young woman winked and her mouth curved into a broad smile, that kind of self-assured, knowing smile that meant she knew damn well Evie had been admiring her. Christ, she looked young, but Evie was spectacularly bad at guessing ages. Maybe she was mid- to late-twenties. At least, Evie *hoped* she might be…

Stop it. She tugged the ball from Kirby's mouth, fixed it into the ball launcher, and tossed it again. She was in no position to be coveting anyone. Evie's heart ached as the reality of her current home situation pushed for attention. She was usually good at keeping it at bay during work hours, and when she played with the dogs, her focus was purely on them. But seeing the hot young woman had derailed her usual train of thought. Evie could admit she was hot without doing or thinking any more

3

about it though. She was trying to get her life back on track, but she couldn't blinker herself to the women around her. That would be impossible. And stupid. She was human. She couldn't turn off the part of her that loved confident, butch women. It hadn't worked for her as a teenager, and it wouldn't work now. *But* she could control herself…no matter how sexy the eye candy.

Kirby dropped the ball at her feet and sat beside her. His giant tongue hung from the side of his mouth and he panted furiously. Evie knelt down and rubbed his chest, and he grumbled appreciatively. He'd been at the kennels for two months now while his owner was away on business. Evie couldn't understand why anyone would have a dog, only to leave it for great swathes of time while they jetted around the world. Evie wouldn't entertain the notion of having a dog since she was at work all day Monday to Friday, and the poor thing would be alone for twelve hours a day.

She checked her watch. Kirby's allotted exercise time was almost over. "Last one, boy." Evie stood, scooped the ball up, and launched it again. Kirby tore after it at full speed, leapt into the air, and caught it mid-bounce. This time, he stayed the sixty metres away and dropped to the ground to chew the ball.

"And they say dogs can't tell the time." It had only taken Kirby three visits before he seemed to realise his out-of-pen time was limited. Now, every time his half hour was about to expire, he'd refuse to come back and Evie would have to traipse across the field to retrieve him. She couldn't blame him. A German shepherd needed two hours of exercise a day, ideally, or they got a little crazy and destructive. Limited exercise was okay for a week, maybe two, but longer than that wasn't fair to the dog. Sarah didn't do long-term kennelling for that precise reason, and she'd told Evie that the client hadn't made it clear that's what he needed. Each week he called to say he was still abroad and needed Sarah to keep Kirby "one more week." If he'd stopped paying the fees, Evie would've thought he'd abandoned the poor mutt, but Sarah confirmed that hadn't happened.

She pulled the lead from her back pocket as she drew closer. "Come on, Kirby, don't make this difficult for me."

Kirby pushed up from his back legs, as if he were ready to pounce on her—or dart away as she reached for his collar. There was a mischievous twinkle in his eye.

"Kirby…" Evie employed her serious voice, and he sat back on his haunches. At least his errant owner had trained him well before leaving him to pine away at the *Hound Hotel*. She clipped him into his lead, walked back and popped him in his kennel, then she made her way through the building to retrieve Ariel, a cute little Yorkshire terrier she'd become quite attached to even though she'd only seen her once.

As she drew closer to Ariel's temporary home, she saw the young woman in the indoor area of the adjacent kennel. So, she owned the new quarantined dog, Java. Evie faltered. Maybe she should exercise Tuna instead; he was on her rota too. But she couldn't ignore Java's mum, could she? And why should she? The two of them were engrossed in an adorable reunion, and Java planted wet, sloppy puppy kisses all over his mum's face. Hopefully she wouldn't see Evie.

It wasn't to be. She turned as Evie leaned down to open Ariel's gate.

"Hi," she said and smiled, still cuddling the hell out of Java.

Evie swallowed and nodded. "Hi." She should say something else. Anything else would do. "So, you're Java's mum?" She shouldn't have said "mum." Some people got weird being referred to that way, the ones who preferred to be called owners instead. That was something else Evie couldn't fathom. Dogs weren't property. They were life companions.

"Yep."

Her smile widened, and Evie's breath caught. This little butch was a cutie, though close up, Evie could see she wasn't exactly little. Five eight probably, tall for a woman. Evie loved tall women. There was something special about looking *up* into her lover's eyes. The woman scooped Java up, but he wriggled furiously in her arms until she released him. He immediately got to chewing on one of the trainers still on her feet.

She stuck her arm partway through the hole in Java's gate. "I'm Ash."

Evie hesitated only a moment to look at Ash's tanned hand before she offered her own. Ash took it gently but confidently, and the heat shot through Evie's hand to an even warmer place. God damn it, she was reacting like one of the kennel bitches on heat. And yet, she didn't pull her hand away, and Ash held it firmly, along with her amused gaze.

"And you are?" she asked when Evie didn't respond.

Evie extricated her hand finally and laughed. "Sorry, I was miles away. I'm Evie."

Ash smiled again. Such a beautiful smile that lit up her eyes and quite possibly, everything around her. Evie wouldn't mind seeing that smile more often.

"Do you work here every day?"

Ash's question could've been innocent enough, but she'd placed both hands on the gate and leaned against it, getting as close to Evie as she could, it seemed. And her eyes hadn't left Evie's face. Heat flushed up Evie's back and tingled at her neck as if Ash's hand had wrapped around it. No one had been this blatantly forthcoming for a long time. She hated to admit that she liked it. And what harm could it do, really? Ash was probably one of those new-style lesbians that would happily flirt with any woman, regardless of whether she thought they were straight or not. And the line was so blurry these days. Almost every woman Evie knew back at the hospital, staff or detainee, had been involved with another woman at least once. It was becoming like a badge of honour…or perhaps it was just how the world was evolving and becoming less caught up in the strictness of sexuality. Not that she minded.

"Are you okay?"

Evie had drifted with her thoughts and not answered the question…again. "I'm sorry. No, I only come here once a week to exercise the dogs for a few hours. I work at the hospital up the road."

Ash looked puzzled, as if she knew the area but couldn't place a hospital. It was a common mistake. Most people thought it was a prison. "Horston Secure Hospital."

"Oh…"

And most people had *that* reaction when Evie told them where she worked.

"Are you a prison officer?" Ash asked.

Her temporary stumble fell away and she easily resumed her laidback demeanour. And Evie didn't miss the flash in Ash's eyes as she asked her question. Prison. Handcuffs. Sexy sex.

"It's not a prison, it's a hospital," Evie said a little more harshly than she perhaps should have, but she grew tired of having to explain the difference. Which was unreasonable of course, because it sort of *was* a prison for some people. Patients couldn't come and go as they pleased, and every door in the whole complex was bolted, or secure, or locked electronically. And it *was* the place where they sent people who were a grave and immediate danger to the public, often through the criminal justice system.

Ash frowned and tilted her head slightly. "But there *are* serial killers and cannibals there?"

She smiled again, a more mischievous one, as if she knew she was pushing Evie's buttons.

"Well, I'm not a prison guard, I'm a doctor." That was the easiest explanation, but it was work she didn't want to talk about. It was work she came here to get away from. Evie looked at her watch, conscious she was wasting Ariel's exercise time. "I'm sorry. I have to walk Ariel." She took a step to the side and began to unlock the little terrier's gate.

"You say sorry a lot, doc."

"I hadn't noticed." A blatant lie. She was always apologising. If she fell to sleep, she woke with sorry on her lips. "Sorry." That one was deliberate, and she ducked down to clip a Ariel into her lead so that Ash didn't see her smile. "Hello, lovely Ariel. How are you today?" Evie tickled under Ariel's chin and the little dog yapped excitedly. "Enjoy the rest of your visit with Java," Evie said as she walked back toward the field, trying not to take one last, lingering look into Ash's sparkling eyes.

"So, you're here every Friday?"

It was all Evie could do not to turn back to answer Ash's call, but she'd had her flirtatious playtime and it was time to get back to the dogs. "Wouldn't you like to know?" Evie rolled her eyes at her cringeworthy response and carried on walking. She might not see her again anyway. Most people with dogs in quarantine only had the time to visit once a week, and Evie couldn't be that unlucky that Ash would always visit on Fridays. Or would it be lucky if she did?

Chapter Three

I *would* like to know, actually. That's why I asked," Ash whispered. She didn't bother to resist watching Evie's butt swinging down the corridor until she was out of sight. Java scrambled at her leg, and she returned her attention to him. "Sorry, boy. Mummy got distracted with the pretty lady, didn't she?" She squatted down, tumbled Java onto his back, and rubbed his chest. "You'll get used to that, but you'll always be my top boy, don't you worry."

Java wriggled until he was free and launched himself at Ash's chest. She caught him and scrundled his furry body until he freed himself again and tore through the opening to his outdoor area. Ash crawled through the hole and followed him. She could do with some fresh air. Her nostrils were filled with whatever sweet scent Evie had been wearing. A doctor. Wouldn't she be a catch? Except Ash had crashed and burned. Evie clearly didn't want to discuss her work, but still Ash pushed and Evie left abruptly. Ash had made such a non-impression that she hadn't even warranted a backward glance.

She looked down at her clothes. She wasn't dressed to impress, she was to dressed to crawl around a kennel floor with her amazing new companion. Ash would rather have met Evie when she was more suitably attired, to give her at least half a chance to show off her best side.

Ash reached back into the covered kennel, pulled her flight jacket out, and put it on the floor to sit on. Java immediately jumped onto it and began to make a bed. "Cheeky pup, that's my spot." She picked him up, sat down, and leaned against the breeze block wall. Java settled on her outstretched legs when she pulled a Dentastix from her jeans pocket and waved it in front of his nose. He used his paws to grab her wrist and hold it in place while he got some purchase on the bone. Ash laughed at his dexterity. "I'm not going anywhere."

She looked up and through the ten or so other outdoor kennels, she could see Evie taking a slow walk around the field. Ash doubted she'd be that long before she bought the little dog back. Had she called it Ariel? After the soap powder or the Disney princess? Either way, surely a dog that size couldn't need much exercise. Heck, weren't they the dog of choice for celebrities to carry around in their handbags?

Ash thought about Evie's parting words. "Wouldn't you like to know?" She could interpret them either way, as a lack of interest or a flirtatious tease. Ash decided she'd go with the latter and give it another try when Evie returned with Ariel. Or maybe she shouldn't. She liked older women but they didn't always like her. Ash remembered the Audi that Evie had arrived in. She'd love to go for a spin in it. That could be her angle. Stop with the immature flirtation and try to get into Evie's head through a shared interest. Ash could show she was mature to someone that sophisticated. She'd learned some tricks from previous encounters with older women.

"Ouch!" Ash pulled her hand away and inspected the damage. Java stopped chewing and looked up as if it weren't *his* razor-sharp puppy teeth that had dug into her skin instead of the chew bone. Unperturbed, he went back to munching his way through the stick. Ash wiped the blood on her jeans and began to stroke Java's ears while she continued to part watch Evie. She was just a shape at this distance, but Ash was still strangely mesmerised. Why had Evie been so reluctant to talk about her work? Ash regretted her overt sexual innuendo when she'd asked Evie if she was a prison guard. So cliché, and Evie had promptly shut down after that. Perhaps she got sick of being asked about the high-profile criminals in her "secure hospital." But that kind of thing fascinated Ash, *and* so many other people, otherwise there wouldn't so many serial killer TV shows, movies, and books. Ash had only recently binge-watched *Dexter* for that same reason.

"What do you think, Java? Should I try again or leave her be?" Java stopped chewing his bone, scampered up Ash's chest, and licked her nose. Lucky he was a puppy and still had fresh breath. The mint flavoured bone helped too. She nuzzled her nose into his chest and wrestled him onto his back. "Submit!" He did nothing of the sort and nipped at her furiously, trying to get away. When he was back on all fours, he ran into the indoor kennel and reappeared with a tennis ball in his mouth. He trotted over to her but didn't relinquish his prize.

"Drop it." She may as well start some training early. If she waited until he came out of quarantine, Java might need the pet version of Supernanny.

He didn't drop it.

"Drop it," she said, slightly more forcefully and pointed to the ground in front of his furry little feet.

He looked down to where she'd pointed and then back up to her as if to say, "What're you pointing at?"

"Drop the ball." She laughed at herself. As if adding "the ball" would make him understand what she wanted him to do. She made a grab for the ball with one hand and the rest of his body with the other. She pulled him into her and wrangled the ball from his mouth. "Good boy," she said and tossed the ball along the thirty feet of his run to the end gate. He bounded after it, snaffled it up, and ran back to Ash.

"Drop it."

He chomped the ball and didn't give it up. Ash grabbed him again, and after a little more trouble than the first time, emerged with his ball. "Good boy."

Ash shivered as the sun dipped behind an ominous-looking cloud. "Let's go inside, little guy." Ash took her coat from under her and pulled it on, glad for the instant protection it gave her from the sudden drop in temperature. Java followed her as she crawled back into the much warmer indoor area that benefitted from a heat lamp overhead. She leaned up against the wall on the same side as the entrance so they could continue their game.

After another ten or so tries, Java still hadn't quite got the idea, *and* he'd got wise to Ash catching hold of him when he brought the ball back indoors. She held him in a tight bear hug, trying to tug the ball from his mouth, all the while imploring him to drop it. She finally yanked it out. "Good boy, Java."

"I don't think that's the way training is supposed to work."

Ash looked up to see Evie standing by Ariel's gate. "Are you a doctor or an SAS assassin? How did I *not* hear your heels on that floor?"

"It's hard to hear anything over the noise you two are making," Evie said as she opened the gate and guided Ariel inside.

Evie's words sounded terse, but her smile and slight eyebrow raise told Ash she was teasing. "My turn to say sorry, then?"

Evie shook her head. "Absolutely not. I'd much rather—"

Yap.

Ariel's piercing bark made Ash jump. She hadn't expected such a loud noise from such a small dog. And her timing couldn't have been worse. What would Evie much rather…do? Hear? Ash knew what she'd liked to hear from Evie's mouth, a soul-lifting orgasm. She squeezed her thighs together. Ash would have to play this much smarter if she ever wanted to get to that place.

"Oops, sorry, Ariel. Let's get you back in your kennel."

There was that sorry again. Why did a woman like Evie think she had to apologise so much?

Evie unlocked the gate and popped Ariel inside. "She knows she gets a treat after her afternoon exercise."

Evie relocked the gate and disappeared from view for a moment, presumably while she gave the demanding little dog her treat. Ash threw the ball through to the outdoor area for Java once more and stood. "I *would* like to know," she said as Evie straightened up.

"Know what?"

Evie's eyes flashed. She knew damn well what Ash was talking about, and that look only served to fan Ash's fire. Maybe she could be interested after all. "I'd like to know if you volunteer here every Friday?" Ash stepped closer to the gate, but Evie took a step back.

"I have another dog to walk," she said and took another step.

Ash almost didn't pursue it further. The signals were getting too confusing. Then she remembered that Evie was the one caught staring at *her*. Evie had declared her interest before Ash had even said a word. "Come on, put a girl out of her misery. Do I get to look forward to seeing you and my wonderful dog on the same day every week?"

Evie sighed. Her apparent lack of confidence with Ash didn't fit with the rest of her sleek demeanour. Ash loved confident women as much as she loved older women, but Evie's hesitance hinted at a vulnerability that called to Ash, called to her own desire to protect a woman in the most old-fashioned way.

"If I answer this question, will you stop asking me questions?"

Ash nodded. "Yes."

"And if I tell you, will you stop bothering me?"

"Only if you want me to."

"Then, yes."

"Yes, you work every Friday, or yes, you want me to stop bothering you?"

"That was another question. You said you'd stop asking me questions." Evie crossed the corridor to another gate around the corner and out of sight.

Ash laughed and shook her head. She knelt back down to Java and rubbed his pink puppy belly. "This one's gonna hurt, Java."

Chapter Four

Sarah clicked the mouse and turned Ariel's exercise cell to green on her spreadsheet. "So, did you and Ashlyn have a nice chat?"

Evie narrowed her eyes. "How do you know we talked? Have you installed CCTV and not told anyone?"

Sarah gave Evie a light shove and winked. "I didn't know until you just admitted it. But when you looked over at us, your tongue was hanging out like Kirby's does after you've exercised him."

"Ha." Evie shoved Sarah back and flopped into the chair beside her. "Was I *that* obvious?"

Sarah nodded and patted Evie on the knee before returning to her computer screen. "I'm afraid you were, love. If it's any consolation, Ashlyn did ask about you."

Evie leaned forward in her chair. "Really? What did you tell her?"

Sarah laughed. "Not much. What should I have told her?"

"Nothing, if you're following the Data Protection Act like any good employer would." Evie sipped at the chamomile tea Sarah had made her after she'd finished exercising five of her residents.

"Then what would you have liked me to tell her, had I not been doing that?"

Evie nibbled her lip and looked up at the ceiling, thinking about her answer. She noticed a patch of damp in the corner. "How long has that been there?"

"Stop trying to change the subject. And more to the point, what did *you* tell her when you were having your cosy little chat under the heat lamps?"

Evie scrunched her nose up and sighed. She'd been all over the place. A little flirting. A little cold shoulder. Some encouragement. Some ice queen. If Ashlyn had *her* gaydar on, it would've been too confusing to read. Evie wouldn't have blamed her if she'd given her a questioning look and backed off…but she hadn't. She'd pursued her. How fast could she make a week go by before she got to see Ashlyn again? "I told her I was a doctor at Horston. She asked if I was a prison guard, but she may have well asked if I had some handcuffs by the bedside table."

"Ooh, kinky. Nothing wrong with some slap and tickle, I say. If Harry got his nose out of those fishing books for a second, I wouldn't say no to a little sesh with a pair of cuffs and a blindfold."

"Sarah!"

"What? Don't be such a prude. You have to mix things up if you want to stay happily married for more than a couple of years, you know?"

"No." Evie straightened in her chair as if to prove Sarah's point. "I wouldn't know."

"And that, my dear, might well be the problem. But I haven't seen you interested in any of the other hotties that have come through these doors since you started with us. That's four years. That's a lot of sexy women."

Evie harrumphed. Sarah and Harry had quite the modern kind of relationship. "You'd know."

Sarah wiggled her eyebrows and smiled. "And *that's* another way to keep a marriage alive."

Evie put her hands over her ears and shook her head. "Spare me the details of your mucky little threesomes."

"There's nothing mucky about them. I like my women and men clean, thank you very much." She pointed her finger at Evie. "And they're not always threesomes. We both get to have solo time with other people too."

"Oh-kay. I get the picture." Evie laughed. She loved how honest Sarah was about her and her husband's sex life and relationships. If only everybody was as open as them, the world might be a more accepting place.

"Ha, you wish." Sarah nodded toward the door which led to the kennels. "But we digress, doctor—and don't think I don't know your games of deflection—what else did you and the hot little butch talk about?"

Evie looked away briefly. Despite her best intentions, every time she'd gone back to get a different dog to exercise, she'd ended up chatting to Ashlyn... Ash. And Sarah was right, she was hot, and she was exactly Evie's type. But there were so many other things and people to consider. Evie wasn't footloose and fancy free anymore. She couldn't just sleep with anyone she wanted to and to hell with the consequences. Those days, as enjoyable as they'd been, were over. She had responsibilities, and her son was the biggest responsibility of all. "It was small talk, mostly. Java is adorable though, isn't he? What's the story there?"

"You mean, you didn't ask?"

"No." Evie shrugged. "It never came up."

"What about all the data protection stuff? Surely I shouldn't be telling you anything about Ash and her cute little monster."

"Monster? Why monster?"

"You should see him when we go in to clean his kennels. He's always trying to jump on the mop or brush, doesn't matter which. And when he gets hold of them, they're toast, I tell you. He's still got his puppy teeth, and those little things are razors. Slash through anything, they do." She smiled broadly. "That's why I call him the monster."

Evie tucked her hair over her ear and tried again. "So, where's he from?"

"You won't report me to ICO for disclosing private client information?"

Evie shook her head. Now she was desperate to hear the story.

"Well." Sarah pushed her chair out from the desk and scooted even closer to Evie than she'd already been. "Our Ashlyn is a bad girl, apparently," she whispered.

"Really? How so?" Damn it. Now she was truly lost. Why couldn't Ash be a choir girl type? Wasn't it about time Evie was interested in a nice butch who wanted a quiet life?

"She turned up at the Port of Calais in a rental car with Java in the front seat. No microchip and no pet passport. All she had was proof that Java had been given a rabies vaccination on the same day as she'd travelled."

"What?" Evie couldn't believe it. The law was clear. It had been changed to make it easier for people to travel with their pets between countries, so why would Ash have risked her pup's life? "What on earth was she thinking? Java could've been destroyed."

"Maybe that's a question you could ask her next Friday? It not's my place to ask her something so antagonistic."

Evie pushed her chair back and looked over toward the kennels. Ash certainly had her intrigued. "Oh, but I can?"

"It'd beat small talk, wouldn't it?"

She couldn't argue with that. "Does she only come on Fridays?" Evie picked up her cup and finished the last dregs of her tea.

"This is her first visit, but she said she was planning on coming at least three times a week."

Visiting times were Monday to Saturday from two to five. What kind of job did Ash have that gave her the flexibility to come here that many times a week? Unless she didn't have a job at all. Evie reined in the judgement before she made it. She had no idea what Ash's situation was…but she definitely wanted to know. And that was a problem. "Where does she live?"

"Now *that* I can't tell you. That would be breaking your data laws."

"Calm down, Sarah, I didn't mean her postal address. A vague area will do. You're out in the middle of nowhere here. I wondered how many miles her round trip was."

"Are you going to offer to pick her up in your fancy car?"

"You're incorrigible. Come on, a general idea is all I'm asking for. I don't have the time to stalk someone."

"Mm, I suppose you're right there. I believe she lives in the city."

Evie raised her eyebrows. "Goodness, that makes it about an eighty-mile round trip." She smiled. "That's dedication."

Sarah touched Evie's knee lightly. "And it shows how loving she is."

Evie shook her head. "You're extrapolating from loving a pooch to loving a human? That's a stretch, even for you."

"Not at all." Sarah looked indignant. "There are studies that show animal lovers are far more compassionate to their fellow humans than people who don't like animals…and people who don't like animals are usually psychopaths. Although I don't have to tell *you* that."

"Not all my patients are psychopaths, Sarah." A high percentage were, but she wasn't telling Sarah that.

"Maybe not. But ask any of your psychopaths if they like animals, and I bet they all say they don't. Go on, do a study for me for next Friday."

"I'd like to see the studies you're talking about. I have a feeling you're making them up. And I'm not asking my patients anything of the sort." Evie didn't want to encourage Sarah's broad brushstroke attitude to the people at her hospital.

"I'm sure I saw it on a David Attenborough programme once. And if he says it, it must be true."

"And I'm sure David Attenborough has never done a programme on psychopaths!" Evie glanced at her watch and sighed when she saw the time.

Sarah jutted her chin toward Evie. "Time to go back to the hell hole?"

Evie laughed. "It's not that bad." Although she did have a child killer coming in direct from sentencing, and a lot of people wanted him sent to hell, so on this occasion, Sarah might be right. She placed her cup on the table and got up from her chair. Sarah stood and they hugged for a few moments longer than usual. Evie didn't retreat from the intimacy, cognisant that she needed some form of physical contact with another adult, even if it was only platonic. The door opening interrupted the hug, and Evie pulled away as she saw Ash come in and close the door. She didn't miss Ash's look of surprise, or was it disappointment? "Say hi to your hubby for me." Evie lifted the countertop to escape before she said anything else stupidly unsubtle.

Sarah gave her a knowing look and laughed. "And I'd say the same thing if you had anyone to go home to."

Oh my god, Evie mouthed at Sarah then turned and headed for the exit. "See you next week."

"Thanks, Sarah." Ash walked through to the reception. "I'll see you tomorrow."

"Lovely. The little monster will love that," Sarah said and smiled.

Ash got to the door first and pulled it open for Evie. "After you."

Great. Another ticked box. As old-fashioned as it was, Evie did love having doors opened for her, especially by a woman like Ash. "Thank you." The autumn sun had gone completely, and Evie shivered as the cold wind whistled into her open jacket and wrapped around her body.

"Good job your Audi has heated seats."

"How do you know it does?"

Ash gestured toward Evie's car. "A warm bum is the least you could expect when you're spending seventy grand on a car."

"And how do you know that's my car?" Evie asked, and Ash smiled that damn perfectly cocky smile.

"I saw you pull into the car park and—"

"And you ogled me when I got out?" Evie couldn't stop her presumptuous words.

Ash tilted her head. "What if I did? How could I not 'ogle' a woman like you?"

Evie laughed, shook her head, and began to walk to her car. "Do those kinds of lines usually work for you?" Evie didn't need to ask. Ash's lines were working on her, which was worrying.

"You tell me." Ash rushed ahead of Evie and opened the car door. "Those proximity keys could be dangerous. If I were a kidnapper, I could've pulled you into the car and driven away before anyone had chance to stop me."

Evie dropped slowly into her seat and swung her legs in, careful not to touch any part of Ash. "*I* would've stopped you." She pulled the door closed, pressed the engine start button, and it roared into life. Ash hadn't moved from beside the car. *Pull away. Don't say another word.* She retracted the window and Ash leaned in.

"But do you want to stop me?"

Evie looked at Ash's hands on her car door. They looked so strong and capable. What would her fingers feel like, dragging under Evie's skirt and up her thigh? She knew what her answer should be. Her life was far too complicated to play with Ash, as beautifully handsome a butch as she was. She knew she should say that she wanted Ash to stop, that she should stop, that she was far too young for her, that they wanted different things from life. That a decade between them at this age may as well have been twenty. "No."

Ash took her hands away and grinned. "I'll see you next week."

She turned and walked away. Not a hurried, it's autumn and it's fucking cold walk. No. A slow enough and deliberate enough walk for Evie's gaze to drift to Ash's bum. Evie had always been a butt girl, and Ash's didn't disappoint. Her baggy jeans were tight in exactly the right place and gave Evie a very pleasant memory indeed to keep her warm until next Friday.

She put the car into reverse as Ash reached the battered little jalopy Evie had seen earlier. It took all her reserve not to look Ash's way again. *What the hell am I doing?*

Chapter Five

I want you here at least thirty minutes before the club starts, Ashlyn. You've got to help me get everything set up."

Ash nodded at her new boss, Bev, who hadn't been part of the interview panel. If she had, maybe Ash wouldn't have taken this job. She couldn't say exactly what it was that didn't sit right, but there definitely was something about Bev that was going to make their working relationship difficult. "No problem, I'm sorry." Though Ash was certain that the woman who'd called her to say she'd got the job, said she should be there at quarter to ten, not 9:30 a.m. "What do you want me to set up?" Ash gestured to the hall, empty aside from a pile of athletics mats, several stacks of chairs against the wall, and a pool table pushed into the corner.

"Organise the mats on the floor for the young people to sit on," Bev said and stalked from the room.

Having no manners didn't help. Where was the harm in asking nicely? "Will do." Ash jogged over to the mats and began pulling them two at a time from the pile. She'd quickly counted twenty, so she dragged the first two into the far corner of the hall and laid them out. At six by three feet, Ash estimated they'd cover most of the floor area, and that it would take her four minutes at most. Quite why Bev needed her there half an hour before a two-hour session was unclear.

Ash was about finished when she saw a little head peek around the corner of the outdoor fire exit. "Hi, are you here for Bright Stars?"

He nodded and took a small step forward into the doorway.

Ash smiled. "Do you want to come in?"

He shook his head. "Bev doesn't like us coming in until exactly ten."

So, her new boss had a big thing about time *and* was mean to the kids she was there to work with. Good to know. Ash approached the young boy and leaned against the doorjamb. "What's your name?"

"Izad."

"That's a cool name." Ash squatted so she didn't look down on him. He was a skinny kid and looked about nine years old. The club was for secondary school kids though, so Ash had to be wrong.

"My dad gave it to me. It was my grandpa's name. He's from Pakistan. But my dad's not. He was born in England." Izad stood a little straighter. "*I'm* from England."

A heavy hammer knocked hard against Ash's heart. Izad had spat most of his sentences out excitedly and rapid fire, but the way he deliberately paused and said his final statement hinted that the kid had already experienced the *less* pleasant side of this green and pleasant land. Tigley was a multi-cultural area of the city where the commonality was poverty and disadvantage. The kids shouldn't have to deal with racism too.

"I don't know where I'm from," Ash said. She pushed away from the door and sat on the edge of the concrete steps. Izad joined her, as she'd hoped he would.

"What do you mean? How can you not know where you're from? I know where I'm from. I know where my dad's from. And I know where my mum's from. She's from England too. I *even* know where my nana and grandpa are from."

Ash grinned widely. If the rest of the kids she was going to be working with were anything like Izad, handling a bad boss would be worth it. "I don't know my mum and dad, Izad, and I don't know where they're from either." She thought about the latest Disney movie that might work for explanation to a kid Izad's age. Trying to explain you were unwanted and unloved might be honest, but it wouldn't be the appropriate way to go. "Have you seen *Frozen*?"

Izad bounced up and down. "Of course! I've got both of them on DVD at home."

He jumped up and launched into the standout song, *Into the Unknown*, complete with actions. Izad had a great voice and hit the high notes well; Ash could see why he was at the drama club. When he'd finished the whole song, he sat back down beside her.

"What do you think?" he asked.

"I think you're a little star in the making," Ash said, relieved that he'd obviously pushed aside the orphan issue to display his considerable talent. "Have you had singing lessons?"

He shook his head. "Not yet. This is raw talent. That's what Mum says." His eyes darkened a little and he looked sad for the briefest of moments. "My dad says I get my singing from my mum. His singing in the shower is terrible. But Mum says I should follow my heart. I don't know what that means. My heart is here." He pointed to his chest. "It doesn't go anywhere. It's in me. I can't follow it anywhere, can I?"

Izad looked at Ash as if she could provide a more satisfactory answer to his question, and she laughed. His logic was faultless. "Follow your heart is something people say when they mean you should do what you *feel* is right, what makes you happy. Does singing make you happy or sad?"

He frowned as if she'd asked him the most stupid question in the world.

"It makes me happy. I love it. I'm always singing. Mum says I was singing before I was talking. And if I get sad, I can make myself happy by singing."

"*That's* what your mum means."

"What if me singing doesn't make other people happy?"

"Ashlyn. What are you doing? Why didn't you come and tell me you'd finished getting the mats ready?"

Bev's voice rankled like nails down a chalk board. She pulled an "Oops, I'm in trouble" face to Izad and stood. "Sorry, Bev. I was talking to Izad."

"Oh." Bev came to the door. "I didn't see you there, Izad."

Okay, so Bev was *that* kind of person. She addressed Izad in a much friendlier way than she'd thus far extended Ash's way. At least she wasn't a complete bitch to everyone. Ash took a deep breath. *Breathe in yellow. Breathe out black.* She'd wanted this job desperately, and now she had it, Ash was going to do everything she could to keep it *and* enjoy it, regardless of Bev's best efforts. Ash wasn't going to let a live version of the *Horrible Boss* movie play out…if she could help it.

"Would you like to come in, Izad?"

Her sing-song voice sounded forced. Why had Bev ever chosen to work with young people? She'd be far more suited to a job in a funeral parlour. The dead didn't care how you spoke to them.

Izad tilted his head at Bev, then looked at his phone. Ash guessed he was checking the time.

"It's 9:57," he said and didn't move.

Bev laughed and managed to make that sound disingenuous too.

"That's okay," she said. "You can come in and write your name on the register." Bev stepped out of the doorway and gestured for Izad to enter.

He seemed unconvinced and looked at Ash, possibly for confirmation that it was okay for him to go in after being told for many months he couldn't come in until ten. Ash shrugged lightly and nodded. "Let's go. It's cold out here."

Izad hugged himself as if he'd become aware of the bitter weather and needed no further convincing.

"Okay."

Without looking at Bev—though Ash could feel her small eyes burning holes in her skull—she followed Izad to the pool table where an open folder was laid on the protective wooden top. He wrote his name down, eleven under the column for age, and a "1" in the box under EO. He'd obviously done it plenty of times before. Two older girls came in, and Ash recognised the first one as Ally, the young person from her interview panel.

She smiled broadly, ran over, and threw her arms around Ash. "Ash! Yay!"

Bev gave Ash a disapproving look, so she gave Ally a short hug back before drawing away. Ash didn't know whether it was a jealousy thing or a safeguarding thing and wished she'd been given an induction rather than being dumped straight into service delivery. She felt desperately unprepared and like Bev was waiting for her to slip up. They'd never met, but it seemed clear to Ash that Bev didn't want her here. Maybe she'd wanted someone else for the job and was pissed off that she hadn't been involved in the recruitment process. Ash would try to find out. She wasn't playing on a level field and didn't know why. That kind of uncertainty messed with her head.

"Hey, Ally. How are you?"

"I'm good. Katie, this is Ash. Ash, this is Katie." Ally gestured toward the girl she'd come in with.

"Hi, Katie. It's great to meet you." Ash smiled and tried to ignore the intense disdain radiating off Bev.

Katie smiled. "Hi, Ash. Is that short for Ashley with a 'y'?"

"Close. Ashlyn with a 'y'. Are you Katie with a 'y' or an 'ie'?" Ash asked. She glanced at the register after Ally had filled her name in and saw she'd marked a "3" in EO. Now it clicked: ethnic origin.

"I use 'ie.' Are you a good singer?" Katie asked as she completed her name in the register too.

"She is. And she's acted too." Ally saved Ash the trouble of answering for herself. "And she plays the drums, and the piano, and the guitar." She turned to Ash. "Did I miss anything?"

Ash laughed and shook her head. "Wow. That's impressive. You remembered all that from the interview?"

"Yep. They're the main reasons why I wanted you to get the job." Ally pulled Izad into a hug and he giggled. "You'll be able to help Izad make his dream come true. He wants to be a singer and an actor…oh, and a model." She ruffled his hair, and he struggled to get out of her grip.

"No, Ally! Don't touch my hair! It took me ages." He swatted her arm and ran to the window to fix the mess Ally had made.

"Also," Ally said and lowered her voice to more of a whisper, "none of the other people who wanted the job were anywhere near as cool as you." She scrunched up her nose as if she'd smelled something unpleasant. "And the only boy was ugly and weird."

"That's enough, Alison," Bev said and opened the cash tin beside the folder. "Has everyone got their money?"

As the three young people parted with their pound coins, a few more kids trickled in. Ally introduced Ash to all of them.

"Okay, then, let's get started," Bev said. "Everybody find a space on the mats and lie down, and make sure you can't touch anyone else."

The young people dispersed, but Izad tugged on Ash's shirt.

"What's up, little guy?" Ash squatted down again. The combination of him being small for his age and her height made it impossible to have a quiet conversation unless she knelt down, and the way he'd tugged at her made Ash think he didn't want everyone to hear what he had to say.

"Can you really make my dreams come true?"

His brown eyes looked so full of hope and expectation that Ash wanted a genie to swoop down and make any and all of Izad's wishes come true.

"I can help you with your singing, but you're the one in charge of making your dreams come true."

Izad frowned and looked thoughtful for a long moment. "I'm in charge," he said and then threw himself onto the mats.

Ash laughed and glanced around the room at the motley collection of young people. Mean boss or not, she already loved her new job.

Chapter Six

Evie hadn't had the time to think about meeting Ash at the kennels. As soon as she returned to the hospital on Friday, the new patient intake immersed her in all things Horston, and analysing her own behaviour had been the last thing on her mind.

Now though, as she attacked the pile of ironing in her wash basket, she remembered Ash saying that she'd see Sarah the next day—today. The start of the weekend seemed a good opportunity to take the time to go over the week in fine detail, as was her habit. Overthinking. If it were an Olympic sport, she'd be the champion of the world. Evie hadn't asked how old Ash was, but she'd now decided that she was in her early twenties. And with Evie at thirty-two, a decade between them may as well be thirty years.

She remembered how she'd been at that age, all hormones and little sense. She'd enjoyed her university and medical school years and squeezed as much fun as she could out of them. She'd been dedicated to making a success of her learning and career, definitely, but at eighteen, she'd also attended the funeral of her best friend and that had forced her to re-evaluate her priorities. Life could be taken away in an instant, and her friend's death made living every moment to its fullest Evie's top priority.

Ash was probably doing exactly the same, and why the heck shouldn't she? She was an attractive woman, the kind who appealed to a wide range of women-loving women, and gay boys, no doubt. Especially with that tight ass of hers.

As Evie thought about it now, she'd somehow lost sight of her own joie de vivre. Her adopted motto of living for the moment had slowly diluted as the reality of adulting had set in. Which was in no small part due to accidentally becoming pregnant. Evie, a mother. Being responsible for bringing new life into the world was something that had never been on her agenda. She embraced her independence and her desire to experience the world and all it had to offer. And raising a child played no part in that plan.

Yet here she was, doing exactly that. Sure, it was on a part-time basis, and he only stayed with her every other week, but the responsibility didn't dissipate with distance. Whether she saw him every day or not, she was a parent, and she had to behave like a parent and do parent-like things.

Which meant curtailing her exploits with women. She hadn't slept with a guy since Tal, the one who got her pregnant at twenty-one, and she had no desire to. University had been the time to explore her sexuality, and she'd quickly discovered men weren't for her. But she had tried it to be sure. She wasn't one to say she didn't like anything until she'd tried it.

But her attraction to women was impossible to control and far harder to limit. Since Von, her last faux-par, Evie had begrudgingly elected to satisfy herself with her own company and a drawer full of sex toys.

She drew the iron over a pillow case and closed her eyes briefly. Von had been more than a small mistake. Evie had been so desperate for an intimate connection that she'd been oblivious to the signs of addiction. It was an oversight of such epic proportions that she'd shared it with no one. Harriet, her closest friend, led the jet-setting, busy life of a global consultant—an occupation Evie had her suspicions was a secret synonym for superspy—and they rarely had the opportunity to be in the same room. They video-called and messaged often, but it wasn't the same. And there was part of Evie that saw her inability to recognise Von's addiction as a professional and personal failure, and therefore, she wanted to admit it to no anyone.

She put the iron aside, folded the pillow case, and placed it on the sofa. She missed Harriet. They talked for hours and it still wouldn't be enough, and Harriet's advice was always spot on. What would Harriet have to say about Von? She would kick Evie up the arse, for sure. Although if Harriet had been nearby instead of gallivanting around the globe to some exotic country or other, Evie would probably never have got involved with Von in the first place. Harriet had a knack for sniffing out the crazies and steering Evie away from them.

She paused her ironing, flicked the TV on, and selected reruns of *Friends* for company. She'd watched every episode so many times that she could say much of the dialogue before the actors did. It was something to watch that took little concentration, leaving her mind free to wander.

She refocused on the problem at hand, although Ash wasn't a problem really. They'd enjoyed some harmless flirting, and Evie had allowed herself to get a little carried away thinking about the possibilities. But it would, and could, go no further. If Ash wasn't in a relationship now, she probably would be by next Friday.

That's the way the lesbian scene worked in your twenties. She laughed. For some lesbians, it was the way it would always work. Evie had thought she would never settle down, and now she was sure of it. Not only did she have her own standards to meet, her kid had expectations too. He didn't know it, of course. But it was way too much hassle to vet a woman to be in the kid's life. Especially with his dad's parents in the background, persistently prodding Tal to propose and make them a "real" family.

Thankfully, Tal knew better and had never suggested they marry for the sake of their son. He maintained he'd known Evie was a lesbian before she did and said their one night together was like having drunk sex with his best friend. Except they'd not been drunk. And once she'd analysed it, Evie realised she'd instigated the encounter with Tal because she'd felt safe with him, not because she was hot for him.

She'd wanted to be attracted to Tal and to men generally, beyond an appreciation of a fitness cover magazine body. She figured it would be an easier life. But it wasn't to be. Evie loved to be around him, and in many ways, he had become her new best friend, but there was never *that* connection, the spark humans seemed programmed to seek out. She was just glad they'd managed to stay friends after she'd given birth to their child.

Evie checked the time. She had less than half an hour before he dropped the kid with her. It had been six months since the Von debacle, but Tal would still ask if she would be "entertaining" over the weekend. What a super polite and completely British euphemism for hot lesbian sex. Which Tal had thankfully *not* asked to see after she'd realised she was into women, and women alone.

She finished the bedding and headed upstairs. Evie opened the door to her son's room and placed the sheets on his keyboard. He was pretty tidy for a kid his age, but that didn't stop her from keeping his bedroom door closed whenever he wasn't around. Shutting the door when he was with his dad meant she could be more than "Izad's mum," that she could be someone's lover too, even if Evie didn't bring her hot dates or one-night stands home. Ever. She wasn't trying to trick anyone, or make someone fall in love with her and *then* hit them with the bombshell that she had a child. But it was important to feel like herself instead of just a mother.

She stuffed his pillow into the pillow case and allowed her thoughts to drift to her own mum. The stab of melancholy struck hard. Memories of losing the two most important people in her life weren't the best way to enjoy the weekend. But if it hadn't been for her mum, Evie wouldn't have known how to begin to have a relationship with her own child.

And she was grateful for that. As much as she bitched and whined about being a parent, she also loved it and wouldn't change her past for anything or anyone. She'd never been one for rocking chair regrets and she stood by every decision she'd ever made, right or wrong. Having a child wasn't one of those bad decisions she was *happy to live with*, it was a happy accident she'd come to embrace and revel in.

Evie finished making his bed and sat on its edge, trying to back track and understand how she'd ended up thinking about her son's journey into her life instead of her original focus of Ash. Their interactions had been fun, and Evie had enjoyed the attention from the young buck. She probably would again next Friday if their paths crossed. But that's all it was. A bit of fun, and that explained why Evie's train of thought had quickly moved from Ash to other people. Her ill-fated liaison with Von had shaken Evie's confidence in her ability to judge people, and it had put her sex life in the background as a result.

And when she could bring that important part of her life back to the fore, it most definitely couldn't be with someone fresh out of university with their whole life ahead of them. She would have to find someone who was happy to share her with her son. Someone who wouldn't begrudge spending hours watching Disney movies or standing out in the freezing cold on the side line of a football pitch lambasting the amateur referees. *Or* Evie would have to compartmentalise the two parts of her life and try to keep them separate from each other. She wasn't sure how that would work. She still knew who she was outside of being his mother, but she'd always *be* his mother. He was part of her, and maybe she couldn't be part of something else without him.

The doorbell chime pulled Evie out of her head, and she rushed downstairs to open the door.

"Izad!" She opened her arms, and her son jumped into them and wrapped his own around her tightly. It had been seven days since she'd last seen him, and the week had dragged without his company in the evenings.

"Momma, I missed you," he said, his voice muffled somewhat in Evie's hoody.

"I missed you, kid." Evie looked up at Tal and smiled. "Good week?"

He nodded as he came in and placed Izad's small duffel bag on the floor. "Pretty uneventful for a change. He's starting something new at the drama club, but he'll tell you *all* about it, I'm sure."

Evie's smile turned into a grin. Their kid did have a flair for the dramatic. "No doubt." She inclined her head toward the kitchen. "Do you have time for a cuppa?"

"Always. I'll get the kettle on."

Tal headed down the hallway and Izad finally released Evie from his grip.

"Dad's got a new girlfriend," he said, grabbed his bag, and ran upstairs without another word.

At least one of us has.

Chapter Seven

"Seriously? You're not staying out tonight?"

Ash shrugged at Kirsty, her roommate and teammate. "We've got a match tomorrow."

"We have a match every Sunday during the season, but that doesn't normally stop you enjoying yourself on a Saturday. What gives?" Kirsty punched Ash on the shoulder. "You already got someone coming over and don't need to work for it?"

Ash laughed and picked up her drink. "I hardly ever have to work for it." Which wasn't the case at all, and she preferred it far more when she had to put in more effort than a "come get me," look. But as a relative newcomer to the city's scene, she had enough single—and some, not so single—women on her trail. Finding company for a night of dancing and beyond was relatively easy but not something she craved.

"So, do you?"

"No." Ash took a sip of her Corona and placed it back on the beer mat. "I'm tired. It was my first day at my new job today."

Kirsty shook her head and held up her hand. "Running around and playing with kids all day is *not* a job."

"Wow, I haven't heard *that* before. I want to relax with some movies and ice cream. I want to not think about what a bitch my new boss is, who also made me late to visit Java." Ash didn't want to admit it, but Bev's regular snipes and digs had worn her down, and she'd only been at work for three hours. If it was a regular nine-to-five job, Ash wasn't sure she'd be able to tough it out.

"What did she do?" Kirsty looked concerned and leaned forward in her seat.

"I don't know…lots of things." Ash ran her hand over the back of her head. It certainly hadn't been the kind of first day she'd hoped it would be. "Disapproving looks, lots of comments, and she never asked nicely for me to do anything. It was boot camp but without the sexy women in uniform to compensate."

Kirsty tutted and gestured toward Ash. "Is it because you're gay?"

"I don't think so." At least, she thought not. "I think *she's* gay so that'd be messed up."

"Then that's it. It's like being at primary school when you like someone but instead of telling them, you bully them."

The thought of Bev being into Ash was an unwelcome one. "God, no. She's about twice my age, at least. And she's not my type at all."

"You mean she's an ugly oldster?" Kirsty laughed and downed the last swallow of her beer.

"I didn't say that. It's more her attitude that's ugly."

Kirsty raised her bottle. "Another one?"

"I'm only half way down this one, thanks."

Kirsty stood. "Hold that thought."

Ash watched Kirsty swagger away and people-watched. Some pretended not to watch Kirsty, but others were blatant and didn't care whether their ogling was noted or not. Ash recognised many of them as regulars, and some as previous lovers, and all of them were on the hunt for some weekend entertainment.

Kirsty returned with a fresh beer and flopped down into her chair. "Do you see the hot girl at the big speaker?"

Ash nodded but didn't look in that direction. Ash had seen her when they first walked in and the girl had raised her eyebrows and licked her lips. It may have been deliberate or it may have been a subconscious reaction to the two of them, but she'd made it clear she appreciated both Ash and Kirsty over the past half hour with surreptitious glances and not so coy smiles.

"What are you going to do about it?" Ash asked, because she didn't have the energy or inclination to do anything herself.

Kirsty flashed a wicked grin. "*Or* what are *we* going to do about it?"

Ash laughed and shook her head. "Not tonight, pal. She's all yours."

Kirsty pushed out her bottom lip. "Oh, come on. It's been a while since we played together." She took a swig of her beer and winked at the girl.

"That was a one-off… She's all yours."

Kirsty huffed. "Fine. But first you have to tell me more about this bitch boss of yours, your first day at work, and your visit with your unexpected fur baby."

"And then I get to go home and relax?" Ash knew the answer before Kirsty opened her mouth. The opportunity for a hook-up with the cute girl would trump Kirsty's need to keep Ash out all night.

"Okay, if you're going to be a grump about it." Kirsty grinned to show she was joking. "Tell me more about your ugly boss."

"It was like she wasn't happy that I got the job. She was snappy and downright nasty whenever she said anything to me. And I was thrown right in at the deep end with no induction about procedures or anything." Ash became aware of her wild hand gestures and busied herself with the beer label instead. "For example, some of the kids were filling their own details in on this paper register in a big folder, and Bev was filling it in for some other kids. And it had codes for their ethnicity…" Ash scrubbed her hand over the back of her head again. Recalling the morning out loud got her raging. "But I had no idea what they were. Other than bloody basic. All kinds of white kids from various countries were threes, and it seemed like Asian kids were ones. And all sorts of black kids, including bi-racial, were twos. A kid came in late, and Bev told me to fill the register in for him. Based on what I'd seen, I put him down as a two. But in the break, she looked to see what I'd written and blasted me for assuming he was a two instead of asking him. But when I asked what he was, she said he *was* classed as a two." Ash lifted her beer and drank. Maybe talking about this wasn't such a good idea. This one tasted nice, and she worried that she might not be able to stop.

"What did you say?"

"What could I say? She found fault with everything I'd done and said up to that point. I'm on a probationary period for three months. I don't want to get sacked from my first job after uni, do I?" Ash took another drink from her bottle, smaller this time. She wanted to go home and forget most of the day.

"Can you go to her boss?" Kirsty asked.

"The chief exec?" Ash shook her head. "I don't think so. Not yet. She's got to keep it up for me to have a real complaint, I think. And I don't know how long she's worked there, or what the relationship is between her and the big boss. They could be best buddies for all I know."

"Shouldn't your boss have been on the selection panel for your post?"

Kirsty had a point. Not having a say in the recruitment of the person she was supposed to be working closely with did seem strange. "Maybe there was someone up for my job that she was related to or friends with. Could be she wasn't on the panel so the process was fair." Ash thought about how Bev had shut Alison down when she'd mentioned a guy they'd interviewed.

"That could be why she's being pissy with you. If that's the case, you'll wear her down with your charm eventually. All you have to do is show her you're the best person for the job, and the selection panel made the right choice."

Ash nodded. She hoped it could be that simple. She'd had a great time with the kids, and there was such a lot of potential to work with young people who needed that kind of intervention. They were exactly the reason she'd not gone on to further study. "Fingers, toes, and pubes crossed."

Kirsty wrinkled her nose. "You can be so gross sometimes."

"Pot, kettle, black. All I'm saying."

"How was the rest of the job?"

"It was great, Kirst. All the kids were brilliant, and some are super talented." She thought about Izad and his impromptu *Frozen* performance. He'd connected with her instantly.

"Cool. Any kids you'll be coaching who should be on *The Voice*?"

"For sure. This one kid could be on the stage in the West End right now. And he's super sharp and cute too."

Kirsty leaned across and gave Ash a light shove. "You're not supposed to have favourites."

"And I don't. I'm just saying that he's got that special X-factor." Would Izad be allowed to explore his gifts fully? Some parents could be restrictive about letting their kids charge into creative careers.

"And the surprise addition to our household? How's Java?"

"Bev kept me back for an hour after I was supposed to finish so I only got to see him for two hours." Part of her had hoped Evie would be there, but she hadn't been. Ash pulled her phone from her pocket and tapped on a video to show Kirsty. Ash had stupidly hoped she might see Evie again, that she couldn't possibly wait until next Friday to see Ash. She was like a silly teenager with a crush, but it didn't stop her craning her neck to see who came through the gates every time they opened. Every time, she'd been disappointed to see only another visitor, the owner, Sarah, or another member of Sarah's team.

Kirsty watched the video and frowned. "Does he have something wrong with his legs?"

Java dragging his legs slightly had concerned her too. "I hope not, but I don't know yet. I'm going to make him a set of hurdles tomorrow before the match. I'll take them in on Tuesday and see how he gets on. I'm hoping that all he needs is some muscle and strength building up." She drifted to the memory of him tied up

in the middle of the desert, left to die. Her heart ached and raged in equal parts.

"I'm looking forward to meeting the little bugger," Kirsty said and handed Ash her phone.

Ash smiled and flipped through a few photos before slipping her phone back into her pocket. "I can't wait to bring him home."

Kirsty gestured toward the cute girl, still at the speaker and still alone. "Speaking of bringing people home."

Ash drained the last of her beer and stood. "Better act fast before she goes home with someone else." She pulled Kirsty into a bro hug and slapped her on the back. "I'll put my earbuds in so you don't wake me."

"Don't wait up…unless…you know."

Ash shook her head and headed for the door. "All yours, pal," she called over her shoulder.

Chapter Eight

Evie watched Izad tear up the stairs before heading to her kitchen. "Who's the lucky girl?" She opened the fridge and took out the milk and a bottle of water.

"He's told you already?" Tal clicked the kettle on and pulled a couple of mugs from the cupboard.

"What do you think?" She hitched up on the marble worktop and leaned back against the wall.

"He's not met her yet."

Evie was familiar with the tone in Tal's voice. "So, it's serious. And he will?"

He turned and looked at her with that serious expression she'd come to know almost as well as her own.

"I do like this one."

Evie smiled. *This one.* He made it sound like he'd gone through hundreds to get to her. "Tell me about her."

He popped a tea bag in the pot. "I want you to meet her first."

"Have your parents met her?" Evie asked, not sure why that mattered. It wasn't as if they were in competition for Tal's secrets.

He glanced away and busied himself with putting honey in their mugs. "No. There's no point…if…"

Evie raised her eyebrows, unable to contain her surprise at Tal's implication. *If I don't approve?* "Okay. I'll meet her. When did you have in mind?"

"Tonight?"

Evie laughed, then stopped when she realised he wasn't joking. "You know I can't do tonight. It's the final for *The Voice.*"

"Oh, I forgot about that." Tal pushed at the kettle as if trying to get it to boil faster. "He was so excited about the results last week, I thought it was all over."

"Did you watch it with him?"

"I was on the settee by his side. Does that count?"

"No, it doesn't," Evie said. "Can you name *any* of the wannabes left in the competition?" She waited for his response, which was a shake of his head. "Can you name *any* of the judges?"

Tal lifted his hand in the air and looked a little smug. "Ah, I know two of them."

Evie was unconvinced. "And they are?"

"The great Sir Tom Jones." Tal drew an arc in the air with his right hand. "And the inimitable Will.i.am," he said with a flourish of his left hand.

Evie laughed. "How dramatic. Now we know where Izad gets his flair from."

Tal harrumphed. "I don't think so."

"You know what they say; he has to get it from one of us." *She gets that from me.* Evie remembered her mum always attributing one talent, habit, or another to either herself or Evie's dad. Evie was fifteen before she realised she wasn't *only* the sum of her parents' parts. But that realisation didn't affect their relationship, and she'd give anything to hear her mum say those words again. She swallowed against the push of melancholy and threatening tears. They'd made so much of the last few months, but they'd never be enough.

"Then he gets all the good stuff from you and all the bad stuff from me. Isn't that the way it works?"

"Only when we're arguing or he's being naughty." Evie grinned at the memory of her mum saying those words too. "Unless of course, he's actually developing his own personality and talent and this one has nothing at all to do with either of us."

"It has to start somewhere, I guess."

The kettle boiled, and Tal filled the tea pot before turning to Evie again.

"So, if it can't be tonight, when can it be?" Tal asked.

Evie didn't want to be a pain, but the thought of dinner with Tal and his new love was far from appealing. More so because she'd be on her own, as usual. She knew the best thing would be to get it over and done with as soon as possible. "What about Sunday night? Izad always goes to bed early after doing some extra reading for school. We could do dinner at seven, if that works for you both."

"I'll check with her now."

Tal took his phone from his jacket and quickly tapped out a text message. Barely a few seconds had passed before a reply came in. The way he smiled when he read it confirmed to Evie that he was well on his way to falling for her, and that made their imminent dinner even more daunting. She couldn't quite believe that Tal was entrusting his future happiness to her impressions of the woman. They'd always agreed to be open with each other about new relationships and potential people entering their son's life, but this seemed a little like Evie had the final say.

"She's free tomorrow night," Tal said and opened the calendar app on his phone. "Where would you like to eat?"

And there was the upside. Evie loved eating out but rarely got to do it. Nevertheless, she did keep up with all the new restaurants opening in the city. "There's a new steakhouse called the Lace Yard I'd like to try. They do halal chicken too. How about there?"

Tal wrinkled his nose. "Patrie is vegetarian. I'm sorry."

"Patrie? That's an unusual name."

Tal shrugged. "Her parents are French."

Exotic. "I see. Perhaps Patrie should choose where we eat. Getting a good vegetarian dish is easier than it ever used to be, but sometimes you can still end up with a plate of vegetables." Evie had given up meat for a girl at university, but it hadn't lasted long as the girl went back to meat *and* men. Evie enjoyed medium-rare steak far too much to keep it up, but it was long enough to constantly be frustrated by a lack of vegetarian options.

"You don't mind?"

Tal sounded dubious. She raised her eyebrow. "Why would I mind?"

"Because you like to be in control of everything." He smiled, then turned away and began to pour the tea.

He wasn't wrong. And she *would* rather have chosen the restaurant, but occasionally letting someone else make a decision didn't hurt…much. When Tal offered her the mug of tea, he was smiling and probably wondering why she hadn't defended herself.

"Not *everything*. And not *always*." She took the tea and tapped him lightly on the cheek. "But don't get used to it."

"No chance of that."

The thunderous sound of Izad charging down the stairs made Evie chuckle. She watched as he turned at the bottom, almost slipping on the rug as it moved beneath him, as he always did, and jogged up the hallway toward her.

"Your water is on the worktop, Aladdin," Evie said and pointed to where she'd placed it on a coaster.

"I wish your rug *would* fly, Momma." Izad retrieved the bottle and drank half of it down in one go. "Thanks, Momma. Did Dad tell you about his girlfriend?"

Evie smiled and nodded. "Indeed, he did."

"Have you seen her photo?" Izad replaced his bottle on the coaster and walked over to Tal.

"Not yet. I found out her name though," Evie said.

"*Patrie*," Izad said in his best French accent. "Very fancy, I think." He reached toward Tal's pocket but was batted away.

"Oi, I don't think so." Tal backed away and pulled his jacket closed.

"Come on, Dad."

Izad persisted and jumped up on Tal's back, but Tal grabbed him and flipped him upside down.

"She's pretty, Momma."

"Good. But where is it most important that she's pretty?" Evie asked.

Tal turned Izad around to face her, and she could see the blood flushing his cheeks.

"On the inside, Momma."

She smiled, glad to hear that some of her respecting women lectures were being heeded. "Maybe you should put him down before he cracks his head on the stone floor?" Evie didn't coddle Izad—the odd fall and scrape were character building—but she didn't fancy a trip to A&E on a Saturday, when it would be filled with early drunks and serial hypochondriacs.

Tal rolled his eyes and carefully returned Izad to his feet. "My boy's tough, you know."

Evie laughed, thinking of their earlier conversation. "So, he's your boy when he's tough, but my boy when he's crying?"

"Absolutely." Tal nodded. "Or the other way around, probably."

"Show Momma the photo."

"Which one?" Tal asked.

"The one with the pretty lipstick," Izad said.

Evie exchanged a quick look with Tal. Was Izad noticing lipstick colours because he wanted to wear it, or because he liked how it made a girl's lips look? How was she supposed to find out which it was? Should she take Izad to a cosmetics counter and see what happened? Should she let him choose his own colour? God, parenting was hard.

Tal shook his head but smiled at the same time. Though they were separated, Evie was glad she wasn't trying to raise a little human being completely alone. It might be the most rewarding job in the world, but it was also the hardest, and there was no official bloody manual to help.

Tal flipped through his phone, found the picture Izad had specified, and passed it to Evie. She took in the short, curly brunette with dark brown eyes framed by thick, well-groomed eyebrows, and nodded approvingly. "Wow, she's beautiful."

Tal snatched his phone back. "Don't get any ideas."

Evie grinned. "As if I would."

Izad looked confused. "What do you mean, Dad?"

"Nothing, Iz. Nothing at all."

Izad narrowed his eyes the way that he did when he was sure that he'd missed something of vital importance.

"Momma, what does Dad mean?"

"He's joking, kiddo," Evie said. "He thinks I might steal his friend."

Izad furrowed his brow and wrinkled his nose in the exact same way his dad did. "Can't you share her?"

Tal shook his head vigorously. This was going to be an interesting explanation. Evie shot Tal a look of amusement at how he might be about to handle Izad's question. "Yeah, Tal, why *can't* we share?"

Tal raised his eyebrow and looked exasperated, before he turned back to his son. "Iz, you know how you've got toys that you don't like to share with anyone?"

"Momma says girls aren't toys, Dad."

Evie had to stop herself from laughing. Her son was becoming a true feminist, and she couldn't be prouder. Tal glared at her.

"I'm not saying Patrie is a toy, Son."

Izad crossed his arms and nodded. "Good. Because Momma says that it's bad to think like that." Izad looked over his shoulder and smiled broadly at Evie.

She gave him a thumbs up sign. "That's exactly right, kiddo."

Tal held his hands up. "Okay. Do you have a friend at school that you like to be with on your own?"

Now it was Evie's turn to look questioningly. She shook her head. Tal was going down a strange path indeed.

"I like spending time with Aisha most of all." Izad looked a little sheepish. "And I like it best when it's just the two of us."

First lipstick, now he had a girlfriend whose time he liked to monopolise. Today was turning out to be a veritable cornucopia of parental hurdles. But at least he appeared to grasp that it wasn't an approved way of thinking about his friend.

Tal sighed. "When you get older, you find people that become more than friends, and you like to spend time alone with them. They're special friends, like your Momma and I were when we had you."

Izad gasped. "But you're still special friends, aren't you?"

Tal blew out a long breath and ran both his hands through his hair. "We're still good friends, Iz. You never have to worry about that. But we're not *special* friends."

"Is Aisha my special friend?"

Tal looked over at Evie and mouthed, "Help."

Evie jumped off the counter, dropped onto a breakfast bar stool, and patted the one next to her. "Pop your bum on here, trouble." In many ways, Izad was way ahead of his years, but in others, he was yet to learn. She was in no hurry for him to grow up.

Izad took a long look at his dad before joining Evie. Izad's neurodivergence made him exceptional in many ways, and his way of processing information was so logical that it sometimes made explaining things slightly more challenging.

"Do you remember Toni?" Evie wasn't sure if he would. Izad had only been two when she came on the scene and four when she left. She'd been the only relatively long-term relationship Evie had ever had, and the only one who'd ever had the privilege of meeting Izad, but that was before Evie had decided the bar had to be set much higher for Izad's sake. She glanced across at Tal and could see he was uncomfortable at the mention of her name.

"Your girlfriend?"

"Yeah, that's right. Another phrase for girlfriend is 'special friend.' Your dad was joking with me, pretending that I might want Patrie to be my special friend instead of his."

"You might when you meet her," Izad said. "She *is* beautiful."

Evie laughed and ruffled his hair. He squirmed away.

"Momma, you know I don't like anyone touching my hair."

Evie held her hands together. "Sorry, sweetheart. But, back to Patrie. Even if I did like her, it wouldn't be right to want her to be my special friend."

"Your girlfriend?"

"Yeah, that's right. Because she'd already chosen your dad, and we don't share special friends or girlfriends. Does that make sense?"

Izad wrinkled his nose and moved his mouth around, deep in thought. "What happened to Toni?"

"We decided we didn't want to be special friends anymore." Evie glanced up at Tal. In truth, it had been far more complicated and volatile an ending than that. And it had been the start of their pact to put Izad ahead of their personal relationships.

"What if Patrie didn't want to be Dad's girlfriend anymore

and chose you instead?"

"That's not going to happen, because Patrie only likes men as special friends." She glanced at Tal, and his nod confirmed her presumption.

"How will I know who I want to be *my* special friends?"

Evie clasped Izad's hands in her own. "When you're old enough, you'll know. Just like I did, and just like your dad did." And she hoped that day would be a long, long way away.

Chapter Nine

A sh's satnav proposed the day's journey was going to take fifty-nine minutes. She shook her head. When she'd been given the kennel's number after a few hours in a holding area at the Port of Dover, Ash had called to find out exactly where the authorities were taking Java. Sarah had asked where Ash lived, then told her that she usually made it into the city in forty minutes. Ash liked speed in all forms and pushed her little Clio to its sporty limits, but on all five previous rides, the fastest time she'd made was fifty-three minutes.

Maybe Sarah had a helicopter or a direct cross country route to the city or even a regular police escort at ninety miles per hour. Whatever it was, Sarah had unwittingly issued a challenge, and Ash was determined to make the journey in forty minutes.

Of course, the time and distance wouldn't have made a difference anyway. She'd fallen in love with the pup with his broken tail, scruffy brindle coat, and soulful brown eyes, and she'd travel for as far and as long as was necessary to see him as often as she could over the next four months.

Ash pulled out of her drive and headed for the main road out of the city. She still couldn't quite grasp what she'd done, but as far as she was concerned, she'd had no real choice. There was no way she could have ever left Java as she'd found him: tied up in the middle of the desert to die. She'd made no attempt to find his previous owner. The callous bastard didn't deserve to be reunited with him anyway, and she'd dismissed the idea that he'd been stolen and left out there deliberately as far-fetched. More likely Java had been one too many in a litter, or even the only one in an unwanted litter, and had been cruelly abandoned.

She didn't want to think about what might've happened if she hadn't taken that strange walk out into the middle of nowhere. Meeting Java was fate, something Ash believed strongly in. Pure and simple, their stardust was part of the same soul group, and they'd crashed together as soon as they could. She didn't share her beliefs with anyone, and she knew they were contrary to the life she'd experienced as a kid. She'd had no soul group growing up. She'd been discarded, much like Java, and maybe that was the reason that she'd been strangely drawn to a hike into nothingness that morning. Maybe she was drawn to a kindred spirit, even if he was a dog. In her experience so far, dogs were far preferable to human beings any day.

Ash stopped at the roundabout and waited for the ambulance to swoop past, sirens blaring. She didn't know if that sound was her real first memory, or if it had been put there by the constant retelling of the story of how she'd ended up in her foster home. By all rights, Ash should be closed off emotionally and unwilling to trust anyone. But she'd been lucky and after some dubious care, at fifteen she'd ended up with a pair of first timers who were the best foster parents the system could offer.

She closed her eyes tightly against the memories. She didn't want to think about that now. Ash exited the roundabout and worked her way through the gears and up to sixty fast. The speed limit was fifty, but she and her trusty satnav knew where the stationary speed cameras were, and it wasn't a hot spot for mobile camera units. A lack of roadside cover didn't give the police many hiding places to catch unsuspecting motorists.

The swift gear changes reminded her of the almighty bruise still on her left thigh from Sunday's match. That defender had been a vicious bitch of the highest order. And she was a shirt-tugger, something Ash passionately hated. Ash had asked at one point during the game if she couldn't wait until the end of the match to swap shirts like a normal footballer. Looking back, it hadn't been Ash's cleverest retort, and the next time the woman scythed Ash down, she'd gone in studs up on Ash's thigh, cutting her game short.

Ash rubbed the injury with her left hand. Between the arnica she'd taken and the daily massaging, she'd managed to get rid of most of the bruising before training last night, but it had hurt like hell on the three-hundred-yard shuttles Brian had made them do. God, she hated those shuttles. Ash liked to run *with* the ball away from defenders and toward the goal, not randomly between orange plastic cones. Yes, it made her fitter, but it did nothing for her enjoyment or temper.

Evie popped into her head, and Ash wondered if she played any sports. She was quite short and curvy. Ash bet she'd played hockey or netball at school and probably at university too. Unless she was too focused on her studies to care about sport while she was there. Becoming a doctor was no easy task. Ash smiled. She wouldn't mind Evie examining every part of her body. Ash kept herself in decent shape between the football and climbing, so she was confident she'd pass any tests Evie might have for a lover. That's probably where the hellish shuttles might prove their worth.

What *would* it take to keep a woman like Evie happy? And did Ash have whatever that was? She was probably torturing herself unnecessarily. Evie had been flirty enough last week, but maybe she was being polite. For all Ash knew, she could be straight and playing along with her for coming on too strong.

She *had* come on too strong. She knew that, and she'd kicked herself every time she thought about their few interactions through Java's gate. Evie probably didn't know how to handle her onslaught. Although Ash was sure Evie responded positively to their final chat about Ash kidnapping her. She'd gone beyond regular flirting with that. Evie had paused and seemed to consider whether or not she would've stopped Ash from bundling her into her car and driving her away. What Ash would give to get in that car for a ride…both kinds.

She turned her radio up in an attempt to flush the errant thoughts from her mind, but it didn't work. She'd let herself get carried away with possibilities that were never there. What would an accomplished, successful doctor want with a youth worker fresh out of university? And behind the flirting, an iron gate dropped down occasionally, maybe when Evie got too close to actually enjoying herself?

She shook her head and checked her speed. In her musing, she'd gone down to fifty. She pressed her foot on the accelerator and got back up to sixty. Her satnav had only dropped a minute from her arrival time, and there was an amber stretch of road up ahead. She decided to ask Sarah for her magical forty-minute route when she got there. Not that Sarah would let Ash in before one anyway. She'd made her wait on Tuesday and Wednesday when Ash had got there ten minutes early. Which was fair enough, otherwise why bother having an opening time at all?

But that didn't stop Ash wanting to get in to see Java for as long as she possibly could. She was glad that she could fit in plenty of visiting days around her new job. The three clubs she'd done this week had gone well, and she'd met nearly fifty children and young people. Bev had continued to be a bitch at each session, but Ash had chosen to ignore her as much as possible and get on with her job. She still hadn't had a proper induction, and it didn't look like one was forthcoming. Part of Ash's job was supposed to be admin, so she had plans to get one created as soon as she was given the space to do so.

She'd briefly checked out the space that may or may not turn out to be her part of the office. Bev had gestured in that general direction and muttered something about it being Ash's desk. The PC on there looked like it had been reclaimed from a recycling tip and the printer beside it looked like a thirty quid special from Asda. She'd be able to get stuck in next week. The first week was always supposed to be a gentle introduction and light duties anyway, wasn't it? She wasn't counting her first job pre-uni when she'd worked nights at a nursing home. She hadn't been on light duties on her first week there. It took four of them to put one patient to bed. Ash shuddered at the recollection. The poor lady had been abandoned by her family too, and her legs were so thick with dirt, flies had laid their eggs and maggots had been eating their way through it. Ash had spent a lot of her spare time with her.

Another abandoned soul. Ash was beginning to see a pattern.

Whatever. Next week was a new week, and Ash would work so hard that Bev wouldn't be able to find anything to complain about or pick faults with.

The amber traffic disappeared from her route, and her arrival time was now showing as 12:55 p.m. *Damn it*. Evie had arrived at 12:50 p.m. last week, and Ash had been able to secretly enjoy her catwalk from car to the kennel door. She hoped she could get there early enough to see that again this week too. And the next week. And every Friday for the next four months. So, she had fifteen weeks of snatched chats and brief good-byes before Ash would never see Evie again…

Unless, of course, she stopped being such an over-sexualised jerk and simply tried getting to know Evie. There had to be a secret entrance through that iron gate she brought down. Ash convinced herself that there'd been enough interest emanating from Evie that it was worth pursuing. If she didn't give it a shot, if she didn't at least try to win the fair lady's favour, she'd regret it. Even if Evie politely refused, or even if she accepted but it went no further than a couple of dates, Ash would have gone for what she wanted and not chickened out.

Not knowing what could have been was far worse than the temporary pain of rejection. She'd adopted that way of thinking early on, after spending the first sixteen years of her life trying to understand why she'd been discarded by her biological parents. It was the *not knowing* that ate away at her soul, vied for attention in the darkest of nights when she was unable to keep her brain occupied, unable to stop from asking *why*? She wouldn't knowingly cultivate another instance in her life where that could happen again. No half chances. No what ifs. Always follow through. Always investigate the tiniest of possibilities.

Ash pulled into the kennel's driveway at 12:51 p.m. to find Evie's car already parked in the exact same spot as last week, despite the car park being relatively empty. It made sense. If Ash had a top of the range, pristine new Audi, she'd either have it bubble wrapped every time she parked or pay for someone to walk around and keep anyone else from parking anywhere near it. Doctors at crazy hospitals must make a good living to afford a ride like that. Maybe she should've stayed on at university and pursued psychiatry instead of getting into the job market.

She pulled her trusty Clio into a space far, far away from the gleaming bodywork of Evie's car. Through the side window of the kennel's office, she could make out Evie's silhouette. She quickly turned off the ignition, grabbed her giant backpack of Java goodies, and got out of the car. She began to jog across the gravel, but the bruising and last night's shuttle runs soon stopped her.

Evie was gone by the time she opened the door, and Sarah looked at her knowingly.

"Java's a lucky pup having such a dedicated mum. This is the third time this week, isn't it?"

Ash nodded. "I'm intending to come four times a week, if that's okay?"

"Of course it is, Ashlyn. I'd be happy if you came six times a week." She glanced over her shoulder in the direction Evie would've gone. "If only Evie could come more often too."

Ash frowned. Were they still talking about her visiting Java or had the conversation taken a different direction? If it had, Sarah was definitely giving Ash the thumbs up to go after Evie. She grinned. That meant they'd been talking about her. Ash straightened her jacket. "I'll have a go at convincing her."

Sarah laughed. "Good luck." She got up from her chair and opened the door to take Ash through to Java.

Ash hoped she didn't need luck, but she'd take it. She wanted to get to know Evie, and she couldn't do that through metal gates. No, she needed to ask her on a date.

Chapter Ten

Evie walked briskly up the path toward the kennels, keen to get some quality canine company. It had been a hellish week at work. The new patient from last Friday hadn't settled in quite as well as hoped, and between sedations, they'd managed little progress. They'd also had picket lines outside the hospital. People were angry and wanted the woman in a prison. Some weren't satisfied with a prison at all and wanted the death penalty brought back. The woman's crimes were heinous, and being a mother herself made it harder to draw professional boundaries, but Evie could never get on board with the death penalty. She hated kennels that put perfectly healthy but unwanted pets to sleep: the leap to humans was unthinkable.

The one thing that had kept Evie moving through the week had been going home to Izad every night. His young babysitter, Dawn, picked him up from school and helped him with some of his homework before Evie returned each evening around six, if the traffic wasn't too obstreperous. Dawn always made him a quick snack but nothing too heavy so that Evie could eat dinner with him every night. It seemed a simple thing, sharing a meal with her son, but it was time she treasured and would relinquish for nothing and no one. It was time she would miss next week, and the gloom usually crept in on Friday, knowing the evening's meal would be their last together for another seven days.

In fact, she had nothing at all to look forward to until a week on Saturday, when Tal would drop Izad off again after his drama club. She shook her head and opened the gate to Amelia's kennel. Strange name for a dog but each to their own. The origin of people's names often interested her. Had parents researched the name they'd given to their little cherub? Like Portia. It was a name Evie had considered before she knew the sex of her baby. She'd thought she couldn't go wrong with something so Shakespearean. Beautiful, intelligent Portia. And the actress who also bore the name was an inspiration too. But no, when Evie did her due diligence, she found the name derived from a word for a pig. Evie discarded it immediately.

After a quick cutch and a tickle behind her ears, Evie clipped Amelia onto her lead and wandered off toward the exercise field, comfortingly lost in her reminiscence and already miles away from thoughts of work.

When she'd discovered she was having a boy, she started the naming process all over again. And again, being a lover of the classics, she thought of Byron, only to find that it meant cow shed in Old English. It was around that time that Tal stepped in and suggested his grandfather's name, Izad. An internet search revealed it meant loyalty and support, two things Evie was in need of at the time, so she happily acquiesced to Tal's request. And it suited him from the moment she first held him in her arms. Now she couldn't imagine him having any other name. And Anglo-Saxon monikers would have been as disingenuous as the phone customer service reps from Pakistan called Dave, a ploy to make English people more comfortable that Evie despised.

Evie released Amelia from her lead, and she trotted off merrily toward a trail of sniff spots around the football pitch-sized field. Sarah had told Evie that Amelia wasn't a fetch kind of dog. Apparently, she was far too sophisticated for that kind of nonsense, and it showed immediately. She seemed like more of an investigator, moving from sniff to sniff like the canine version of Sherlock Holmes. Evie had read that dogs could glean all kinds of interesting information from their explorations, including whether the object of their interest was male or female, top dog or subordinate. But could they tell other things? Were they able to leave coded messages? Was there talk of escape from the kennels? Did they let other dogs know they had the best owners who served them steak and cheese for dinner every day?

The large metal gate leading to the kennels banged shut and Evie jumped from her musings as she followed Amelia around the field. She looked up to see Sarah escorting Ash toward the kennels' building. Both of them waved, and Evie responded in kind. Sarah continued up the path looking forward, but Ash kept her gaze on Evie. She tripped on a crack in one of the paving stones and stumbled. Evie laughed then covered her mouth. Ash smiled and waved again before concentrating on where she was putting her feet.

"And that's why you should always look where you're walking, Amelia." Evie finally looked away and re-joined Amelia, who'd made good headway up the field. "Steady, little one. I can barely keep up."

Amelia glanced backward at the sound of her name but didn't stop. She was obviously tracking someone of great interest. Evie thought about the dogs that came to the kennels. The cages were lined up, fifteen in one row and fifteen opposite those. Sarah or Harry closed the doors to their outdoor play area around ten in the evening and reopened them at six a.m. What did the occupants of the cages get up to in those eight hours? Did they argue? Converse? Have staring competitions? Fall in love? Was love at first sight possible for dogs? And if they *did* fall in love, what heartbreak they must experience to be separated so abruptly from their soul mate…and how long did it take for them to recover and pursue the next great smelling companion?

Maybe she should've been a veterinarian instead of a psychiatrist. Animals weren't inclined to reprehensible behaviour unless trained to do it, and Evie had always preferred their company to most humans. The only thing stopping her having one was her lack of time at home, and unfortunately the hospital wasn't inclined to let anyone bring their pets to work. Which seemed a missed opportunity to Evie. She certainly had some patients who would benefit from contact with a dog. There'd been plenty of research that reported all sorts of physiological benefits simply from stroking a dog. But the board weren't interested in alternative forms of therapeutic intervention, so her dream of having a pup would stay just that unless her home situation changed dramatically…she'd settle for a lottery win since her personal life was currently stalled.

Unlike Tal's. Patrie, his new girlfriend, had certainly made a big impression on him, fast. They'd all had a pleasant meal on Sunday at a fancy new vegetarian place in the city. Evie's dish of toad in the hole was made from more than serviceable vegetarian sausages with plenty of flavour. They were tastier than the real thing, so Evie had asked the chef for the brand and promptly ordered some in her next Waitrose home delivery that week. Izad had loved her version of veggie bangers and mash and proclaimed it his new favourite dish.

Food shopping was something she didn't like to do when she had Izad at home. She didn't like to waste their time together, and he abhorred grocery shopping. Clothes shopping was another thing entirely. *That* was a love they shared, and she indulged him terribly. But the boy had such good taste and could put together a fashionable, colour-coordinated outfit in minutes—for him or her. And he looked good in everything. Of course, she was his mum: she was supposed to think that *and* tell everybody all about it, but he was the proverbial clothes horse. He could easily be a model when he grew up and out of his spotty face and braces phase.

Evie drifted back to Tal and Patrie. She was nice enough, and Tal was clearly besotted with her. Some part of his body was in contact with Patrie for the duration of the evening, to the point that Evie began to think there was some sort of invisible thread holding them together. Patrie seemed equally taken with Tal, and every time he spoke, she gazed upon him as if he were a Greek god bestowing his precious time on her, a mere mortal. It was sickening of course, because she was alone and completely out of place. As soon as Patrie excused herself to go the bathroom after the main course, Tal asked what Evie thought and if she approved. *Yes, she's lovely. Yes, I think Izad will love her. Yes, I'm happy for him to meet her.*

What else could she have said? Her first impressions of people were usually solid, and she couldn't help but like Patrie. She had a good job, she was polite, and seemed respectful of Evie's relationship with Tal and their son, and how important he was to both of them. If she was some sort of horrific axe murderer, it certainly wasn't immediately apparent, but Evie's relatively recent experience with Von had shaken her belief that she might have been able to spot it even if Patrie was homicidal.

So, what did that mean for her love life? Tal had bluntly asked her about it during the meal. Stunningly obtuse of him, really, and Patrie had jumped to Evie's defence to shut down his questioning. But Evie said it was okay, because sharing a son meant they had to be open and honest with each other. She should've choked on the words, since Tal knew nothing of the Von debacle. Nonetheless, he wanted to know how Evie could possibly be single. He knew well enough her passionate side and didn't understand why she wasn't dating. And she had no intention of telling him why she'd faltered. Open and honest relationship be damned.

But maybe it *was* time to think about looking for someone to share her life with. She was the wrong side of thirty now for the kind of sex life she'd been used to. Endless dates and one-night stands seemed somewhat unbecoming in her fourth decade on the planet. Evie wasn't sure she knew *how* to date. Maybe there was a manual. She didn't fancy dating apps, though she knew of several married couples who'd met online and swore by their efficacy. But she didn't understand how algorithms were supposed to interpret an individual's emotions and experiences and match them to someone else's. She supposed it took a lot of the work out of the whole process. Made the sifting easier—*if* people were truly honest on their profiles. Perhaps that's where the success lay. Only the ones who were themselves online, instead of some special, Photoshopped ideal were destined to find true happiness.

Evie's watch buzzed to signal she should leash Amelia and head back for Kirby. Another week and another excuse from his owner meant Evie would get to exercise her throwing arm today. Maybe tonight, after she'd tucked Izad into bed, she'd Google the bars and clubs in the city. Evie and Sarah hadn't been out for a while, and she could see if Harriet was home for the weekend, though it was unlikely.

She called Amelia and popped her on her lead before gently jogging back to the kennels. If she was serious about getting back into bed with a real woman instead of her Wonder Woman soft toy, she'd have to get back to some real exercise.

Evie came to a halt after about twenty steps, already uncomfortable from her bouncing breasts. Who was she kidding? She hated exercise, and she especially hated running. And without a torturous sports bra, it was especially disastrous.

She looked down at Amelia, who seemed to be regarding her sudden dash with suspicion. "Fine. Speed walking will have to do."

Chapter Eleven

O kay, little guy." Ash placed the home-made hurdles in the centre of Java's run. "Time to see if you've got a problem or you're just being a lazy boy." She positioned the stick on the bottom rung, four inches from the floor and walked back to where Java lay on her coat, munching a rawhide bone. The part he was chewing had turned white and was leaving sticky residue all over her jacket. "So, I'll be washing that tonight then."

Java looked up briefly, his mouth wide open like he was laughing, before returning his attention to the tasty treat. Ash assumed it was tasty, since it seemed to be his favourite kind of munchie, second only to tripe sticks. And boy, did *they* stink. He wouldn't be eating those sitting on her, that was for sure. She'd never get that smell out of her clothes. Kirsty had already banished the giant tub containing the offerings to the garage, declaring it offensive to her nose. Ash was glad that the odour didn't seem to last too long on Java's breath though. She enjoyed his exuberant kisses whenever they were reunited. She hoped the combination of teeth brushing and regular Dentastix would prolong his fresh, puppy breath. Ash's foster mum had a dog with breath that would beat back the hounds of hell, and she *never* wanted Java's to get like that.

Ash grabbed the bone from Java, shoved it in the pocket of the giant rucksack she'd bought to carry the hurdles, and dropped the bag to the floor. Java scratted at the pocket and refused to come to her calls, so she picked it up and used a carabiner to clip it to the metal roof of the run, well out of his jumping range.

She picked up one of his tennis balls and got his attention. "Ready?"

Java gave Ash's bag one last look before he made a jump for her hand. She pulled it away. "Wait." Ash threw the ball the length of the run, ensuring that it bounced over the hurdles in the hope that Java would follow.

He didn't.

Instead, he ran alongside the hurdles, retrieved the ball, and ran back, again without using the hurdles, and straight past her into his covered area.

"Java!" He appeared at the small three-foot square opening

with the tennis ball jammed in his mouth, lifting his head up and down as he tried to chomp on it. Ash managed to grab his collar. "Drop it." Ash pointed at the floor. Java looked down at where she was pointing but didn't give up the ball. "Drop it."

More chomping and immeasurable cuteness.

"Drop it." Ash used her other hand to grasp the ball and tried to tug it from his mouth, but he wasn't letting up easily. She repeated her demand, but he was oblivious either because he hadn't made the connection between her words and what she wanted him to do, or he was being wilfully disobedient. Ash reasoned it was the first option since she'd only just started training him.

She got on her knees and repeated the command to no avail. *Fine. New tactic.* Ash licked his nose. He dropped the ball immediately and leapt at her chest, knocking her onto her back.

"Looks like his training is going well."

Ash looked up from the floor to see Evie in the next kennel along, staring down at her through the chain link. Ash sat up and grinned. "English *is* his second language. I reckon I have to give him extra slack for that."

Evie laughed and nodded. "Really? Where's he from?"

"Spain. Long story." And one Ash didn't want to share with Evie in this environment. "What are you doing in Kirby's run?" She didn't care what Evie's answer was. She was just glad Evie was there at all and that she had the opportunity to speak with her.

Evie pointed to something Ash couldn't see from her position on the floor as Kirby reared up on his hind legs and pressed against the fencing. Java took a few steps back, placing Ash firmly between himself and the huge dog. Kirby looked distinctly uninterested, dropped to all fours, and trotted down his run.

"I'm getting his favourite ball. He's very particular." Evie gestured toward Ash's hurdles. "Nice work. Are you getting him ready for the Canine Olympics?"

Ash moved from sitting to a kneeling position on her coat, still sticky on the floor. She pulled Java into a bear hug, and he began to lick and nibble under her chin. "Ouch! Teeth!" She took another rawhide chew from her back pocket and put it into his open mouth. "Nothing so grand, sorry. I was worried about his back legs." She patted his butt. "He drags them around instead of walking. I'm hoping that building some muscle will solve the problem." Hoping wasn't a strong enough word. She was praying he didn't have some congenital defect that could've been the reason for him being left in the desert to die. She'd happily build him a skateboard and harness if that came to be the case, of course.

"That's impressive." Evie put her hand against the metal fencing. "You're obviously quite talented."

The desire to place her own hand against Evie's rushed through Ash's mind. "Thank you. It's my first attempt at athletics' equipment. The best I'd done before this was a bed."

Evie raised her eyebrows. "You built a bed?"

She sounded impressed. Ash nodded. "Yep, from wood I reclaimed out of skips and building sites." She regretted giving the extra detail the moment the words left her lips. A doctor wouldn't be impressed by someone she might see as a thief, even if the wood had been discarded.

"Not an Ikea fan then? I thought it was compulsory to kit out all students' digs with flat pack furniture."

Ash registered the subtle acknowledgement to her age and the teasing out of her education. Was age the reason Evie had blown hot and cold last week? "I'm not a student. I'm a fully-fledged member of the UK work force now."

"But you *were* a student."

Ash tugged at Java's chew, averting her eyes from the intensity of Evie's gaze for a moment. Ash saw all kinds of possibilities there, and the realisation was both disconcerting and intriguing. Could it be that Evie was part of her soul group, and she'd been destined to find her? She resisted smiling outwardly at the romantic notion, sure that Evie would find her ridiculous. "You sound sure of that. What are you basing your assumption on, Sherlock?"

"The way you speak, for starters," Evie said. "Plus, everyone's at university now. It delays the path to adulting quite nicely."

Evie winked, making Ash's heart skip. She shrugged. "Fine. You're right. I finished in June."

"Was your degree in carpentry or did your dad teach you how to make things?"

The question caught Ash off guard, and she looked away. They weren't even on a date, and it was already getting too personal. "I don't have a dad."

Evie's expression changed, softened from flirty to concern.

"I'm sorry." Evie held up her hands. "I didn't mean to upset you."

Christ, she must've blurted that out with more bluntness than she'd thought. *Are there tears in my eyes?* Ash blinked them away, shrugged, and shook her head. "It's okay. It happens." She sighed at the glibness of her response. What happens? Shit happens? Parents tossing their new-born baby away like rubbish happens? People asking personal questions happens? Evie nodded and gave her a small smile. Ash didn't want Evie's sympathy; she hadn't told her for that reason, though she wasn't quite sure why she'd told her at all instead of just telling her what her degree *was* in.

Kirby jumped back against the fence with an orange ball in his mouth and growled through it. Java whined and then barked back. Evie ruffled Kirby's mane and gently pushed him back. The dog's impeccable timing saved Ash from further accidental disclosures.

"I think that's Kirby expressing his boredom," Evie said.

She smiled and Ash again saw something in Evie's eyes that went beyond passing interest. That's what Ash wanted to see, anyway. She could be misinterpreting Evie's tender bedside manner. "Looks that way." Ash tapped her watch. "He knows you're on a schedule and doesn't want to miss his exercise time."

Evie looked like she wanted to say something, but the moment was overwritten with another growl from Kirby.

"Drop the ball."

Kirby did as Evie requested, and she scooped it up with the launching stick thing she picked up.

"Maybe you could train Java for me?" Ash asked, keen to move back into safer, less personal territory.

"I'm no expert. And I think you're doing fine." Evie turned and began to walk out of Kirby's run.

Ash smiled, unsure whether Evie had been complimenting her or knocking her back. She wouldn't know unless she came out and asked Evie outright, would she? Ash was no good at this cat and mouse game.

By the time she'd taken a deep breath and decided to ask Evie on a date, Evie was already locking up Kirby's gate from the other side, and the opportunity had passed. Ash swivelled around to Java and chuckled his chops. "I bet you'll be a lot smoother with the ladies."

He put his paws on her shoulders and licked her nose.

"You think I should try *that* approach?" She shook her head. "I get the feeling she's going to need a more sophisticated style, little guy." Ash looked along the kennel runs to see Evie and Kirby

at the field, and her body flushed with warmth despite the relative cold of the afternoon. There'd been *something*. Something else unexpected. When she'd first met Evie, the physical attraction had been instant. But today, there had been more. There had been something she'd failed to see last week, but this week it was as if there was a Ready Brek glow around Evie to make sure Ash *saw* her, *really* saw her. She took it as a sign that she had to ask Evie out, regardless of the potential rejection. Ash had that same pull in Spain and it led her to Java. Was this the same force? Or had she unknowingly become so desperate for an intimate connection that she was over-romanticising their meeting? After a lifetime of not belonging, had Ash's latent need to belong finally surfaced? There was only one way to find out.

Chapter Twelve

Evie returned Kirby to his indoor kennel area and locked it safely behind him. She smiled at the noises of Ash and Java playing, but she couldn't get past the hurt in Ash's eyes when she'd responded to Evie's clumsy question about her carpentry skills. And she couldn't dismiss her sudden desire to want to know the story behind her pain. Not in a therapeutic way, though the early childhood trauma still clearly distressed Ash, but from a personal interest. Pain had a way of maturing someone beyond their years, and Ash's vulnerability had called to Evie in a way she was unfamiliar with.

Evie wanted to know more, and not only about Ash's pain, but about Ash in general. What *had* she studied at university? What was the story behind bringing Java into the country? How had she learned to make things from wood? What had happened in her childhood that she'd ended up without a dad?

Ash had seemed so cocky when they'd first met a week ago—and she probably still was—but there was definitely more there. More to be explored. More that Evie found herself drawn to. She had no intention of getting intimately involved with Ash but getting to know her couldn't hurt. And it would help Evie get back on the dating scene, wouldn't it? No doubt, Ash wouldn't be looking for anything serious and maybe she'd turn out to be good friend material. Evie could certainly do with more of those. Harriet was a good friend, but she was hardly ever around.

Evie hung Kirby's lead and was about to head for her next pooch when Ash poked her head through into Java's indoor area.

"Hey."

Evie smiled. "Hi again." She laughed when Java shoved his head between Ash's arms and bashed his head under Ash's chin. "That looked like it hurt."

Ash crawled through and stood, rubbing the affected area. "His head is like a rock."

Java jumped up at Ash, clawing at her jeans. She pulled a rawhide stick from her pocket and gave it to him. He settled in his bed, chew positioned firmly between his paws, and chowed down.

"He's got a big appetite for a little dog."

"He's a little guy, but he's got a mighty attitude. And I don't know anything about his lineage, so he might turn out to be bigger than Kirby."

She saw something fleetingly cross Ash's eyes but didn't pursue it. Evie didn't want to upset her again. "His paws are quite big. That's usually a good indication of how large a puppy will turn out to be." Evie nodded toward a content-looking Java. "He's got a broad chest too, a little like a Staffy."

"I thought he might have some Staffy in him too, especially with his brindle coat," Ash said. "But then, he's got a long body and has pretty short legs too, sort of like a dachshund."

Evie smiled. "I noticed his legs; they're like Victorian bath tub legs when he's stood to attention, pointing in opposite ways."

Ash laughed. "That's a great way of describing them. I'm stealing that." She moved a little closer to the gate before she ran her hand through her hair. "Listen, would you consider going on a date with me…or, you know, a get together where we talk about dogs' legs and their fur all night…"

Evie's heart pounded against her chest as Ash's question hung in the air. "I'd like that."

Ash sighed, and the relief on her expression was clear, which surprised Evie. She hadn't thought of Ash as lacking confidence or self-belief, but she was obviously prepared for, and possibly even expecting, a no.

"Really?"

"Really. Would you rather I declined?" Evie couldn't resist the opportunity to tease. There was something particularly sexy about a butch on the back foot, probably because it was so unusual.

"No. God, no. I…I wasn't sure what you'd say." Ash shifted from left foot to right and back again and glanced at Java.

"Well, I've said yes, so when are you thinking?"

"Tonight?"

Evie shook her head. "Sorry, I can't do tonight." She wouldn't allow this new focus on her personal life to push her time with Izad aside. Friday nights were always Disney movie night with popcorn and ice cream, though she could never understand why Izad always chose vanilla when they were so many other flavours to choose from. His eclectic taste in fashion definitely did not extend to his taste buds.

"Oh…how about Saturday?"

Evie smiled and nodded, wanting to quickly reassure Ash that she did want to meet up with her and hadn't said yes with no intention of ever making plans. She so disliked when people did that. She found it disingenuous and would never do it herself. "I can do that." Evie gestured toward Bobby's kennel. "I have to get on." She pulled a card from the back pocket of her jeans and handed it to Ash through Java's gate. "Text me a place? I don't know the city scene that well anymore."

Evie mentally kicked herself for showing her age as Ash took her card, but then forgave herself; she didn't want to hide it. There'd be no point, particularly since Evie wanted to be friends with Ash. And being upfront about being in her thirties would probably put Ash off from pursuing anything beyond an initial date too. This date would get Evie back onto the scene *and* gain her a new friend to explore it with. It seemed like a perfect fit.

Ash examined the card and tapped her finger on Evie's name. "What kind of doctor are you, by the way?"

She shook her head. "We've got to have something other than dogs to talk about on our date. Ask me again tomorrow night." Evie gave Ash a parting smile, thinking that her profession would be another reason for Ash to stay away from an intimate relationship. Evie had discovered that people often found it hard to be with any kind of psychiatrist or therapist for fear of every move and emotion being overanalysed.

***

Evie closed the door softly behind her, not wanting to disturb Dawn and Izad from his homework. They were seated at the dining table by the bay window, and Izad looked studious from his side profile, his brow creased in obvious concentration and not a small amount of consternation. He looked up when her foot fell on the creaky floorboard by the entrance to the front room, leapt out of his chair, and ran over to her.

"Momma!"

He threw his arms around her waist and hugged her tightly. Evie wrapped her arms around his shoulders and pulled him near. She kissed his head and closed her eyes, breathing him in. She never got tired of his exuberant greeting and hoped it would always be this way, though she suspected it would not. She thought he might have grown out of it when he began secondary school, but so far, his affection hadn't lessened, and he seemed more than happy to greet her the same way whether he was at home or at school with his friends. As of yet, he'd affected no cool pretence that meant he didn't hug his mum or tell her he loved her. And he still claimed she was his best friend. What was that saying? A son is a son until he gets a wife. A daughter is a daughter all her life. If that turned out to be true—wife, husband, or other—Evie had plans to enjoy his unfiltered love while ever he was prepared to show it.

"Hey, little guy. How are you?" Evie looked up and smiled at Dawn, who smiled back.

"I'm okay." Izad loosed himself from Evie and stepped back. "But I'm bored of factors and primes."

"Is your homework nearly done?"

He nodded.

"Yes, Evie," Dawn said. "He might not like those numbers, but he's exceptional at them."

"Super." Evie put her hands on Izad's shoulders. "How about you finish up your homework then come and help me in the kitchen with dinner?"

"What are you making?"

Evie smiled. "Will that make a difference on whether or not you come and help me?"

He nodded. "Yes, it will. You might be making something simple where you don't need my help, but you'd like my company." Izad grinned to show he was joking and walked back to the dining table. "I'll be with you soon, Momma."

"Don't rush it," Evie said as he returned to his seat. He looked over at her and shook his head as if she'd accused him of some unthinkable action.

"I know, Momma. I don't rush homework so I don't make mistakes."

"Good boy." She half turned to head toward the kitchen, then turned back. "Would you like to stay for dinner, Dawn?"

Dawn shook her head. "Thanks, Evie, but we had toasties when we got back, and my boyfriend's taking me out to a restaurant later."

"Sounds lovely." Evie dropped her work bag on the end of the stairs and walked down to her kitchen, relieved that Dawn had other plans. Evie had been looking forward to a solo night with Izad but felt obliged to invite Dawn. Izad liked her though, so it wouldn't have been too much of an imposition if she had accepted Evie's invitation.

She poured herself a small red wine and began pulling

ingredients from the fridge. She lined them up on the kitchen island and placed various sizes of pots behind each of them for when she'd chopped them up. She took the spring onions, wiped each one with a wet piece of kitchen roll, and quickly chopped them. She'd deliberately chosen a meal she could prepare quickly so she and Izad could be eating within half an hour of her getting home. Then they could relax and tuck into some ice cream with the new Blu-ray she'd bought for Izad as a surprise.

When she topped and tailed the garlic, Ash popped into Evie's head. Would her breath still stink of garlic tomorrow night for their date? She laughed. She was getting ahead of herself. A date was one thing, but why was she thinking of kissing Ash when she had no real intention of going any further? This would be one of those dates where both she and Ash would quickly realise they were better off as friends? One kiss wouldn't hurt though, would it? Ash had such a lovely mouth. It'd be a shame not to find out if her lips were as soft as they looked. Perhaps she could do that *before* she told her that she was a psychiatrist *and* a mother to totally scare Ash off from thinking anything serious could develop between them.

She had to admit to a certain excitement about Saturday night. Her usual Saturday routine after Tal picked Izad up for his drama club entailed a short trip to the gym for a yoga session or a swim, a takeout coffee from Costa, and an afternoon of paperwork. The evenings often saw her order a Thai takeout, thus negating the limited benefits of her workout, and an evening of binge-watching streamed TV series while munching on salted popcorn. Her current vice was *Elementary*, though she wished that they'd had the balls to make Sherlock a woman instead of Watson. Kristen Stewart perhaps, provided she kept her hair short. It would've been a great part for Sharon Stone two decades ago. She had the Holmes-like intelligence *and* the looks. She'd never seen Lucy Liu with short hair. Evie could possibly get on board with that casting.

The smell of fresh garlic rose to meet her nostrils, and she realised she'd digressed from her original thoughts of Saturday night. She hoped she hadn't completely lost her rhythm. She used to love dancing when she went clubbing at university and the occasional nights out once she'd had Izad. Unless Ash was one of those "too cool to dance" types she'd been bemused by the last time she and Harriet had gone out to a club. The DJ had played some awesome tunes, but no one under thirty moved, not even a toe tap. All the girls with their long hair under reversed baseball caps had shocked her too. Where had all the butches gone?

Well, Ash certainly slotted rather nicely to that category, so at least they weren't extinct. She hoped that Ash would give her the full tour of the city scene so she could explore them with Sarah or Harriet for more suitable prospects. Ash was sexy and intriguing, there was no doubt, and she was clearly an intelligent young woman. And if she was seven or eight years older, Evie's outlook on tomorrow night's possibilities would be entirely different.

But Ash had said she'd finished uni last year. Unless she'd had a gap year and/or studied for a Masters after an undergrad degree, she was twenty-one. *Crikey.* Twenty-one: the age Evie had been when she fell pregnant with Izad.

Evie took a long swallow of her wine. She'd set boundaries tomorrow, and they would become firm friends. Ash would be a good wingwoman and help get Evie set up with someone more suitable, someone her age. The worst that could happen would be a drunken fumble. And that wouldn't be so bad. It was flattering that Ash found her attractive, and it made her feel good, wanted. She'd enjoy it while it lasted…which would be one night. Wouldn't it?

Chapter Thirteen

I thought you'd decided you weren't going out on pre-match nights anymore?"

"We don't have a game tomorrow, dipstick." Ash shook her head.

"Ah, that's good news for both of us then," Kirsty said.

"And anyway, I didn't have much choice." Ash pushed past Kirsty and grabbed her eau de toilette from her bedside table. She sprayed her neck, pulled up her shirt and sprayed her stomach, then added a couple of dashes to her wrists.

Kirsty waved her hand in front of her nose. "Jesus, do you want to bed her or knock her out?"

Ash snapped her head up. "Too much?"

Kirsty shook her head. "Nah, mate. I was joking." She wafted her hand through the air. "You smell divine."

Ash laughed at Kirsty's attempt at the Queen's English. "Fuck off."

Kirsty put her hand to her chest as if she were mightily offended. "What do you mean, you didn't have a choice? I thought you asked her out?"

"I did." Ash opened the top drawer of her desk and pulled out her Armani watch, a graduation present from Nat and Rich, her final foster parents. "But she couldn't do Friday, and I couldn't wait until next week in case she changed her mind."

Kirsty flopped onto Ash's armchair and put her drink on the table beside it. "Is she *that* flaky?"

Ash wrinkled her nose. "No, not at all. Well…I don't know. The first time we met, she blew hot and cold. I think it might be an age thing. I think she might be worried I'm too young for her."

"But you like the cougars?" Kirsty picked up her mug of coffee and sipped it.

Ash grinned. "Always have. I thought you knew that." She and Kirsty had spent many a night at university on the scene, and Ash had always gravitated toward the more mature ladies. Women her own age had no idea about anything. And Ash wanted to learn *everything*. "They're so much better in bed than younger women. Less fumbling. And they tell you what they want; they don't expect you to figure it out."

Kirsty tilted her head and looked unconvinced. "Isn't working it out part of the fun?"

Ash shrugged. She sat on the edge of her bed, adjusted the time on her watch, and strapped it on. "Why waste the time? She could be well on her way to a fourth orgasm by the time you've figured out how she likes it." Ash pulled on her boots and zipped the sides. "No, that's not for me. I like a woman who knows what she wants and how to get it."

"So how old is she?"

"I don't know."

"Where does she live?"

"I don't know."

"What does she do for a job?"

"I don't—"

"Jesus, Ash. What *do* you know? She could be a serial killer escaped from prison for all you know."

Ash grinned again. "You should see her. If she *is* a serial killer, that would be one hell of a way to die." She stood and tucked her shirt into the front of her jeans. "Anyway, you interrupted me. I don't know exactly what she does for a living, but I do know that she's a doctor at Horston."

"The prison?"

"The hospital prison, yeah." Ash recalled the distinction Evie was at pains to make.

"Kinky. Now I'm starting to see the attraction."

Ash picked up her discarded socks from the bed and threw them at Kirsty's head. "I'll ask her if she's got any prison guard friends for you."

Kirsty batted the stinky socks away. "Prat. They nearly landed in my coffee."

"They might've made it taste better." Try as she might, Ash couldn't get the appeal of coffee. She used to drink the instant stuff all the time in one of her foster homes, but now it tasted like the bad times and desperation of her childhood. The smell of it used to twist her stomach in knots, but she'd learned to control that particular Pavlovian response. Studying psychology had its own personal benefits soAsh hadn't yet succumbed to the lure of a therapist to deal with her childhood issues.

"If you think age is an issue, how old does she think you are?"

"If she's done the basic maths, she probably thinks I'm twenty-one. Twenty-two at most." Ash went to her drawer of belts and chose one in black. "But she doesn't know that I didn't start uni until I was nineteen or that I swapped degrees partway through and had to start again." She threaded the leather through her jean loops and pulled open her buckle drawer. She picked up the Alton Towers Oblivion ride buckle with an orange arrow pointing to her crotch. It wasn't quite the subtle, mature approach she intended to pitch at. She showed it to Kirsty, who laughed and shook her head. Ash tossed it back in the drawer and chose the buckle with a monochrome bird in flight instead.

Kirsty shifted in the armchair and draped her legs over the edge, making herself comfortable. "Why do you think she even agreed to a date if she's got a problem with how young a boi-toy you are?"

Ash shrugged. "Curiosity? Boredom? I don't know. I'm just glad she did."

Kirsty's brow furrowed. "You seem serious about this one, but you've hardly spoken to her. You'd been with the last one for two months and didn't shed a tear when you broke up…what's the big deal with the doc?"

Ash fixed the buckle on her belt while she considered Kirsty's question. Soul group. Fate. Destiny. All of which applied to Ash's thinking. None of which she'd share with her friend. "I don't know. A feeling." She ran her hand through her hair. "Something different, you know? Haven't you ever felt an immediate spark with anyone?"

Kirsty laughed and nodded. "Every. Single. Time. With every single girl. Anyone I see more than twice, I think it could be forever."

Ash smiled. She hadn't seen what forever could look like yet. She unscrewed the lid on her hair wax, worked some onto her fingers and through her hair. Surf hair or preppy? Which one would Evie prefer? Ash stopped for a moment. No. She was going to be herself, not who she thought Evie might like. There'd be little point in trying to be something and someone she wasn't. Inevitably, Evie would end up disappointed…just like all those early foster parents who wanted a quiet little girl to dress up in frilly pink dresses.

"Aren't you going out tonight?"

Kirsty grinned. "Steph's coming over. I have an evening of candles and Netflix planned."

Ash looked at the ceiling, trying to recall if she'd met Steph. "Which one is that?"

"The one *you* passed over last week before you went home for a quiet night on your own."

"You're welcome." With her first visits to see Java, her new job, *and* distant thoughts of Evie, Ash had been way too pre-occupied last week to even consider the girl who'd shown interest in both her and Kirsty. "Have you been talking all week?"

Kirsty nodded. "Almost all day, every day. I've not talked to anyone else this week."

"Wow. Must be serious."

"Could be forever." Kirsty half laughed. "She's cool. I like her a lot."

Ash opened the wooden box containing her leather straps and bracelets and chose a black one to go with her watch and belt. "You must do, to invite her home so soon."

"So, you're not going to get dumped and be home early, are you?"

Ash walked over to Kirsty and gave her the bracelet after unsuccessfully trying to get it on herself. "Why? Are you planning on having sex in the lounge?"

"I'm hoping to at least start there…" Kirsty fixed Ash's bracelet and pushed her hand away.

"I suppose I should be grateful the sofa's leather so you can clean up after you've finished." Ash checked her final look in the full-length mirror on the back of her door. "What do you think?"

"You're someone's wet dream. I don't know whose, but someone out there likes that kind of thing." Kirsty waved her hand up and down in Ash's direction.

Ash picked up her discarded tank top, balled it, and threw it at Kirsty's head. "You're a bad friend."

Kirsty caught it and tossed it on the floor. "I'm a great friend, and you will be too if you don't come home until at least two a.m."

Ash raised her eyebrows. "You can only last until two? No stamina. Not surprising you're still single."

"Ha fucking ha."

Ash opened her wardrobe, pulled out her beat-up black leather jacket, and slipped it on.

"You're going full butch with the plaid lining, eh?"

Ash shrugged and gestured to her shirt. "At least I've gone with a block colour." She picked up her phone and checked it for any messages, half-expecting Evie to get cold feet and cancel. Relieved there were no flashing lights or envelopes in the top corner of her screen, she slipped her debit card into the back of its case and put it in her jacket pocket. She took some cash from her wallet, folded each note individually, and put them in the back pocket of her jeans.

"How *old* is she that you think you need to carry cash?"

"*I* like carrying cash. It's too easy to spend on a card and not realise how much you've blown." Ash patted the money in her pocket. "Just because I've got a job doesn't mean that I'm flush." In truth, she was far from comfortable. She'd had to sell almost everything she had of value in the months after university and before landing her position at the youth club. Her semi-acoustic guitar and her lightweight mountain bike had all been sacrificed for food money. She'd have been in a far worse position however, if it weren't for the fact that Kirsty's rich parents had purchased her a house to celebrate her first-class degree *and* she'd landed a graduate position with Fosters, one of the top architecture firms in the UK. Kirsty insisted on Ash not paying rent until she got a job. After that, Kirsty checked what the national average percentage of wages Brits spent on rent, and said that Ash could pay a fifth of her monthly salary but only after a three-month grace period of still paying nothing. Ash had joked that Kirsty was a bad friend when really, she was the best friend Ash had ever had or could ever ask for. And not only because of her generosity with money either. Her heart was huge, though she didn't let too many people know that, and Ash was grateful for her friendship.

Ash ran her hand across the back of her head, aware that she'd drifted into soppy thoughts she shouldn't share with Kirsty because overt shows of affection made her desperately uncomfortable. Which was why Ash sometimes did it just to mess with her. "You're the best, you know that, right?"

Kirsty sighed and shook her head, before pushing up from the armchair and heading for Ash's door. "You had to ruin it and be all sentimental, didn't you?"

Ash moved toward her. "Come here. Let me give you a hug."

Kirsty pushed her off. "Get away from me, you sap." She opened the door and paused. "Have a great night, and remember, don't come home before two." She closed the door behind her.

Kirsty's swift exit made Ash laugh. She was fully mindful that she'd deliberately cultivated a soft centre to rail against the cold and unfeeling person she *should* be after a childhood lacking in love and affection. Nat and Rich had changed all that and helped her to manage her own emotional transformation, something the psychology books said was impossible. It was something Ash had thought impossible too, but they did everything they could to show her love, to value herself, and to know her own worth. They'd been the greatest gifts Ash had ever received, better than any number of presents that she never got under countless Christmas trees in numerous foster homes. Then at university, she and Kirsty bumped into each other, literally, in a queue to join the LGBTQ student group, and Ash began to believe that she was finally starting to find the right people to journey with, and her foster parents hadn't been a blip on her otherwise shit-littered path of life.

And then there was Evie. Ash hadn't been looking to find forever, nor had she been burying herself in transient trysts. Now she laughed at herself. Maybe she was getting too syrupy sweet. Evie seemed like an amazing woman, and Ash wanted to get to know her. Tonight would be a good start. What came after that, Ash was happy to let destiny decide.

Chapter Fourteen

I'm sure you can't have been stood up, so can I buy you a drink while you wait for whoever is stupid enough to be late?"

As pick-up lines went, it wasn't the worst Evie had heard. She tapped the side of her wine glass, its contents as yet untouched. "I already have a drink, but thank you for the offer." She glanced at her watch. *8:55 p.m.* "And not late yet." She was careful to avoid the inclusion of Ash's pronoun, and her instinct to do so unsettled her. She wasn't one to hide her sexuality, but it seemed strange meeting in what appeared to be a regular bar in the middle of the city, and she didn't want to invite any trouble on her first night out in a while.

"Well, could I sit here until your date does show?"

She took a second to appraise him. Smart shoes, designer jeans, big name shirt, and a suit jacket. He certainly wasn't a thug, and his presentation suggested restraint and style. She supposed she could stand for him to chat with her while she waited for Ash. "Sure."

He hitched up onto the bar stool, drawing Evie's attention to his lack of height. When he was sat, he appeared to be about as tall as she was, perhaps a smidge taller if he straightened up a little. He ordered a fancy whisky the bartender had to retrieve from the top shelf and didn't take the change from a twenty-pound note.

"Is this a first date?"

He sipped at the fine-looking amber liquid that slid down the side of the glass.

Evie nodded. "Yes. I'm out of practice though. I haven't dated much since my son was born." The child. Usually a perfect rebuff and reason for anyone looking for a no-strings evening to immediately retreat.

"How old is he?"

Evie raised her eyebrows, vaguely impressed that he hadn't fallen off his stool in his hurry to move onto the next possible target. "Twelve."

He nodded as if he knew all about children. "You've been blessed so far. Wait until he hits his teenage years." He pointed to his glass. "That's when you find yourself turning to more of this stuff."

Evie laughed. "You sound like you're speaking from experience. Do you have children?" Evie looked beyond him to the front door and glanced again at her watch. *8:59 p.m. Am I going to get stood up on my first date in a decade?*

"Oh, yeah. I've got three. And they're all teenagers. I weep for the days when they couldn't speak and when they believed I was their hero."

A faint whisper of sadness passed across his eyes, and Evie's therapist-radar kicked in. Probably cheated on the wife in a moment of whisky-fuelled weakness, and his kids now hated him. A quick glance at his left hand showed he was still wearing his wedding band though, so he hadn't given up or his wife was thinking about giving him a second chance, and he wasn't hiding the fact that he wasn't actually single. "Do you still love your wife?"

He moved his right hand to his left and twisted his wedding ring around his finger several times before answering. He smiled, but it didn't hold much affection. "I do."

"But you made a bad decision one night?"

"Hey, Evie. Sorry to have kept you waiting."

Evie looked up from the man to see a vision of sexy butchness in front of her, dwarfing both of them. She gulped. An actual gulp. Rough, funky hair, skinny jeans, tailored shirt, big belt buckle, and leather jacket. If Evie were an artist, she couldn't have drawn a better wet dream of a woman.

She checked her watch to see it was exactly nine p.m. Ash wasn't late at all. She was perfectly on time, looking…well, looking perfect.

The man looked up too and his smile broadened. He slipped off his stool and gestured for Ash to take it. "*You* are a lucky woman," he said and raised his glass toward Ash.

Ash stepped aside to let him out. "I know it."

She said it with such conviction that it took Evie by surprise. She reached out and touched the man's arm. "Don't give up. There are too many hearts at stake for you to go absentee."

The man smiled. He finished his drink and put his glass on the bar. "I'm going home right now." He nodded slowly. "Thank you. Have a good night."

Ash rested against the seat he vacated, and Evie watched over her shoulder to see if he did head home. Sure enough, he headed out the door. She turned her attention back to the vision barely twelve inches away and hitched her feet up on the bar stool. This was going to be a fun night.

"Do you know him?" Ash asked after she'd ordered a drink. "Surely you didn't think I wouldn't show and you brought someone with you to keep you company in case?"

Evie wrinkled her nose and shook her head. "Of course not. He asked if he could sit and talk while I waited for my date." *My extremely hot date.*

"Had you been here long?"

Ash took a long drink of her bottled beer. What would those lips feel like wrapped around her breasts? She pushed away the base thought and tried to concentrate on Ash's words instead of her body. She was more than just a sex object. She was going to be a good friend. That was the plan, wasn't it? "Just a few minutes."

"I'm sorry. I should've been here before you arrived." She glanced away. "Forgive me?"

Evie furrowed her brow, thinking Ash was joking, before she quickly realised she was being completely serious. It had been a while since Evie had been around a butch woman. It had been a long time since she'd been thought of and cared for in that distinctly old-fashioned and charmingly chivalrous manner.

She'd missed it.

"I forgive you, as long as it doesn't happen again." The words were out before Evie could stop them. They were a promise that this could happen again, and the flash across Ash's eyes showed she recognised that. And she looked excited about it too. The night was young. Plenty of time for Ash to discover that dating someone a decade older wasn't as much fun as she thought it was.

Unless, of course, it was a lot of fun. Why couldn't it be? Why *had* Evie got it into her head that ten years was too great a distance between two lovers? Ah, it was the easy go-to excuse. Far simpler to blame it on age than her job or her son. Or perhaps it was because she didn't want to be one of those people who tried to hold onto their youth by dating someone far younger, like some dirty old man. But Evie was thirty-three, not sixty-three. She resolved to stop thinking about it so hard and let the date with Ash run its course. She had to think about a prospective partner's suitability for Izad as much as for her, for the next six years anyway, and in all likelihood, Ash wouldn't fit. *Stop overthinking.*

Ash waved her hand in front of Evie's face. "It's not a good sign if I'm boring you already."

"Sorry, I—"

"Was miles away." Ash nodded. "Yep, you do that a lot. Is it me or do you have a Walter Mitty life going on in your head?"

Evie laughed at the 1940s literary mention though she suspected Ash's frame of reference might come from the Hollywood movie. "Are you calling me meek and useless? That's not how a first date turns into second date, Ash. A young buck like you can't be out of practice."

Ash's cheeks flushed adorably. She shook her head and held up her hands, clearly mortified at Evie's suggestion.

"Oh my God, no. No, of course not. It was the daydreaming…" She ran her hand across the back of her head and continued to shake her head. "I didn't mean to… Oh, fuck."

Evie raised her eyebrows and laughed again. Ash was endearingly nervous, something she certainly hadn't seemed when they first met, and it was tremendous fun teasing her. "I have a tendency to overthink everything, and when I'm doing that, I disappear into my head and everything around me goes silent and soft, like a photograph…and apparently that looks like I'm daydreaming." Evie surprised herself with her honesty, but Ash still looked like a rabbit caught in headlights. Evie reached out and put her hand on Ash's legs. "I'm messing with you. You haven't offended me at all."

Ash looked down at Evie's hand and seemed appeased…or distracted. Her thigh felt solid, and Evie left her hand there.

"Football."

Evie glanced up at the large TV screens dotted around the bar, but they featured music videos, not sport. "Rachel Daly."

Ash looked confused. "What?"

"I thought we were playing word association." Evie smiled. "Rachel Daly is an English footballer who plays for the national team *and* in America."

Ash smiled and nodded. "She does. You like football?"

"I like *women's* football. I'm not interested in watching a bunch of men dash around a field falling over each other."

Ash's smile turned into a grin, and she sat up a little straighter on the bar stool. "Do you like to watch the game?"

"Yes. I watch the international games."

"Who's your favourite player?"

Evie dropped her head back and cast her eyes toward the ceiling, making a pretence of thinking about her answer when the name came to her instantly. "Can I only have one?"

Ash nodded, her eagerness obvious.

"Ashlyn Harris."

Ash laughed and shook her head. "A goalkeeper? No one chooses a goalkeeper. I have a feeling you're not choosing her because of her ability on the field."

Evie removed her hand from Ash's leg and pressed it against her heart. "Why ever would I choose her if not for her playing prowess?"

"Oh, I don't know. Something to do with how hot she is, maybe?"

Evie pressed her lips together and raised her eyebrows. "You think she's hot?"

Ash looked quizzical, as if Evie were asking a blind man if he'd like the gift of vision.

"Absolutely."

Given that the footballer was approaching her mid-thirties, it looked like Ash had a thing for older women in general. "I prefer her with short hair though."

Ash grinned. "Of course you do."

"Meaning?"

"Meaning maybe you have a type…meaning, I *hope* you have a type."

Ash twisted her fingers through her hair and smiled. She managed to convey knowing, cocky, and wistful all at once in that smile. Evie thought about twisting her own fingers through Ash's hair. She swallowed hard. "How did we get onto football?"

"You seemed impressed with my thigh when you put your hand on it. I was saying they're hard because I play football. Now I wish I was a goalkeeper."

Evie reached for her drink and took a sip, needing the cool white liquid to drop her temperature some. "What position do you play?"

"Left wing."

"So, you're left handed?" Evie recalled a ridiculous article she'd read years ago about left-handed people having better sex because their pleasure came from the right side of the brain. More sensual thinking apparently equalled more pleasure. She'd never slept with a leftie before. Were they able to *give* better sex too?

Ash narrowed her eyes. "Yeah…why? You're not some

religious nut that thinks being left-handed is related to the devil and black magic, are you?"

"I'm not, actually, but that's a pretty damning judgement of religion, right there."

Ash smacked the heel of her hand against her forehead. "Am I two for two on offending you? Are you religious, and I've wronged you again?"

Evie shook her head and laughed. "Not at all. Well, I'm not *not* religious, but no, you haven't 'wronged' me. You surprised me, that's all."

Ash blew out a breath and stood up. "If it's okay with you, I'm going to leave, come back, and start again…if you'll let me?"

Evie caught hold of Ash's wrists and pulled her back down. "There's no need. You're doing fine." As she'd moved Ash, she came close enough to feel Ash's warm breath and smell a woody cinnamon scent she couldn't place but liked a lot. The combination of both went directly to her sexual sensibilities, and she pulsed in appreciation. She looked up into Ash's eyes and sighed lightly when Ash licked her lips, as if readying them for a kiss. Evie half closed her eyes, and then remembered where they were.

With the strongest show of self-control she'd perhaps ever managed, Evie pulled back from the magnetic draw of Ash's mouth. "Not here." She caught two men smiling at them in her peripheral vision. They weren't being lairy or even leering, but she didn't want to be anyone's wank-bank fodder.

She heard Ash's breath catch and saw the disappointment clear in her eyes.

"But somewhere?" Ash whispered and slipped her hand through Evie's hair and around the back of her neck.

The sensation travelled south faster than she could have anticipated. Ash's touch jolted through her like lightning. Had it been so long, or did Ash simply have a magical touch? "Yes," Evie whispered. *God, yes.*

Chapter Fifteen

A sh burst out of the pub doors and gulped the cool night air into her lungs. Evie made her so hot, she might spontaneously combust on the spot. She could still feel Evie's hand on her leg as if she'd seared through Ash's jeans and branded her. She held the door open for Evie to sashay through, and Evie slipped her arm into the nook Ash had offered her. She pulled Evie in tight to her side and immediately liked the way she fit, so close.

"Where are we going?"

Down the nearest alleyway. Ash held back the response and grinned. "Do you like to dance?" She led the way, taking a short cut down a side street. When Evie nodded, Ash continued, "We've got a great new club. It only opened two weeks ago. Fantastic mix of old school classics and thumping new tunes. You'll love it." *Fuck.* Had she managed to offend Evie again? She certainly seemed to be doing a bang-up job of trying to. Evie had shown she was interested, and the age thing Ash had thought was an issue hadn't been mentioned at all until now. Ash kept her eyes fixed on the pavement ahead, not wanting to acknowledge yet another foot-in-her-mouth incident. She was usually so relaxed when she was out. What was it about Evie that made her so nervy?

Ash loved the strength and quiet confidence that came from older women, from their lived experience, their simple knowing. Obviously, not *all* older women had that. She wasn't naïve enough to think every woman in their mid to late thirties had the mystery of life figured out and had reached Buddha-like calm. But she was undeniably attracted to the ones who did fit that criteria. And Evie ticked every box so far.

And damn, she'd wanted that kiss right there and then. She couldn't believe she'd managed to pull herself away but then she always liked to be on the receiving end of that control and confidence. It wasn't the same for younger women or women Ash's age. She'd happily take control there, but here, in these situations, she submitted gladly and willingly to anything a woman like Evie might desire.

"The last time I went to a dance club, no one was dancing."

Evie's response broke into Ash's wandering thoughts, and she cursed herself for disappearing, however briefly. She wanted to savour every moment of this date and having internal conversations with herself didn't figure into giving Evie all the attention she deserved. "Some places are like that, as if it's uncool to have fun and sweat through your make-up." Ash gestured toward her face. "I don't tend to have that problem. I found too much foundation was making my skin blotchy so I stopped using it altogether."

Evie snapped her head toward Ash. "What?"

Ash shook her head and laughed. "Just checking if you were listening. I've never worn make-up in my life. Unless you're talking about face paint, but that's a different story. I can do a super cute butterfly, if, you know, you're ever going to a butterfly-themed party."

"Actually," Evie said and squeezed Ash's arm, "that's useful to know. I go to animal-themed parties all the time."

"Really? Do you have a favourite go-to animal? Or do you have to be different at every party?"

"Secretly, my go-to animal is a killer whale, but it's difficult to do. All the Google pictures have kids with the whale on their cheeks. They don't actually *become* the whale, and it's important to me to fully inhabit the animal. And the size of the fins on the whale costume make it rather hard to drive or fit in a taxi. So, I have to settle for conventional animals like tigers and pandas…I don't know if a butterfly would suit me."

Ash stopped walking and pulled Evie close to her. She moved Evie's hair over her ear and cupped her face in both hands. "I think you have a face shaped perfectly for a butterfly masterpiece."

Evie looked at Ash, her desire clear, and pushed against her. "Perfect for a butterfly?"

Ash let out a shallow breath and leaned in so her lips brushed against Evie's. "Not just for a butterfly. Perfect for anything… You're perfect." Ash pulled back enough so she could focus on Evie's eyes. Even in the darkness of the dimly lit street, Ash's need reflected back at her. The blackness of Evie's pupils drew her in, tempting her to forego all pretence of dating decorum and sink straight into the strong sexual urge that surged through her and begged her to take Evie to bed.

Evie licked her lips and diverted Ash's attention. Her plum-coloured matte lipstick accentuated the seductive lines of her mouth, and Ash drew her fingers from Evie's cheek and dragged them lightly over Evie's lips. Evie closed her eyes briefly, her answering desire declared in the deep exhalation of breath that carried the warm scent of the wine Evie had consumed. Evie slid her hands inside Ash's jacket, and she raked her nails across Ash's back. Trails of fire remained though the night air did its best to cool her skin. Evie moved her hand lower, and Ash gasped when Evie unexpectedly squeezed her ass. Evie opened her mouth slightly and nibbled on Ash's fingers, her tongue sliding lightly over Ash's fingertips.

Ash swallowed hard and breathed deeply through her nose. Every cell in her body screamed for deeper contact, yearned for a more intimate connection. Her mind distantly called for her to rein in her impulses, but the din of her body's cry for pleasure echoed louder. Her impatience won out. "We don't…have to go dancing." There. She'd made her need known, and Evie could make the call.

Evie reached up, wrapped her hand around Ash's neck, and pulled her down so their lips finally met. Probing and gentle, Ash ran her tongue over Evie's lips and into her mouth. Evie sucked Ash's tongue into her mouth as their kiss deepened, became harder and more urgent. Ash tasted wine and want. She slipped her hand through Evie's hair, drew her fingers through its length until she reached the base of her spine. She rested her hand there though she was desperate to explore, craving to slip her hand beneath Evie's blouse, aching for skin-on-skin. The kiss engaged every synapse in her body to fire jolts of electricity across her nerves, declaring their absolute arousal.

"I can't take you home," Evie whispered against Ash's lips.

Nor could she take Evie to her place. Ash's hopes sank like a leaden anchor to the bottom of her sea of desire. Even if Kirsty hadn't been entertaining and hadn't expressly asked for Ash not to come home until two a.m., Ash couldn't take Evie home. She was a doctor, a sophisticated woman with class and style. Ash didn't want to sully that with their first encounter in a shared house. Ash imagined Egyptian bazillion count sheets and a super king-size bed, a duck down duvet, and soft pillows.

"And I can't take *you* home… I have a roommate." Ash's confession covered her in shame, both for not having her own place *and* for not being grateful to have her place with Kirsty. Without her, Ash would've been couch-surfing at her foster parents' house, and with their new baby, that was the last place she wanted to be. She'd been a burden to her real parents, and she'd long ago vowed never to be the same to anyone in the future.

Fuck. The realisation hit her that Evie's words didn't necessarily mean what she'd taken them to mean. *I can't take you home* could equally have meant *I won't take you home*, as in "You're moving too fast. Slow the fuck down," or "I don't sleep with someone on a first date." Or worse yet, "I won't *ever* take you home because my husband lives there."

"I'm sorry…" Ash struggled to find the words. The heat from the moment they'd shared dissipated into the unforgiving night air, forever lost. She'd messed everything up by letting her pussy rule her head, and Evie was already in the process of letting go. "I shouldn't have… Do you still want to go dancing?" *Please God, say yes. Tell me I haven't sabotaged something that could've been special.*

Evie shook her head and pulled back. *There she goes*. Ash closed her eyes, the soft burn of threatening tears pushing to escape.

"I don't want to go dancing now," Evie said. She stepped back, pulled out her phone, and began to tap away at the screen.

Ash thought of things to say, but none of them made their way out of her mouth. They seemed too trite, or too throwaway, or too intense. She couldn't rewind the night and start again. She'd blown her chance with this exceptional woman out of the water within twenty minutes of a first date. That had to be some sort of record. It was one she'd certainly never be proud of.

"There's an Uber on its way," Evie said without looking up from her phone and continuing to poke at it.

"That's the beauty of a big city, I suppose." Ash zipped her jacket, more from reaction to the sudden lack of heat between her and Evie than the evening's temperature. She wished she'd finished that beer. It may have gone some way to quieting the growing noise of disappointment in her mind.

Ash heard the quiet whirring of an electric engine as its bright headlights turned into the narrow street. Evie held up her hand, and the car came to a stop beside them. Defeat and failure settled in her heart with a sharp ache, but ever the gentlewoman, she opened the rear door for Evie to get in. Ash saw the flash of Evie's leg revealed in the thigh-high split in her skirt, and other parts of her ached for the clumsy loss. She closed the door gently and stepped back, waiting to watch the taxi drive away with the sexiest woman Ash had *ever* had the pleasure in kissing. She looked up at the clear, midnight blue sky that twinkled with a thousand bright stars. If it had been a movie, the heavens would've opened and she'd already be soaked to the skin, mourning her loss with the tears of clouds.

The whir of the car's window pulled her attention back to Evie. Ash didn't feel she deserved even a polite good-bye, but as she was about to lean in, Evie looked out, her brow furrowed and a puzzled look on her face.

"The taxi driver might not be in a hurry, but I am," Evie said.

Ash was sure she now sported a puzzled look. She shrugged. "What do you mean?"

Evie let out a short laugh and shook her head. "I mean, why aren't you in the car already?"

Ash smiled at the offer. Evie truly was a lady. "That's okay. I'll head back to the bar." *To be a cliché and drown my sorrows.*

Evie narrowed her eyes, then laughed longer this time. "I think you misunderstand my intentions, handsome. I called the car to take us *both* to a hotel."

Ash tilted her head. "Wha—"

"Get in the car. Now."

Evie's window retracted, and the reality of the fantasy clapped Ash on the forehead. "Ohh." Ash jogged around to the other side of the car before Evie changed her mind. She jumped in, buckled up, and was about to speak when Evie grabbed the collar of Ash's jacket and pulled her hard into another kiss. All the tension that had knotted itself into her muscles when she thought Evie was blowing her off, softened and she became the human equivalent of marshmallow in Evie's hands. She groaned into Evie's mouth, vaguely aware of the car pulling away, and responded with gusto as her relief settled in that the night *wasn't* over, *and* it was fast forwarding to a hotel. Ash's wish that their first night together be cushioned in elegant luxury might be about to come true after all.

Evie wrapped her hand around the back of Ash's neck again, and Ash sighed deeply into the overwhelming feeling of being claimed. Evie's other hand pushed against Ash's chest and squeezed her breast. This was a lover who knew exactly what she wanted and how to get it, and Ash's body thrilled in Evie's expertise.

Evie broke away. She somehow managed to pull a handful of hair at the back of Ash's head, eliciting a throaty moan. So, this was what it was like to feel ravished. Ash would've laughed at the thought, but all her emotion was concentrating in her core.

It was as if every last drop of blood was coursing its way to her pleasure receptors, in anticipation of imminent release.

"You are devastatingly sexy." Evie's voice was raw and sexual. She shook her head lightly. "What have you done to me?"

Ash swallowed and her breath caught on the tail end of Evie's whispered words, taken away with the erotic, almost poetic notion. "Nothing compared to what I'll do if you let me."

Chapter Sixteen

Evie closed the hotel room door, double locked it, and slid the security chain into place. She turned around to find Ash waiting in the narrow hallway, partially lit by the bathroom lights streaming through the glass separating it from the bedroom. Her face was partly in shadow, and her expression was searching. Evie couldn't have made it any clearer. She'd ordered a taxi and booked a hotel. She had to have Ash, and she couldn't—wouldn't—wait. She didn't want to give herself the opportunity to be sensible and change her mind. She didn't want to think about the aftermath and what this might mean for the friendship Evie had envisaged.

Ash held out her hands, and Evie stepped forward and took them, happy to lead. She pressed her body against Ash's and pushed her arms above her head, glad for the four-inch heels that almost levelled their height difference. Ash's answering sigh indicated she too was happy for Evie to lead. She leaned in and ran her tongue from the hollow of Ash's throat and along her collar bone. Her skin was so incredibly soft, and she tasted sweet through a light sheen of perspiration. Evie opened her mouth and gently sank her teeth into Ash's neck, the temptation too great to resist. She felt Ash soften, as if her knees might fail her, and she pulled back to face her. Ash's eyes were half-lidded, and she looked…captured, and contentedly so.

Evie raised her eyebrows. The evening seemed to have taken a turn into unfamiliar territory. She could roll with that. She stepped back and leaned against the wall. "Take off your jacket." Her own command made her pussy jump in response, as did Ash's immediate and slowly deliberate compliance. Her expression altered, her questions seemed to vanish, and the look in her eye told Evie everything she wanted to know… Ash was ready to play. Without breaking eye contact, Ash pushed forward from the glass wall, shrugged out of her leather, and let it drop to the floor.

Evie flicked her eyes to Ash's torso, covered with a graphite button down, her sleeves rolled up to her elbows. "Open your shirt."

Ash smiled, her confidence seeming to return with each

instruction. She looked down and began to unbutton her shirt slowly. Evie appreciated the time she took. First sex was often rushed and the delicately desirous details lost in the fervour to achieve satisfaction. Evie had enjoyed her fair share of those conquests. Taking the time to slowly discover, to properly explore, tended to be the purview of longer-term intimacy. And yes, there was something to be said for instant gratification and the animalistic ardour of fast sex, but from the moment Evie's eyes settled on Ash in the half-light of the hotel room, she was determined to make this last. She pushed away the intrusion that she wanted it that way since she suspected it would be the only time she and Ash came together like this. She didn't want to think about anything other than Ash right now. How she looked. How she felt. How she moved. Evie wanted to learn it all.

Ash pulled her shirt from her jeans, revealing virgin skin unblemished by tattoos, something that seemed rare these days. The small breasts Evie had enjoyed groping earlier were hidden beneath a graphite-coloured bralette with Calvin Klein emblazoned in large, grey-heather block letters across a wide, elasticated band. Her stomach was flat, and Evie noticed the beautiful bird on her belt buckle. Evie glanced lower at Ash's crotch and a pang of desire fizzed through her body. *Did she have something…more tucked away in her jeans?*

"Take off your boots and socks." Evie wanted to be taller than Ash, even if only by virtue of her heels. She said nothing and acknowledged the instruction with a smile that showed how much she was enjoying herself. She bent to her feet and removed both items, taking far less time than she had with her shirt. She tossed them toward the door and stood straighter again, waiting.

Evie took a moment to check out the room. She knew from previous dalliances here that the chain hotel included a large, wingback chair positioned off the corner of the king size bed in all their *Go* rooms. They also had secrecy glass between the bedroom and bathroom that could be clear should one wish to enjoy watching their lover shower.

Evie nodded toward the wingback. "Go and sit in that chair."

Evie heard Ash swallow. She seemed to hesitate for a moment—had she tired of the game? But she did as she was bid with a grin. She settled into the chair and spread her legs wide. The pull to go to her, to sink to her knees, undo her jeans, and press her mouth to Ash's centre was strong, almost too strong. But Evie had started something, and she was fascinated to see

where it went.

She walked slowly toward Ash. She wanted to drive her insane with need, desperate to touch Evie but know that it wasn't allowed…not yet. She glanced at the plush leather chair with its chrome arms tucked under the desk and almost giggled at the thought of using that chair instead and tying Ash's wrists so she was physically unable to touch Evie. The night *was* young. Maybe later. She passed Ash with her back to her and felt Ash's hand graze across her butt. She turned around, tutted, and shook her head. "No," she said simply, at which Ash looked like she might melt in the chair. Evie had to grit her teeth and turned back around quickly to stop from smiling at Ash's reaction to the reprimand. Evie had no idea how the evening had taken this turn. Perhaps it was instinct. Whatever it was, it certainly felt right and rather natural, but she was in slightly unfamiliar territory. Her sex was usually pretty vanilla.

She sat on the bed and inched up so she remained upright, leaning against the two enormous luxury pillows at the headboard. She drew one leg up, bent it at the knee and let her other leg fall to the side slightly. The long slash in her skirt fell open to reveal her naked flesh and, she suspected from the angle, her silk and lace panties. Evie was taken aback by the hungry look in Ash's eyes as she took in Evie's leg from the top of her thigh to the tip of her high heels and back again. Evie saw a slight, almost imperceptible move forward before Ash looked as though she almost pushed herself back into the chair to prevent herself from rising and jumping on Evie. Her desire practically dripped from her, and its intensity was intoxicating. Evie had been wanted, desired, and even needed before. But this, *everything* about this, was different. And as a result, Evie's arousal escalated off any scale she'd ever judged a sexual encounter by.

Evie raised her eyebrows and tilted her head as if to warn Ash that she'd seen her minute move. Ash averted her eyes and glanced to the floor, before returning her gaze to Evie.

"What do you want?" Evie rested one hand on her knee and the other on her thigh, inches away from where Ash's gaze had focused.

Ash looked up and took a short breath. "You," she whispered.

The lustful longing Ash managed to communicate in one word and her accompanying look almost made Evie beckon her over immediately and give her complete access to whatever she wanted, for however long she wanted it. *Almost*. But this clearly wasn't about instant gratification. However Evie had intuited Ash's needs, she knew—could feel it in every cell in her body— that wasn't what Ash wanted. And surprisingly, it wasn't what Evie wanted either. As unacquainted as she was with this kind of sex, and as used to the quick and simple kind as she'd been in the past, this immediate connection and unspoken understanding of Ash's inclinations ignited a passion that she was desperate to explore.

Evie moved her hand onto her silken underwear, and the heat rushed to greet her fingertips. They'd barely touched each other, and she was on fire. "Tell me what you want to do to me." Evie lazily traced small circles through her panties, and she throbbed in response.

Ash glanced at the floor again before looking up to Evie. Was that part of what this was? It seemed like a display of deference. She began to wish she'd listened more carefully to Sarah's tales of her role play with Harry and made a mental note to gently quiz her by text tomorrow.

"I wish to do whatever you would like me to do."

Ash's words were more formal, respectful even. It was as if her response had to be ten words or less, like some Twitter version of sexual foreplay. But Evie liked the economy in her utterances, and she certainly appreciated the hoarse whisper Ash had adopted.

Okay, let's see where this goes. "What would you have me do to you?" Evie echoed Ash's verbal etiquette.

Ash did the thing with her eyes before she settled on Evie once more. "Whatever you would wish to do to me…"

There was something else there, something Ash didn't say… wasn't ready to say? The verbal dance fascinated Evie, and her body was equally enthralled. Her spontaneous decision to call an Uber rather than go clubbing was turning out to be one of her best for years.

"You would let me do…*anything?*" How flexible were the parameters of this play? And could Evie's imagination rise to the occasion? What *exactly* did Ash like and *how* did she like it? Ash didn't answer immediately, and the anticipation was almost unbearable.

Ash looked down. But this time, she didn't look back up so quickly. Was she shy? Embarrassed? Had Evie gone too far?

"Yes…anything," Ash said.

She finally looked up but seemed unable to look directly at

Evie.

Evie parted her legs a little wider and enjoyed the resultant ragged breath that escaped from Ash's mouth. She lifted her hips from the bed and slowly peeled off her panties. She watched Ash carefully, saw her linger on Evie's discarded garment. She gently waved it in the air and Ash's eyes followed it like the pendulum of a metronome.

"Do you want these?" Evie tried to hide the incredulity in her voice. The thought made her feel dirty in a way she'd never experienced…but it was thrilling.

Ash shifted in the chair, as if she could no longer contain her arousal. If she were a man, Evie might have expected her to have adjusted the crotch of her jeans to accommodate growing physical proof of her excitement. Ash pushed her hips forward before relaxing back into the chair with a look that indicated she knew she'd done something she shouldn't have. Evie let it go and waited for her response.

Ash nodded slowly. "Yes. If it pleases you to let me have them."

Evie raised her eyebrows, a sudden wickedness flaring through her mind and body. "It doesn't." She tossed them to the opposite side of the room and Ash looked bereft. "Don't look at them. Look at me."

Her words would have amused her if it weren't for the sexual charge in the room that made even the most vain of demands seem strangely acceptable. And more than that, they seemed required.

Ash's head snapped back to Evie, and she looked suitably chastised, another expression that zipped electricity through her core. What had she been missing out on with regular sex all these years? She didn't want to think about that. It might start her on a train of thought that would lead to over analysis. And she didn't want to analyse anything right now. All she wanted to do was be in this moment. All she wanted to do was *feel*.

Evie wetted her middle finger and placed it back between her legs. She jumped slightly when she rested her finger on her clit, the strength of her reaction testament to her level of arousal. Ash licked her top lip slowly.

"Are you thinking about what I taste like?"

Ash nodded.

Evie continued to work her finger, occasionally drawing it along the length of her pussy lips as she became more and more slick. "Come here."

Ash stood slowly, and Evie tried to decipher Ash's intentions. Did she want to draw out the anticipation for both of them?

"Where do you want me?" Ash whispered.

Evie pointed beside the bed so that Ash would be within touching distance. "Open your jeans and push them down to your knees."

Ash's eyes half-lidded as she unbuckled her belt and undid her jeans. She pushed them down and came back up to a standing position. Evie took a deep breath at the sight of Ash's matching Calvin Klein faux boxers, with decorative buttons and no easy access. Her thighs were large, strong, and solid looking. Evie switched hands, using her left to stimulate herself while she reached for Ash with her right hand. She pushed the soft cotton of her underwear aside and sighed deeply when her fingers slid over Ash's wetness. Her clit was hard, ready. Evie mirrored the motion of her left hand over Ash's warm flesh, and Ash moaned. Her hands remained by her sides, though her fists clenched from the moment Evie began to touch her. Evie wouldn't come this way, not quickly, but that wasn't her goal. She wanted to see how long Ash could stand there, how long it would take to get her off, if she even could.

Evie pressed a little harder with her right hand, and Ash moaned again.

"Please…"

Evie smiled. She hadn't heard such a simple word said with so many potential meanings before. "Please stop? Please carry on? Please do it harder? Softer?" Evie slipped her finger from Ash's clit and ran it the length of her wet lips. "Please what, Ash?"

Ash shook her head as if she was unable to decide exactly what she was asking for either.

"I want to make you cum while you're standing there looking so…" Evie ran her tongue over her lips as she looked Ash up and down, "so delectable. If you have a preference as to pressure," Evie eased off and used lighter circles again, "you should tell me."

Ash swallowed, glanced down at Evie's left hand and back up to her eyes. "What you're doing is…perfect."

Evie raised her eyebrows, not convinced. "Are you sure? When I did it harder, you moaned…" Evie pressed harder again to prove her point and got the same response. "Don't lie to me," she said, a little harsher. Evie saw a flash of panic cross Ash's expression before she settled.

"I like it hard and soft," Ash whispered. "I'll...I'll come for you either way."

Evie smiled. "You will?" She didn't manage to supress the surprise in her voice. When she'd told Ash to undress, Evie hadn't been sure that she'd acquiesce to her demand. She'd known plenty of butch women who didn't like to be touched or only wanted to give. Her relationships with those women had never lasted long. Evie loved the silken softness of a woman at her fingertips. She loved the look in a woman's eyes after she'd orgasmed, the release and raw vulnerability of sharing that moment was something Evie couldn't live without.

Ash nodded. "How could I not come for you?"

Evie sighed at the thought. She wanted to enjoy this hot, sexy butch with her pussy in Evie's hand. She wanted to see if Ash was right, and that she'd come for Evie. She decided to go with harder strokes and became so engrossed that she stopped moving her left hand. She was throbbing intensely anyway, she didn't need her hand there too. Ash looked like she was struggling to keep her eyes open and her legs strong as she moaned softly and murmured Evie's name along with repeated pleas for Evie not to stop.

"Can you come for me standing up?"

Ash opened her eyes. "I've never done it before...but I'm close."

Evie continued her rhythm, Ash's wetness allowing her fingers to slide easily over her hardness. The contrast ignited a passion to please Ash in a way Evie hadn't felt before. She shook that thought away. It was just sex. Hot sex, yes. Unexpectedly fascinating sex, double yes. But still, just sex. And in the morning, Ash could mark it down to experience and would undoubtedly move onto the next woman in her sights. And Evie could get back to looking for a potential life partner. *Ugh.* The concept was almost enough to put her off her stride.

Get out of your head and concentrate on what's in your hand. She pulled herself back into the moment and focused only on Ash. Evie watched her thighs strain with the effort to stay upright; enjoyed the way her stomach tensed and relaxed in time with her breathing and Evie's pace; but mostly, she wanted to capture Ash's face in her memory. The way her lips parted, the way she nibbled her bottom lip, the pure ecstasy in her expression. And she hadn't even come yet. Ash was a woman who knew how to enjoy sex, that much was clear. Evie returned her left hand between her own legs and once again, coordinated her touch to how she touched Ash.

"Please, God, don't stop that."

Evie didn't know whether she meant what she doing with her right or left hand, because Ash's gaze was fixed on what Evie was doing to herself. "You like watching?"

Ash nodded. "You're a goddess," she whispered as her body began to pulse and tense faster.

Ash's change tremored through Evie's fingertips, and she concentrated on maintaining the pressure exactly. Ash's movements quickened, and her throbbing became more powerful. She grabbed Evie's wrist and cried out as her release came. She pressed Evie's hand hard against her core and pulsated in Evie's grip until her breathing slowed, and she slowly opened her eyes.

"You're amazing," Ash said between ragged breaths.

"Want to thank me properly?" Seeing Ash come had intensified Evie's own need for release, and she was desperate to have Ash's mouth on her.

Ash grinned and nodded. "Absolutely."

She began to sink to the bed, but Evie held up her hand and shook her head. "Not so fast, handsome. That's not what I have in mind."

Ash glanced to the floor, in the deferential way she'd done a few times earlier.

"Forgive me…I'm sorry."

Evie tilted her head and raised her eyebrows. "As you should be." She smiled, and Ash grinned in return before briefly looking away again. God, she couldn't remember having this much fun with sex before, and she was still fully dressed but for her discarded panties. "Pull up your jeans."

Ash did as requested, and Evie could see the cogs turning and the competing thoughts racing around behind Ash's eyes and expression. She'd make a terrible poker player, but Evie enjoyed keeping her guessing. She'd think on what kind of person that made her tomorrow. Tonight she didn't care a jot. "Get on your knees."

Ash sighed deeply and swallowed hard, her arousal at Evie's curt commands glaringly obvious. How many women had Ash gone to her knees for in this way? She sank to the carpet slowly and sat back on her heels, waiting. Evie swung her legs off the bed so that she sat directly in front of Ash. She pulled her skirt up over her hips, parted her legs wide, and lay back. Evie said nothing for a long moment. Would the anticipation get the better of Ash's apparent etiquette? Or after wrongly predicting what Evie wanted moments ago, would she patiently wait? Evie's excitement was such that she could smell her own arousal. She knew Ash would be able to see how slick she was. But how long could she make Ash wait, when it was Evie who needed this so badly?

Evie pulled a pillow from the top of the bed. She placed it beneath her head to prop herself up slightly so that she could see Ash. "What are you thinking?" she asked.

Ash licked her lips and nodded toward Evie's open legs. "That I'd like to thank you properly with my mouth."

"Do you think that's what I've got in mind too?"

Ash rolled her shoulders and inclined her head slightly. "God, I hope so."

The knock at the door echoed along the hallway. Ash looked at Evie and frowned. She stood, tucked her shirt into her jeans, and went to see who was bothering them. Talk about bad timing. Ash was in the middle of what might be the most exciting sexual encounter she'd ever experienced. The last thing she needed was some emergency like a full-scale evacuation from a bomb threat. *She* might be the one exploding if her efforts to get her hands and mouth on Evie were about to be thwarted. Ash glanced at Evie, who hadn't moved despite the interruption, and shook her head at the reclining beauty with her legs open and ready. *How did I get so lucky on a first date?*

Ash opened the door to a guy in a suit holding a silver platter with an ice bucket, champagne, two flutes, and a bowl of strawberries on it.

"Oh…right. Not Miss Evie then… I'm so sorry this took so long." He pressed his lips together and shook his head before leaning a little closer to Ash. "We've had a problem with a hen party on the fourth floor," he whispered. "Terribly loud. Upsetting all the other guests. Singing *S&M* at the top of their voices—badly, I might add. Rhianna would be mortified. The other guests might not have minded so much if any one of them could hold a tune, but they sounded like a bag of cats being mangled in a tumble dryer."

He laughed at his own joke and Ash smiled, amused by his camp candour. "That's okay. We've kept ourselves busy."

He grinned and winked, making Ash think they'd checked

into a sex hotel rather than the upmarket kind. *Miss Evie?* Was she a regular here? Was that why she'd said she couldn't take Ash home? Because she had no intention of this going any further than one night of off-the-charts sex? And giving Ash her home address would be inconvenient if she didn't take kindly to the brush off? Ash supposed she couldn't blame her. Jilted lovers could be crazy sometimes. She hoped she hadn't given off a psycho vibe.

"No doubt. So…" He inclined his head toward the tray. "Can I bring this in for you?"

Ash shook her head. "That's okay. I'll take it." She dug into a back pocket of her jeans, pulled out some folded notes, and gave him five quid. She might not have spent much time in hotels like this one, but she knew the drill. It would've been beyond her usual means, but since they'd not ended up drinking all night, it wasn't quite as painful to part with. She shoved the remaining cash away and took the tray from him. "Thanks."

He slipped the note into his trouser pocket and nodded. "Have a lovely evening."

"Will do." Ash used her foot to close the door before she turned around, walked back down the short corridor, and placed the tray on the large desk running alongside the left wall of the room. Evie hadn't moved.

She pushed up on her elbows. "You'd made me forget about that."

"I didn't hear you order it when we checked in." Maybe because it was a regular order whenever Evie stayed here for the night. She was a successful doctor and clearly a woman of means. Her car, her clothes, the way she spoke, all declared an affluent stability. Ash couldn't decide if she were irritated or impressed by it, and had tried to keep her tone neutral. Evie raised her eyebrows as if she understood what Ash was implying.

"I requested it at the same time as I booked the room. High-end places like this tend to be rather accommodating."

Ash shrugged. "I wouldn't know." *But that's not Evie's fault.* She motioned to the champagne, wanting to recapture their earlier connection and dismiss the doubts trying to drag her down. "Would you like me to pour you a glass?"

Evie shook her head. "Not right now." She motioned toward where Ash had previously been positioned. "I'd like you to get back on your knees and put your mouth on me…if the hotel guy hasn't knocked you out of the mood?"

Ash refocused on Evie, incredibly sexual and mysterious Evie. Ash decided to park the questions until a more suitable occasion. Could be that she'd get her answers organically when Evie didn't respond to her texts or calls tomorrow or the next day. But that shouldn't, and wasn't going to, stop her enjoying tonight in all its glory.

Ash came back around the bed, slowly removed her shirt completely, and tossed it onto the wingback she'd been occupying earlier. She peeled off her bra and threw it in the same place. When she turned back toward Evie, her mouth was slightly open, and her eyes expressed her desire perfectly. Ash took a moment to savour the feeling of being so hungrily devoured, and it made her feel incredibly sexy and powerful and…in control.

She reached down and pulled Evie to her feet. "I can assure you, I'm still *very* much in the mood for you." She put her finger beneath Evie's chin and tipped her back slightly, exposing her throat. Something primal stirred Ash's consciousness, and she traced her tongue along Evie's neck before lightly biting her. Evie moaned and rested her hands on Ash's waist, but Ash grabbed her wrists and pushed her hands behind her back.

Evie gasped and pushed her body against Ash's in response. "Who put you in charge?"

"I could say the same to you." Ash crushed her lips to Evie's, swallowing any potential response in a passionate kiss. She sensed the tension in Evie's body melt away and pulled her closer. She released her grip on Evie's wrists momentarily to enclose both of them in her left hand. She used her right hand to draw a line from Evie's collarbone to the opening of her blouse. She broke from the kiss and began to open Evie's blouse, pausing between each button to push the material aside and watch the soft rise and fall of Evie's breasts pressed against her own, much smaller chest.

Ash released Evie's wrists, took the flimsy material of Evie's top in her hands, and slid it gently and slowly over her shoulders, pressing her fingertips into Evie's flesh as she did so. She pulled the blouse off and let it drop to the floor, then quickly worked Evie's bra open and off so that she was completely topless. Ash kissed a trail along Evie's body from her neck down to her stomach and then sank to her knees. She unzipped Evie's skirt and pulled it down to a heap on the floor.

Ash stood and caressed Evie's cheek. "I want you to lay back on the bed," she whispered. Ash waited, hoping the change in dynamic hadn't unsettled Evie or put a dampener on the fire that burned between them. Ash had been enjoying Evie's tentative yet firm commands, but something had turned naturally to put Ash in the driving seat, a position she was more familiar with.

Evie sighed and relaxed onto the bed. "Here?" she asked, bending her legs, and putting her feet flat on the covers, opening herself to Ash in the same position she was in before they were interrupted.

Ash grinned and nodded slowly as Evie put her hands behind her head, as powerful in her nakedness as she had been fully clothed. Ash might be the one giving the directions, but Evie seemed reluctant to relinquish her autonomy. "Yeah, there is perfect." She stood there for a few silent moments to take in Evie's beauty; her soft curves, the ins and out of her contours like the sloping lines of a topographical map, her large breasts and her erect nipples, peaking, begging to receive attention. Then Ash focused on the centre of Evie's sexuality. Her sex was slick with wetness, and the hood of her clit peeked out from a ruffle of dark curls.

"What are you waiting for?" Evie asked.

"Not waiting—taking you all in. I want to remember every line and feature." She looked up to Evie's eyes, trying to see behind the heat of the moment, but she was giving nothing else away. "I wish my brain was like a movie camera, and I could commit all of this to memory so I could close my eyes and play it back anytime I wanted."

Evie laughed. "Pervert. You want your brain to be a porn stash hard drive?"

Ash dropped to her knees, slipped her arms underneath Evie's thighs, and placed her hands on her hips. "You'd make an amazing porn star." She tugged Evie closer, unable to prolong their inevitable coming together, and Evie gasped and smiled. The smell of her, the sight of her. Evie invaded all of Ash's senses and flooded her brain with pleasure, even though they'd barely touched. She licked her lips as she descended toward Evie's inviting heat, thirsting to taste her. She inhaled deeply before allowing her tongue to explore Evie's pussy. The solid hit of arousal sent her spinning into overdrive, and she wasted no time licking and sucking to discover how Evie liked it. She kept her eyes open, careful to watch for any visual clues.

Evie reached down, twisted her hand into Ash's hair, and gripped tightly. "Fast and hard," she said between gasps.

Ash smiled inwardly. *This* was why she loved older women so much. They always seemed far less inhibited and far less inclined to waste time on bad sex. She pressed down on Evie's hips as she did as instructed. She slid her tongue over and around Evie's clit with as much pressure as she could. Evie reached down with her other hand and held the back of Ash's head in place firmly. Ash wasn't going anywhere. She wanted Evie's orgasm. She wanted her release. She wanted her to explode in her mouth and swear that she never wanted another woman to place their mouth where Ash's had been.

Evie bucked her hips beneath Ash's touch, rising and falling, faster and harder. Ash grabbed hold of Evie's wrists and forced them onto the bed, taking control and holding her in place. Evie elicited a low growl in response but didn't fight to release herself. Ash continued her rhythm, her chin soaked in Evie's wetness.

Evie forced her hips upward. "I'm close…don't stop."

Ash barely heard Evie's words with her thighs pressed so tightly against her head, but she wasn't about to stop. Evie's thrusts grew stronger and her pleas louder until she screamed Ash's name and crested her climax, falling still. Ash stopped but didn't move, choosing to appreciate the way Evie's throbbing pulsed slower in time with her breathing.

Ash released Evie's wrists and trailed her fingers over her stomach. She shuddered in response, making Ash want more. She crawled up onto the bed, propped herself up on an elbow beside Evie, and placed her hand between Evie's legs. She pressed her finger into Evie's wetness and slipped in easily. Her moans of pleasure encouraged Ash to go deeper and harder, safe in the expectation that Evie would issue instruction if she wasn't doing it right. She hooked her left leg over Evie's and pulled it aside to allow her unfettered access. She wrapped her right hand in Evie's hair and closed her grip. Evie moaned and opened her mouth, arched backward, and exposed her neck to Ash's mouth. She traced her tongue over Evie's neck, kissed her all the way up to her ear, and nibbled on it.

Evie shook her head and opened her eyes. "No. I don't like that."

Ash blinked to show her understanding and moved her lips back to Evie's neck, pausing to kiss every inch of flesh as she moved downward to her breasts. She took Evie's nipple into her mouth, used her teeth to tease it to become harder. She flicked it with her tongue and tugged on Evie's hair a little. Evie gasped and she opened up, silently asking for more.

Ash was quick to fulfil the request and pushed two more fingers inside her. Evie thrust her hips upward and shouted Ash's name along with a couple of expletives and threats to advise her against stopping. Ash let Evie's nipple go and looked up. She wanted—no, needed—to see Evie's face. Her open mouth and lips swollen with pleasure, her eyes, closing and flicking open occasionally to focus on Ash, communicating her wild abandon to the moment. Ash loved sex for these connections, though the unrestrained delight she sought was rare. People were often too concerned with how they might look in the throes of an orgasm to give themselves up completely. That seemed to be the case for short term trysts anyway. She hoped that such reservations would fade with familiarity and comfort, but she was yet to experience the contentment and peace that a long-term relationship promised.

But she could see something in Evie's eyes. She wanted to believe that she could. Despite the alarm bells that hotel sex with a string of strangers might be Evie's *modus operandi*, Ash wanted to believe that this might be different, that she could be the one who changed all that. She wasn't talking about forever. Ash wasn't that hopeless of a romantic to think that forever could be found after a fifteen-minute conversation and a night of mind-blowing sex. But it could be a start.

A string of barely coherent mutterings drew Ash's attention to what she was supposed to be doing with her hand instead of staring longingly at Evie's face, trying to divine her inner workings. She gave Evie's hair another forceful tug and clenched her thighs together at the resultant open-mouthed gasp of arousal. She thrust her fingers as deep as she could, pressed them to Evie's inner walls, before pulling out and driving back in just as deep. Ash forced the heel of her palm against her clit, and Evie let out a throaty moan that had Ash's pussy responding with its own throbbing beat. Evie threw her arms around Ash and dug her long nails into her back, yelling expletives.

Ash pushed herself back up the bed to kiss Evie, to share her experience. Evie's kiss was as forceful as the sex, and she shoved her tongue into Ash's mouth, the vigour of it taking Ash a little by surprise. She kissed back with as much passion as she could convey, trying to maintain the movement of her hand that was so delighting Evie.

Evie's hip thrusting quickened. She cried out and dragged her nails across Ash's back, leaving trails of burning fire. Her hand closed over Ash's, as if holding her there to prolong her pleasure, and she pulled Ash onto her with her other hand. Ash tried to keep herself form putting her full weight on top of her, but Evie didn't seem to care. She let out short and rapid breaths before she convulsed once more, almost crushing Ash's fingers inside her.

Ash breathed in deeply, the heady scent of their sex surrounding and soothing her senses. Evie relaxed around her hand, so she began to stoke the fire once more.

"Woah, handsome. I'm going to need some sustenance if it's your intention to keep this up all night." Evie ran her fingers over Ash's shoulder, downward to the base of her spine, before she grabbed a handful of Ash's ass and squeezed hard. "Please say that *is* your intention."

Ash grinned and pressed her body against Evie's. "We might need more than a bowl of strawberries for what I've got in mind." She reluctantly pulled herself from Evie's embrace and got up from the bed. She padded toward the desk and in the wall mirror, she could see Evie watching her as she walked. She glanced over her shoulder as she pulled the champagne from the bucket. "Like what you see?"

Evie nodded slowly and raised her right eyebrow. "I do. But I'm going to need to see everything." She motioned up and down the length of Ash's body with her hand. "No more hiding in your jeans. I want to taste every inch of you before we're through tonight."

Ash liked the sound of that immensely. She imagined Evie covering her whole body with sliced slivers of strawberries and taking a painfully lengthy amount of time to eat them from her skin. She unwrapped the foil from the champagne and began to force the cork from its confinement. It shot out with a resounding pop, and the cold liquid spewed upward before dribbling down, the bubbles dancing and tingling on Ash's skin. She quickly poured a glass for Evie and dropped a fresh strawberry in, before pouring one for herself. She turned and went back to the bed, where Evie lounged seductively, looking ready for a glamour magazine photoshoot. Those would be photos Ash would sell her soul for and hang on her bedroom walls to keep her warm on lonely, cold nights.

Evie hitched up toward the head of the bed before taking the proffered glass. Ash climbed onto the bed but sat farther down with her legs folded beneath her so she could continue to look at Evie. Her skin glowed, and she looked radiant and energised from her orgasm, rather than spent. The night still held much promise, and Ash was ready and willing.

Evie clinked her glass to Ash's. "Here's to an amazing night."

Ash smiled and drank to the toast, but a dull ache settled in her gut and pulled for her attention. There was a finality to Evie's choice of words that bothered her. Ash might have said "Here's to the start of something amazing," or "Here's to the first of many amazing nights." She shook it off and tried to enjoy the dry, sweet taste of the champagne. Maybe that would be rushing things, and some women bolted at the first sign of anything serious.

She chose not to respond with her own toast and glanced at her watch. She had hours to convince Evie this could be the start of something wonderful.

Chapter Seventeen

"That would be wonderful. It's been too long again," Evie said as her taxi pulled up at the red light. She glanced at her watch. The traffic wasn't bad, and the driver had been swift enough thus far. "I should be home in ten minutes. Can you be there in half an hour?" Harriet responded that she could, and Evie ended the call. She needed to quickly change, but she *didn't* need a shower. She and Ash had enjoyed a luxuriously long and hot shower, physically and metaphorically, before she left the hotel. It had been an intimate exchange she'd not expected. Showering after sex had always been functional. It served a purpose; to wash away the lingering aroma of the night's activities, to freshen her up for the non-sex related day ahead. Showering with Ash had been more like a ritual. She'd taken such care, lathering every inch of Evie's body slowly before rinsing her off with equal tenderness. She had made Evie feel like a queen being bathed by a particularly attentive servant. Ash had seemed to take such pleasure in the simple act that Evie had shared that feeling by a kind of sensory osmosis. The lack of words they'd uttered throughout the whole process had added to the exquisite experience.

The taxi driver braked hard, honked his horn, and shouted words Evie didn't understand. Nor did she want to. They sounded angry and harsh.

"Sorry, love. Idiot thinks he owns the road."

Evie caught his eye in the rear-view mirror and offered a tight smile and a nod. She noticed his grey hair and heavily wrinkled face. Was his eyesight up to DVLA standards? This was why she hardly took taxis or let anyone else drive her anywhere. If she was going to end up in a fiery car crash, she'd prefer to know she'd done all she could to avoid it. She spent the rest of the short journey watching the road and praying to get home in one piece.

The driver pulled up at Evie's house, having narrowly avoided a further three accidents. Evie noted the driver's name and quickly thumbed it into the taxi firm's contact details on her phone. She definitely wouldn't want another death ride with him. She held her card to the reader in the back of the cab and added a gratuity despite the hellish journey. Perhaps if he made enough in tips, he'd retire early and save some lives.

"Thank you." Evie got out and walked up the long driveway to her house. First stop, fresh clothes. She went upstairs and hurriedly changed into fresh underwear, some comfy yoga pants, and a loose, long-sleeved top. She and Harriet had the kind of friendship with no pretence. She didn't have to rush around the house, vacuuming and cleaning. Nor did she have to dress to impress in her own house.

She went down to the kitchen, clicked the kettle on, opened the small cupboard dedicated to coffee, and scanned her options. It was noon, and she optimistically calculated that she'd had less than two hours sleep. The thought made her yawn hard enough to worry that her jaw might break. Easy decision. She chose the super strong Café du Monde chicory that Harriet had brought back from her last trip to New Orleans. She put a double helping into her one-cup French press and prepared her giant mug with milk and sweetener while she waited for the water to boil. She'd get her first cup in before Harriet arrived.

Did Ash like her coffee strong, assuming she liked coffee at all? Evie couldn't think of a single person she knew who didn't like the dark nectar. She supposed she'd find out soon enough. Which brought her to think about what last night had meant. Perhaps she shouldn't think about it before she'd had her first cup of the day. Her non-caffeinated decisions were never particularly well thought through.

She poured the water onto her coffee and closed the press just as she heard gravel crunch on her driveway. Harriet was early. She filled the kettle again and switched it on before heading to open the door to let her friend in.

Harriet pulled her into a tight hug. "I've missed you."

"No, you haven't." Evie shook her head and laughed. "You're too busy to miss me." They parted, and Evie pulled Harriet in and closed the door.

"That is *not* true. Being insanely busy and insanely missing someone are not mutually exclusive." Harriet nodded toward the kitchen. "I smell coffee, but I want wine."

Evie smiled and shook her head. She led the way. "That can be arranged."

"Don't judge. I'm still on Tokyo time."

Evie turned back form the wine rack and held up her hands. "No judgment here. How long have you been back?"

"Two weeks."

Evie laughed hard. "You're incorrigible."

"Just joking. I got back in the early hours of Saturday and spent the day knocked out from jet lag and tramadol."

"Tramadol? What have you done?" Evie quickly appraised Harriet for signs of obvious injury but saw nothing.

Harriet grinned and wiggled her eyebrows. "Again. Joking. God, you're easy today. Distracted?"

Evie ignored the direct reference to her night out with Ash and pulled a Calvario rioja from the rack, one she'd been saving for a special occasion. Waiter-like, she offered the bottle up for Harriet's inspection.

"Wow, a Calvario?" She inclined her head and gave Evie a serious look. "Are you trying to seduce me?"

"You wish." Evie handed the bottle and a corkscrew to Harriet. "Knock yourself out."

"Won't you join me?" Harriet pulled a large goblet from the glass cupboard.

Evie picked up her French press and began to pour the delicious smelling libation. "Later. First cup of the day. I need this before I collapse." She added a touch more milk and stirred it before bringing the mug to her lips and sipping. "Mm, coffee."

Harriet narrowed her eyes. "First cup of the day…in the afternoon? What's the story?" she asked and poured herself a generous glass of the wine.

"Let's get comfy, and I'll tell you all about it." Because she needed to talk about what had happened between her and Ash, and how quickly it had turned into sex. Amazing, mind-blowing sex. She needed a second opinion to stop her overthinking and overanalysing everything about last night. Harriet's timing had rarely been better.

Evie took her mug and headed through the lounge to the second living room, her adult sanctum sanctorum. She eased herself onto her oversized swivel armchair, careful not to spill her coffee, and shuffled all the way back so her feet were only just poking over its edge. Harriet sat in the identical chair opposite her and took a small sip of her wine before placing the glass on the table beside her.

Harriet pointed to her glass and nodded, licking her lips. "You should've saved *that* for a special occasion."

"We get to see each other so rarely that this qualifies as a special occasion."

Harriet smiled. "Okay, enough small talk. What's going on

with you?"

Evie launched into telling the story. She told Harriet all about how she met Ash and how she'd agreed to go on a date with her, despite reservations about her age—which, no, she still didn't know—and the gap in life experience that created. She relayed the dinner date with Tal and the apparent love of his life, Patrie—who, no, she was not jealous of because she and Tal were a one-time thing as Harriet well knew—and how that made Evie rethink her outlook on potentially sharing her life with someone, which clearly couldn't be Ash even though the sex was amazing.

Harriet tapped her empty glass and got up. "I'm getting the bottle and another glass. This is serious."

Harriet returned within moments, filled a glass for Evie, and replenished her own.

"So…what do you think?" Sharing the events of the past week or so lifted the weight, but it hadn't made it any clearer in her mind.

"Okay. Number one: you can't know whether or not Ash is a serious contender for your future. You went out on a date that turned into sex after fifteen minutes. If you want to know whether Ash could fit into your world properly, you need to spend some time in her company and *not* in her pants."

"But—"

Harriet held up her other hand and shook her head. "No interrupting my flow."

Evie smiled and held up her hands in mock apology.

"Number two: you've already dismissed Ash as a serious contender based solely on her age, which is ageist, short sighted, and stereotyping. Three things I wouldn't have expected from you as a psychiatrist." Harriet inclined her head and pointed a finger toward Evie. "Don't do it."

Evie relaxed back into her chair. Perhaps discussing this with Harriet hadn't been such a good idea after all. "Bossy britches."

"Zip it. Number three: it's great news that Tal has found someone he loves. He's a great guy, a wonderful dad, and he deserves some happiness."

Evie nodded. She certainly couldn't argue with that.

"And lastly, number four: you need to analyse your sudden motivation to find a life partner. Had you got it into your head that you didn't need one or that you didn't deserve one? Had you become so focussed on being a mother that you've forgotten how to be a woman and thus, what you need as a woman?"

"I thought *I* was supposed to be the psychiatrist and you were supposed to be the global consultant-come-international spy?"

Harriet grinned. "I do love that you think me capable of leading such an exciting, double life." She took another long sip from her glass. "This wine is absolutely delicious. We should be eating a medium rare steak with it, though. *Perry's* deliver now, you know." She pulled her phone from her pocket and waved it in the air. "I have their app. Are you hungry?"

Evie raised her eyebrows at the amused denial-not-a-denial. A steak did sound nice though, and Harriet was right, a filet mignon would pair beautifully with the wine. "I'm ravenous. Let's do it." She hadn't eaten since lunch on Saturday and although the shared bowl of strawberries had given her a sugar boost, she'd expended far more energy overnight than she'd consumed. Her stomach growled at the thought of a medium rare steak with creamed spinach and Lyonnaise potatoes.

After asking what Evie wanted, Harriet created the order on her phone. Then she placed it screen-down on the table and turned her attention back to Evie. "It'll be here in three quarters of an hour. That should give us enough time to sort you out."

Evie didn't share Harriet's optimism, but she was willing to give it a try. "Okay, I'm going to take each of your points out of order. In answer to number three, I'm also glad Tal has found someone he tells me that he loves, and I'm happy for him. I have every intention of being supportive. She seems nice, like I said, and as long as Izad likes her, that'll be good enough for me."

Harriet shook her head. "Kids are crafty little shits. You can't base your like of the woman on Izad's reaction to her."

"Why not? He has great instincts when it comes to people."

"That may be. But those instincts will be clouded by the fact that he suddenly has to share his dad with somebody else. He might resent that, and that resentment might manifest in a dislike of Patrie. Tal will have to show him that Izad is no less important to him, and that he's gained another person to love him rather than lost some of the love from his father. You'll need to back him up with that."

Evie moved her head from side to side and rolled her eyes. "Yes, obviously. That's what I said, isn't it?" She laughed, and Harriet joined her.

"Yes, that's *exactly* what you said… Next?"

Evie closed her eyes for a moment to remember the points Harriet had made. "Numbers one and two, or Ash for short. She's just left university and has her whole life ahead of her. I'm settled in my career. I know who I am and what I want from life—"

Harriet huffed. "That's up for debate in number four."

"I know what I want from life. Ash is still a baby, and I *have* one—"

"Izad is nearly a teenager. I don't think you can still call him a baby. Nor do I think you can call someone in their twenties a baby when you're only in your early thirties."

"How come you can interrupt me but I wasn't allowed to interrupt you?" Evie adjusted her shirt and brushed off imaginary dust.

Harriet tipped her wine glass toward herself. "Because I'm the one advising *you* and making sense of the cobbled crap you've jumbled up in your oh-so-clever brain."

Evie blew out a big breath and rolled her shoulders. "Fine. I'm not being ageist or stereotyping, I'm being realistic. I don't think Ash is ready to settle down, and at her age, I wouldn't expect her to be even thinking about it. But most importantly, I don't even know who Ash is. She seems interesting enough, and we had oodles of stunning sex last night, but we've not had any deep conversations about morals or politics or hopes for the future."

"You realise that you've created a circular argument, don't you? You don't know who Ash is and yet you do know what she is and isn't ready for? You can't discard her on that basis. It's illogical…and downright crazy. And you've said the sex was stunning, yes?"

Evie nodded. It wasn't as though she could remember all the sex she'd ever had in her life, but she was certain last night's sex had been the best. And that hadn't been just about how many orgasms she'd had, although Ash had drawn from her too many to count. Nor had it been about how many orgasms she'd taken from Ash, and they too had been numerous. It was the coupling of their minds that made it special. The communication without words, the electricity that sparked and promised more than sex, promised a constant and intimate reconnection, that X factor she'd read about in so many romance books and seen in a multitude of rom-com movies…but hadn't experienced.

"And judging from that faraway look in your eyes, it was the best you've ever had." Harriet sipped her wine. "You owe it to yourself to find out if the rest of the package matches the sexual side of it. *That's* where you'll find the true answer. Not in your head." She tapped two fingers to her chest. "In your heart. Isn't that what you're always telling your boy genius? Follow your heart?"

Evie wrinkled her nose and looked away briefly. It wasn't fair to use her own words against her, was it? Why couldn't this be a *do as I say, not as I do* situation?

"So, you need to spend some time in her company and—"

"Not in her pants. Yes, I know." That wouldn't be so bad. It had been Evie's original intention: to have a wild night of energetic sex, figure out there wasn't enough to sustain a relationship, and then cultivate a solid friendship.

"Which leaves the biggie. Number four. Is your sudden desire to think about settling down a knee jerk reaction to Tal finding happiness? Or have you finally realised that you can be a mother and a lover?"

Evie pinched the bridge of her nose. "You know, sometimes you could just come over for normal friend talk?"

Harriet frowned and arched her eyebrow. "And what exactly does that entail? Talking about the latest fashions and what happened in last night's serial TV show?" She shook her head. "We don't see each other enough to spend time on the trivial stuff. We have to dive straight into the things that are troubling our souls, sweet friend."

Harriet was right, of course. She had that irritating habit when it came to Evie's issues, which was what made her a good friend. "Okay, okay. For once, I haven't overanalysed that aspect of my decision to start looking for someone to share the rest of my life. I don't think it's a reaction to Tal finding someone, but that might have a small influence." She stopped to think for a moment. Did it have anything to do with Tal? "I'm certain that it has nothing to do with Tal himself. He's a big part of my life as co-parent to Izad, but I definitely *don't* have any residual sexual feelings toward him beyond that. He's been a damn good friend for over a decade, and I'd like nothing more than to see him fall in love and live happily ever after." And what about Izad? Where did he come into all of this? "Perhaps I'm scared that we're not doing a good enough job of parenting Izad. I've seen so many couples not give enough time and love to their kids because they're too wrapped up in themselves and their own needs. I don't want to be the reason Izad ends up in his thirties in some therapist's office blaming a lack of parental love for all his problems." Evie closed her eyes and rubbed her forehead. "He's got his own issues without us adding to them, and we're already a splintered family."

Harriet held up her hand. "Woah there, Evie. You and Tal may live separately, but you've always worked together to ensure that didn't impact negatively on Izad. He's got a consistent schedule, which helps him, and he couldn't ask for more love from either of you. Any idiot that saw you all together could see how you both dote on him, and vice versa. You don't get that kind of closeness without earning it, believe me."

Evie took a sip of her wine but barely tasted it. She should've stuck to coffee. And Harriet's words brought a bitter taste to her mouth. Evie had been lucky with her parents, but Harriet had grown up with a cold and distant mother and an absent father. She hadn't meant for this conversation to remind Harriet of memories she liked to remain in the past.

"I've thought about finding someone to settle down with before, but…" *Von*. She hadn't told anyone about her. "I don't trust my instincts anymore."

Harriet leaned forward. "How so?"

Harriet was the only one Evie would ever share this story with, but a lack of proximity hadn't been the only reason she'd not done so. She'd avoided discussing it not just because it was a shameful, professional failure, but because she'd pinned her hopes on Von being that someone special. And all she turned out to be was an addict. It wasn't until now that Evie realised how vulnerable she'd let herself be with Von, and how falling so flat on her face had knocked her back farther than she knew.

She took a deep breath then launched into the whole wretched tale. When she'd finished, Harriet had polished off her second glass of wine.

"I'm sorry, Evie. I wished I'd been here when it was all happening. I wish you'd called me."

"I don't think I knew how much it had hurt or affected me until now." Evie climbed off her chair and poured the remnants of her wine into Harriet's glass. "I need something stronger." She went to her drinks' cabinet, unlocked it, and took out the bottle of Aviation gin Harriet had brought back from a trip to Portland. Having a globe-trotting friend had many benefits.

"Let me get you some ice."

Harriet was out of her chair and on her way to the kitchen before Evie could respond. She brought back a handful of cubes and dropped them into the glass Evie had pulled from the cabinet, before retaking her seat. Evie took time to prepare her drink so she could dissect the problem quietly. She sliced a lemon and added it to the glass, along with a hefty triple of the crystal-clear liquid. She flopped back down onto her chair and wiggled backward.

"I can't live in the past. I know that, before you say it. It's what I'm always telling my patients. Learn from your mistakes and move into your future, lessons learned. I suppose that I'd got so caught up with working and parenting that I hadn't stopped to think about how the Von thing had affected me. Which is strange for me, since my usual go to method of dealing with things is overthinking them to death." She shook her head. "I still have to consider my choices carefully. I can't let just anybody be around Izad, and I wouldn't want him to get attached to someone who had no intention of sticking around. That would be too destructive, and I don't think that's me making excuses for not taking chances. It's what Tal and I have always had in place. No one gets introduced to the kid unless we're properly serious about them."

Harriet had been nodding throughout Evie's soliloquy. "And that makes perfect sense…but…"

"But I can't put my life on hold until Izad has flown the nest. And I have needs that I should attend to, because if I don't look after myself, how can I look after anyone else, especially Izad."

Harriet raised her glass. "Exactly."

"I'm a woman as well as a mother so I shouldn't close myself off to any possibilities," Evie thought of Ash, "however unlikely they might be."

The doorbell rang to signal the arrival of their food order, which was good since Evie had become aware of a gnawing hunger. "I'll get it." She pushed herself out of her huge chair and headed to answer it.

"It's already paid for. My treat since you sprang for the wonderful wine," Harriet said. "But they'll need a tip."

Evie smiled. "You're a star." She went to the front door with a lightness in her step. Harriet stopping by couldn't have come at a better time. They'd chewed through her problems, and Harriet's no-nonsense and well-educated way of looking at the world saved Evie going around and around in ever-increasing circles. She'd open herself up to getting to know Ash. Like that strange advert for fizzy pop proclaimed, what was the worst that could happen?

Chapter Eighteen

We jumped a few steps. I'd like to go back and start with a date that doesn't end with us in bed.

Ash had read and re-read the text, unsure what to make of it. Evie had initiated the fast forward to unbelievably hot sex, so why was she putting the brakes on now? Maybe it was a good thing. Maybe that's how Evie operated. If she discovered early on whether or not potential partners were compatible between the sheets, she saved herself a whole heap of *get to know you* time. It was pretty efficient, really. There was no point falling in love with someone if they didn't satisfy in bed. Ash had passed that test, it seemed, but something about this still bothered her a little.

But it didn't bother her enough to not pursue it further, so there she sat, waiting for Evie in the Snug just before three in the afternoon, two weeks after their spectacular night in a posh hotel. Unusually, and with a predictable grumble from Bev, she'd managed to leave work on time and get home to freshen and change to be here early. She didn't want a repeat of their first date, with some random guy already chatting merrily to Evie before she even got there.

She'd picked a high-backed booth for privacy and comfort. Evie had chosen the venue, and it was the first time Ash had been there. She'd decided she liked it within five minutes of going in. The décor, ambience, private seating, quiet music, and wide variety of food and drink, alcoholic and non-alcoholic, made it a perfect place to spend a few hours getting to know someone better.

Ash sipped her beer, thinking about how she hadn't seen Evie since they'd parted *the morning after*. The following Friday Evie didn't show at the kennels, and Sarah had said Evie had been unable to get away from work. She'd texted Ash later that night to explain she'd had a work emergency, something Ash had been grateful for because her first thought was that Evie was avoiding her.

Two weeks with a few messages here and there, texts with nothing of consequence as if Evie was censoring herself to prevent their fledgling relationship going sexual again. Ash had lost track of the number of times she'd scrolled through to Evie's contact and hovered her finger over the call icon. Fear of not knowing what to say stopped her from following through every time. Kirsty called her an idiot more than once and threatened to steal her phone to call Evie herself. She eventually made Kirsty understand that she didn't want to push too far too soon. That night had been perfect in so many ways that the next time they met had a lot to live up to. Ash didn't want to blow it. She hoped they would slip into easy conversation, and somehow, she'd be able to give Evie proof of whatever it was she was looking for.

She'd kept herself busy with trying to bring in new activities at work and spending the rest of her time with Java. Sarah had advised that she get Java snipped while he was there, but Ash wanted some time to think about it. She wasn't sure she wanted to deny him the pleasure of that particular activity once he was out of quarantine jail. She asked for him to get a fur cut instead, because he was starting to look like a dog version of Russell Brand.

Ash turned her attention back to the entrance. She'd sat so she could watch people coming into the place. Every time the door opened, her heart dropped a beat in anticipation, and her mood fell when it wasn't Evie. She checked her watch again. Evie was late. Ash brushed away the stab of disappointment and ignored the possibility that she was being stood up. She placed her bottle on a coaster and adjusted the pot of coffee she'd got for Evie. Should she have had tea or water instead of a beer? Would Evie read something into her choice? Like the truth of needing a quick buzz to calm her nerves. She waved the waitress over, ordered a Coke Zero, and gave her the half-full bottle of beer to take away. She quickly had a nibble of the walnut cake to take away the alcohol from her breath. That might be taking it too far. How was she supposed to greet her anyway? A hug? A hug and a kiss? A handshake? Should she even stand or would that make it awkward and force Evie into a hug she didn't want to give?

Jesus. Hurry up and get here already. She was driving herself crazy, and that definitely wouldn't be the attractive option Evie was looking for.

Ash watched the door open again, and this time her breath caught. Evie looked stunning and classically casual in jeans, knee-high boots, a simple cable-knit sweater, and an elegant woollen winter coat. She spotted Ash and waved as she came over, her high heels hitting the solid wood floor and making her approach musical. Ash stood immediately. It's what she'd always done, and she couldn't stop herself. A beautiful woman was walking toward her, it was her natural reaction to stand to attention. Only trouble was they were at a booth, and there was no seat to pull out for her. Ash smiled and hoped she didn't look as tongue-hanging-out-bewitched as she felt.

"You look amazing." The compliment sounded trite, but Ash didn't want to gush too much. She didn't yet know if Evie was the kind of woman who thrived on praise and her efforts being noticed.

Evie gave a small smile in return. "Thank you." She gestured toward Ash. "You look handsome. So, are we hugging or being terribly awkward?"

Ash blew out a relieved breath and opened her arms. "I'm up for a hug, if that's okay with you."

Evie laughed and moved into Ash's arms. "I know what you look like completely naked; a hug should be easy," she whispered.

Ash closed her arms around Evie's body and inhaled deeply. "You smell divine. What is that?"

Evie pulled out of the hug, waved the compliment away, and slid into the booth to sit opposite Ash. "It's called Suede Orris. A gift from a friend."

"Your friend has great taste." Ash swallowed the tang of jealousy at a *friend* buying something so special and intimate. It was clearly what Ash would consider expensive. Though she wasn't accustomed to the high life, she could smell class when it wafted under her nose. What bothered her more though, was that she wouldn't be able to afford such a gift without some serious saving or serious not eating.

Ash sat back in her seat as the waitress arrived with her drink. "Second drink? Did I keep you waiting that long?"

Ash shook her head. "I didn't want you waiting for me again so I got here nice and early."

Evie pointed to the two slices of cake beside her coffee pot. "Starting with the sweet stuff?"

Okay, easy conversation. I can do that. "I think the traditional order of a three-course dinner is outdated. I always start with dessert."

Evie winked. "You think we'll make it to dinner?"

"Because you won't be able to keep your hands off me or because you're going to discover I'm not the kind of person you want to date?" Ash's question made it out of her mouth without her permission and made her sound like a conceited asshole. "Sorry…I didn't mean it like that…I…" She shrugged, choosing silence over sticking her foot further into her mouth.

"I suppose either of those options could apply." She gestured toward the coffee pot. "Is that for me?"

Ash nodded. Either answer could have applied, yes, but Evie didn't specify which one did. Her lack of direction didn't help Ash at all. She tried to concentrate on her breathing to regain her composure. She ran through a series of questions in her head about jobs, educations, and family, but two kept rearing their heads. Was her age an issue? Did she always take women to that hotel to see if they were sexually compatible before she tried dating them? Nope, she was keeping those in check. She'd already had a good go at blowing the date again before it had barely begun. Seriously, what was it about Evie that made her so clunky and charmless?

"It's been a while since I dated," Evie said as she poured coffee into her cup. "I don't want this to be a question and answer session, but there's lots we don't know about each other." She added sweetener and milk before stirring the drink carefully. "How do you want to do this?"

Ash laughed gently. "Honestly, I'm terrified that anything else that comes out of my mouth will put you off instantly, and you'll be out of here as fast as your impressively high heels can carry you." There was no point in denying how being around Evie made her feel. Maybe admitting it would give her some leeway and understanding on Evie's part. "I don't know what it is, but whenever I'm around you, I turn into an idiot who has no idea how to talk to you." She shook her head. Wrong play. She'd blown it for sure now.

Evie reached across the table, took Ash's hand, and squeezed it firmly. "It sounds like we're both nervous. How about you tell me about Java and how he came to be in Sarah's quarantine?"

Evie's touch settled her a little. She wasn't hurrying out the door yet. Ash needed to relax and be herself. Like Oscar said, everyone else was taken. If Evie liked it, all good. If she didn't, then it simply wasn't meant to be.

"Okay. I can do that." She took a long drink of her Coke but wished she hadn't sent the beer back. "I went on holiday to celebrate getting my first post-university job." Ash maintained eye contact and was sure Evie winced a little at those words. How old did she think Ash was? "I know, it sounds like I didn't get my first proper job until I was in my mid-twenties, but that's not the case. I had lots of other jobs before and during uni."

"You're twenty-five?"

Evie sounded somewhat relieved, reinforcing Ash's belief that a perceived age gap had presented a problem for her. Ash nodded. "I didn't go straight to uni after A-levels. I needed to make some money first to make it a possibility."

"What do you mean? Did your family not want to finance you?"

Ash sighed against the sadness that surfaced as an unstoppable response to Evie's question. Straight into the deep stuff, then. She leaned back against the booth wall, pulling away from Evie's touch. "It wasn't quite that simple."

Evie said nothing, but her expression asked Ash to continue.

"I don't know my parents. I bounced around various foster homes hoping I'd stick somewhere, but that didn't happen until I was fifteen." She smiled at the thought of Nat and Rich. "There's no way I was asking them to help pay for my education, so I finished school and worked as an office temp for two years to build up some cash. Not enough to cover the degree, but enough so I wouldn't end up in an unmanageable pile of debt that might make me suicidal once I'd graduated."

"I'm sorry, Ash. I didn't realise that talking about Java would result in you opening up about your childhood. Do you want to talk about something else?"

Ash shrugged. "If you do want to get to know me, this is a pretty big part of my life." She laughed but didn't feel the humour. "And it might make you want to run. Orphans can have real attachments issues in their adult lives."

"So, you studied psychology at uni then?"

"How'd you guess?"

Evie tapped the side of her nose and smiled. "Takes one to know one."

"Ah, so you're a doctor of the mind at Horston?" That was another mystery solved. And it explained the fancy car. Psychiatrists could earn ridiculous amounts of money.

"See? Takes one to know one."

Ash shook her head. "Nope. I stopped at bachelor level. I wanted to make a difference with kids before they assimilated and repressed their traumas and ended up in a therapist's office as an adult."

Evie's smile widened. "Wow. That's…that's something." Her

brow wrinkled as though she couldn't fathom such a decision. "Did you enjoy studying?"

That question rankled, and she didn't censor her response. "Do you mean, did I not go onto a masters and doctorate because a bachelor's was about as much as my little brain could cope with?"

Evie raised her eyebrows. "No, that's not what I meant. But you've obviously been asked that question before to react like that."

Ash sighed, embarrassed that she could be so easily and correctly read. "Sorry. Yeah, I have. And they made their mark, apparently."

Evie smiled and shook her head. "People can be assholes. What you've done is commendable. I love that you want to help kids before their problems get too big for them to handle."

Something crossed Evie's eyes that Ash couldn't interpret before she glanced away. "I couldn't help but notice you sounded surprised when my age came up." Since they were swimming in deep waters anyway, it made sense to address it. "How old did you think I was?"

Evie scrunched her nose and fiddled with her mug before answering. "Twenty-one."

"And you were struggling with that? Because you're…"

Evie nodded before taking a long drink of her coffee. "How old do you think I am?"

Ash laughed and wagged her finger. "Oh, no way. I'd never try to guess a lady's age. That's date suicide."

"I turned thirty-two in December."

"Only seven years difference then. Is that still a problem?" Ash held her breath. She wanted Evie to say that it wasn't.

Evie inclined her head. "People change so much in their twenties…but you probably had to do a lot of growing up as a kid that you shouldn't have had to do. Which means, you might not have so much to do as an adult…*or* you're going to make up for those lost years by being an even bigger kid in your twenties."

"Spoken like a true head doctor. But are you willing to stick around and find out which it might be?"

Evie smiled. "I think so, but we have to come back to your job. Now would you get back to Java's story? The suspense is murderous."

"Okay, but you have to tell me something about yourself soon."

Evie waved her hand. "Yeah, yeah. We've got plenty of time for that."

"You say that, but we have a curfew, and time's a ticking." Ash motioned to the giant four-foot clock above the bar. "We can't have your Audi turning into a pumpkin."

"I think they only do that if you don't keep up the payments, and I own mine so I think I'm safe."

Ash raised her eyebrow. Evie *owned* her Audi? That was a serious pile of cash she'd parted with. Maybe Ash had made the wrong decision to not continue her studies. Evie was shaking her head as if she knew what Ash was thinking.

"I'm not rich, no. Ask me about the car later, and I'll tell you the story. Now carry on with yours."

"Fine," Ash said. "But you've got to promise not to judge me for breaking the law."

Evie threw her hands in the air. "That's a big ask." She frowned. "But since you're sitting here today free as a bird, I'm going to assume it's only a light breaking of the law rather than a heavy bank robbing or grievous bodily harm breaking of the law. Still," she picked up a fork, speared a piece of carrot cake, and wafted it in the air, "I'm going to reserve the right to judge you, sorry. Request denied."

"How about you keep an open mind, then?"

Evie nodded as she munched on the cake she'd popped into her mouth. "That, I can do. Continue."

"So, I'm on a cheap holiday alone in Spain. I'm out walking on the last day of my holiday, and I find this tiny little puppy roped up to a stake in the beach," Ash motioned with her hand, "way away from the tourist area. The little guy's been there a while—there's a couple of small, dry poos within reach of his rope—and he's so thirsty that he drinks my Sprite Zero. I check his chain collar and there's a disc on it, but it doesn't have anything inscribed. No telephone number, and not even a name. There's no one else around, so I cut the rope and take him for a walk back into the main village to see if anyone has lost a dog or had one stolen." She made a nought with her hand. "Nothing. Nada. No one knows anything, and no one's seen the dog before. A bartender at my hotel tells me that this happens a lot. Dogs have puppies, and the owners can't afford to take care of them, so they dump them. No one around there cares." Ash looked at Evie, who seemed completely absorbed in her story. The intensity in her eyes stirred memories of their night together, and Ash squeezed hers shut to push the naughty thoughts away. *No sex date. No sex date.*

"Are you okay? Do you have a headache?"

"No, I'm okay. I'm trying not to think about how beautiful you look when you're…" Ash stopped short of the full revelation. "I'm trying to comply with your 'date that doesn't end in sex' rule."

Evie gave her a winked grin. "That doesn't mean I don't want you thinking about it…I know I am."

Ash swallowed hard and let a breath out through her nose. Evie was all kinds of intoxicating, and her being so close without being able to kiss her was excruciating.

Evie jutted her chin. "Come on, handsome. Don't keep me in suspense. Tell me how you're a master criminal."

Ash tried to think of something unpleasant to abate the throbbing in her jeans. *What if I hadn't found Java that day?* It was enough to refocus her on the requested story. "Back to it then. Asking around got me nowhere, so I started to research how to get a pooch back into the UK, because I had no idea what that involved."

"Neither did I until I started volunteering at Sarah's kennels." Evie chopped off another piece of cake with the side of her fork.

"And now you know that you need microchips and pet passports?" Ash narrowed her eyes when Evie wrinkled her nose and looked somewhat guilty. "What else do you know?"

"A little bird might've told me that you showed up to the Port of Calais in a rental car with Java and none of the aforementioned requirements."

Evie pressed her lips into an apologetic smile and looked cute as all hell. There was nothing for Ash to be mad about really, but even if there was, she couldn't possibly be mad at that angelic face. "You might've told me you knew the punchline."

Evie shook her head. "But with this story, the punchline isn't the best bit. Getting to it is." She put her hand on Ash's forearm.

Evie's touch on her bare skin sent a familiar jolt to her core. "If you say so…" Ash took a moment to eat some walnut cake and make Evie wait. She pouted some, which prompted Ash to eat a few more forkfuls. "So obviously I had neither a passport or a microchip for Java, and like I said, it was my last day. I haven't mentioned it was a Sunday, so there were no vets open. Hence, no microchip." Ash shrugged. She could see the look in Java's eyes as clear as if he were sitting in front of her right then. "There was no way I could pack my stuff and leave him." It pleased Ash to see Evie nodding in agreement. "I got a taxi to the airport, hired a car, and drove to Calais without stopping…well, except for pee stops and drinks."

The next part had been a nightmare, but Ash relayed the story making it as captivating as possible. She'd managed to find a vet who microchipped Java and gave him a rabies shot, and his pet passport was issued in a swift five hours. The next obstacle was the twenty-one day ban on travel to ensure Java hadn't already got rabies. So she'd convinced the "pet police" and the UK authorities to let her go through that day on the proviso that Java went into quarantine as soon as they hit UK soil. A quick internet search found Sarah's kennels close to her home, called her, and Sarah had immediately agreed to help out after she'd heard Ash's story.

Evie remained attentive throughout, though Ash worried that she might be boring her. Ash wasn't capable of telling a story concisely. When she finished, Evie looked glassy-eyed, and Ash hoped her heroic tale might be enough to score her a follow-up date.

"That's an astounding adventure, Ash. You should write a book about it."

Ash laughed and shook her head. "I don't think so."

"No, you should. You could write it from the perspective of Java, and he could tell the tale of his time in quarantine with all the other dogs as colourful characters."

"Nope," Ash said. "I'm pretty sure I couldn't even begin to put a book together. I write songs, but they're a lot shorter and take a lot less time."

"You're musical, too." Evie ran her hand through her hair and leaned back in her seat. "You're sporty, intelligent, and creative. Are there no end to your talents?"

Ash didn't know whether Evie was teasing her or not. She resisted the urge to say that Evie hadn't mentioned the amazing sex they'd shared, which could be seen as another talent. But then it was more important that Evie thought there was more to Ash than her flair between the sheets. Otherwise this was going nowhere, and with every moment Ash spent with Evie, she knew that would be devastating. She didn't know where this might go, but she was certain she wanted to find out.

"I play the guitar. Do you want me to write a song and serenade you with it?" What the hell? Maybe a grand romantic gesture was exactly what would win Evie's heart.

Chapter Nineteen

I need the loo. I won't be a minute." Evie pushed her cup away from her and slid out of the booth.

"I'll be here," Ash said and grinned.

There was that gorgeous smile; the one Evie could get used to seeing regularly. "I hope so." She'd seen the toilet sign and headed that way, conscious to sashay her way there. She didn't fall to the temptation of glancing over her shoulder to see if Ash had peered around the booth to watch her walk away. Ash had been sufficiently attentive for Evie to be assured that would be the case.

She glanced at the mirror before entering one of the toilet stalls. She'd been concerned that the odd tear had fallen during several of Ash's stories and that they may have ruined her eye make-up, but everything was in order. Evie had been excited to learn Ash wasn't as young as she'd originally thought. Silly, but seven years difference didn't seem anywhere near as bad as over a decade. There was still a great deal of life experience and change that happened during one's twenties, but Ash was halfway through that, and her personal life experience had made her more mature than the average twenty-five-year-old.

The afternoon was going far better than she'd expected. Over the past two weeks, Evie had vacillated over whether or not to even have this date. After the straight forward conversation she'd had with Harriet, doubts had begun to creep in, and Evie got hung up on the age gap again. Not only that, but she'd all but decided that they wouldn't have enough in common for a friendship, let alone a relationship. In fact, she wasn't sure why she'd fooled herself into thinking that a friendship would happen in the first place. Intimate relationships often blossomed from friendships, but what interests could she possibly share with Ash anyway? Aside from carnal ones. But when that inevitably slowed, or rather, was no longer the primary focus of the relationship, it was the things two people shared an outlook on that nourished that connection.

She returned to the mirror and looked at herself steadily. She'd been enjoying Ash's company so much that she'd deliberately parked the second main topic of conversation, and that was far from ideal. She glanced at her watch. They were two hours into their date, and the end of daylight curfew was a little over an hour away. She'd spent enough time with Ash to be sure there was more than an incredible sexual connection. She was charming, funny, talented, and had a heart of gold. Her career choice and Java's rescue attested to that. The elephant in the room loomed large, threatening to ruin everything that a relationship with Ash could entail.

Oh, well. It had to be done. The question was, how? A little poking around and testing of the water, or a straight forward plunge into the potentially icy abyss? Evie took a deep breath and headed back to their table. Ash had chosen to work with kids. That had to be a good sign. At the very least, it meant she liked them. Halfway back to the table, Ash poked her head around the booth and grinned.

"You ladies take an awfully long time in the loo."

Evie retook her seat and raised her eyebrow. "'You ladies'? Unfortunately, the toilets here are only for ladies or gentlemen. What does that mean for you?"

Ash wiggled her eyebrows. "I'm a woman, and proudly so, but I'm no lady. I guess I'll have to hold it until I get home."

"And where is home?" Evie asked. *Chicken.*

Ash shook her head and crossed her arms. "Nope. No more from me until you share. Otherwise this," she gestured between the two of them, "is a long job interview for a non-existent post."

Evie inclined her head. The post wasn't non-existent. The post was for a full-time lover and possible co-parent. Christ, it sounded too serious when she framed it that way. But there was no other way around it. If she wanted someone in her life for the long run, even a short long run, they had to be more than good with the fact that Evie was mother to a twelve-year-old kid.

"Tell me about your amazing car. Does she have a name? Because obviously, it has to be a she, or that would be an injustice."

"Annie." Her fancy Audi didn't scream family car. Steering the conversation to kids from this was an ask. "And not Annie the Audi because of the alliteration, though that *is* nice."

Ash slapped the table lightly and then pointed her finger as if she'd figured out an unsolvable maths problem.

"After Annie Oakley? Driving her makes you feel like an outlaw."

Evie shook her head and laughed. "Have you thought about

going into marketing? That could be an outlet for your creativity that you're missing… Anyway, she's named Annie after my mum. I'm an only child. My dad died a couple of years ago, and my mum followed him last year." Evie took a breath. The swell of emotion from sharing this still-raw part of her life caught her by surprise. Ash reached across the table and offered her hands. Evie placed hers in Ash's, and Ash gently squeezed them. Warmth flooded her body and began to melt the icy chill that had swept through her as soon as she thought about her parents' deaths. She kept her gaze on their interlinked hands. She'd seen that look of sympathy too many times, and it made it hard to breathe. That Ash hadn't been lucky enough to have a mum, let alone one as supportive and wonderful as Evie's, made it harder still to witness her reaction, so she didn't seek it out.

"She loved cars, and she loved speed. Every year we bought each other one of those racing experiences with the supercars. And every year we drove away from the race track in my sensible hatchback, both saying that we needed to win the lottery so we could afford a supercar for playing around in and keep a sensible car for daily life." Like for running her son to and from school. Evie paused again and concentrated on the feeling of Ash's hands wrapped around her own, tried to tether herself to the ground and not be carried away on the wings of her grief. She thought she had this under control.

"When I went to the solicitors for the will reading, I had no idea what to expect." That was a white lie. She thought that some of the estate might be put into a trust for Izad, but it had never been mentioned or discussed. "Dad had been a teacher and Mum had been a stay-at-home mum. Dad retired early at sixty, and I'd always encouraged them to enjoy retirement. They took holidays and trips all over the world. They ate out a lot. Mum stopped travelling when Dad died, and the eating out turned into a lot of deliveries—she was never much of a cook." She laughed quietly and briefly closed her eyes. What she'd give for a poorly-cooked homemade meal one more time. "I wasn't expecting some huge inheritance—enough for cremation costs etcetera—and I fully expected that they'd released the capital from the house to finance their lifestyle." She shrugged. "Money was never something we talked about. Dad handled everything, and they never asked me for any help or guidance." Evie turned her hands over and placed them on Ash's forearms. "I was partly right. They had sold the house, but there was still a sizeable sum in their bank. One of the stipulations of the will was that I use a large chunk of that to buy our version of a supercar. The month before Mum died, we'd been drooling over the new TT and talking about all the extras we'd have if we could ever afford to have one. We'd looked at a lot of cars over the years, but it seemed right that I bought the one we'd most recently been coveting."

"Can I ask what she died of?" Ash asked gently.

Evie swallowed and offered a smile, but she knew it was a poor effort. "A broken heart, perhaps. They don't know. There was nothing physically wrong with her. No diseases. No aggressive cancer. It was like she'd had enough of life without Dad."

Ash shook her head. "That's sad, but so touching that your mum loved your dad *that* much. What does a love like that feel like?"

"I have no idea." Evie pulled back and picked her mug up for a sip before she continued, "I've been in love a few times, but ultimately, it was short-lived and disappointing."

Ash jutted her chin. "Is that what this is all about?"

"What do you mean?"

"The date with no sex? A quick—but not fool proof—way of finding out if this might be worth pursuing?" She flicked her finger between them to indicate the two of them.

"You're rather blunt." *And rather perceptive.*

"I prefer straight forward and honest," Ash said.

"Have you ever been in love?" The conversation was leaning toward discomfort, so Evie tried for deflection.

"Not really, and definitely not like your mum and dad…but I want to be…one day." Ash looked away and wrinkled her nose.

"What? What is it?" Evie's psychiatrist kicked in. There was something Ash wasn't saying. But she was feeling it deeply, that much was clear.

Ash rolled her shoulders and looked away. "Nothing." She looked at her watch. "Would you like another drink? We've got time for one more before the sun goes down." She winked and wiggled her eyebrows mischievously.

"Only if you tell me what just went through your head."

Ash signalled for the waitress. She came over quickly and took their order.

"Tell me what happened."

"It's crazy." Ash rubbed at her forehead. "You'll think I'm weird."

"Weird is good. It wouldn't do for us all to be strait-laced, by the book, vanilla people. The world would be dull and monotone without the weirdos to colour it in."

"You promise you won't run?" Ash asked. "I mean, this isn't aimed at you specifically. It's just the way I think of life and the people in it."

"Come on. The build-up is making it worse."

The waitress returned with their drinks, and Ash had a hefty slurp of her Coke before she continued. "Have you heard of… soul groups?"

Evie nodded. "I know a little about it."

"Well, it's something I believe in. I believe that there are people and beings you're meant to connect with, that you're drawn to over and over again in different lifetimes. They call to you. People and beings that you search for without even knowing that you're searching for them, but when you find them, they… they fit. They feel right." Ash looked away and shifted in her seat. "I told you it was weird."

Wow. A beautiful butch *and* a helpless romantic. "It's not. I think it's sweet. It's a wonderful idea." Of course, the scientist in her couldn't possibly believe in it, but there were far worse schools of thought to live one's life by. And whilst Ash had said it wasn't aimed at Evie, she was here with her now so she must feel something or, like Evie, want to know if there could be.

"Okay. So, moving on. We've covered some serious topics. Is the next one going to continue in the same vein, or are we moving onto lighter stuff?"

Evie closed her eyes briefly. It was the perfect segue into the big question. "How do you feel about kids?"

Ash frowned then smiled. "I love them. I think they're great. I'm not big on the tiny, snivelling, nappy-filling, crying with no possible way to find out why, kind. I like them best once they get past eight years old. That's when you can start having interesting conversations with them."

Evie's countenance lightened. Ash had brightened considerably once she began to talk about children. She was clearly passionate about them, hence her career choice.

"I think it's great that more and more LGBTQ couples can adopt now," Ash said. "It's been nearly twenty years since it was made legal, but I think it's only taken hold in the past five years or so. It would have been amazing to have had LGBTQ parents. The level of support they could've given me when I began to realise I was a lesbian would've been something else." She sighed and looked down at the table, her sadness clear. "I'd like to have kids one day…you know, when I grow up and am no longer considered a kid myself." Ash laughed. "I've got some living to do though before I can even begin to think about helping a little human be a great human. I mean, it's my job, but I leave the kids at work and go home, you know?"

One day. There it was. Everything Ash had said sounded perfect up to that point. And it wasn't lost on Evie that Ash recognised she was still a kid in some ways, just like she'd said to Harriet when they'd talked all of this over.

"What's up?" Ash asked, reaching for Evie's hands.

Evie pressed her lips together tightly and pulled her hands from Ash's reach. *Friends it is, then.* "I should go." The words were out before she'd given them enough thought. She couldn't leave without explanation. That would only prolong this now unnecessary dance. "Sorry, no. Let me take that back." Evie shook her head and sighed. The letting go. They'd only had one night together and a few conversations. This shouldn't be that hard. And yet…

"Did I say something wrong?"

Ash looked panicked. Adorably so. Evie wanted to pull her into her arms and soothe away the obvious self-doubts she'd inherited from a childhood lacking in love and stability, from not having the right parents there to build her up to believe in herself. That's what Evie had received. And she'd always been grateful for it. "No, not wrong, just…" *Crap.* "I have a child. A twelve-year-old boy that I had when I was twenty-one and fell pregnant after having sex with my best friend *once*." Once. That particular element of the tale always resonated, no matter how many times she told it. Izad was simply ready to be born, or if Ash's stardust theory was correct, he'd been hanging around waiting to be reunited with Evie.

Ash said nothing. She was looking at Evie but seemed to be looking through or beyond her. Evie waited a few moments, waited for Ash to say something, anything, but a long period of silence came and went, and still she remained mute.

"Maybe I *should* go." Since the conversation had ended abruptly, and Ash seemed reticent, perhaps leaving would be for the best. Ash could have some time to process what Evie had told her. When she came out of the apparent shock, perhaps they could talk and consider being friends…or not.

"No, don't go."

Ash reached out again, and this time, Evie allowed her hands to be held. She tried to ignore the jolt of excitement that ran through her at the touch, her stupid body reacting to the memory of what those hands had done to her…and what they would never do again.

"I'm sorry."

Evie waited for more, but nothing was forthcoming. She raised her eyebrow. "What do you have to be sorry for? I'm certainly not sorry I've been blessed with a child." She didn't regret her curt response. She'd had more than her fair share of people telling her she'd ruined her life and career by having a kid at twenty-one. She didn't need someone fresh out of uni repeating the tired old mantra.

"No, I didn't mean that. I was apologising for falling dumb." Ash scratched her head, clearly trying to find the right words and failing miserably.

"There's no need to be sorry for anything," Evie said. "I should have told you earlier. I was going to tell you on our first date, but…" That hadn't quite panned out, and they'd used other methods of communication all night. Evie gathered her handbag and coat and slid out from the booth. "It's getting dark anyway." She motioned out the window to the dusky sky and the city lights beginning to dot the city street with an amber glow. "This doesn't have to be awkward. This was about finding out if we might be compatible, and we're not because my son comes first for me. And that's okay." Evie opened her handbag, pulled out some cash, and put forty pounds on the table. "I had a great time, and I like talking to you… Perhaps we can be friends." Evie began to retreat from the table, discomforted by Ash's repeated streak of silence. "Think about it."

Evie turned and hurried out into the cooling night air, which freshened her burning skin. Was she embarrassed? Ashamed? She shouldn't be any of those things. What was it then? She pulled her coat on, hitched her handbag over her shoulder, and walked briskly to the car park. She glanced over her shoulder more than once. Did she want Ash to come running after her? What could she say that would end the night better?

She shook her head and tugged the collar of her coat closed against the bitter wind. She was being silly. She'd known Ash was going to react that way. She'd predicted she wasn't ready for that level of adulting.

So why was she so angry?

Chapter Twenty

"Thanks, Matt. If you could get the table tennis set up, that'd be great." Ash gestured to the table in the corner of the giant storage cupboard. "We'll put it in the blue room today. I've got the green room organised for the music session."

Matt nodded. "Will do. I'm looking forward to helping you."

"Cool. Let me know when you've done that, and I'll see what else needs sorting." Ash left him to it and jogged back up to the office to get the attendance folder and cash tin. Bev didn't look up or acknowledge her when she entered their shared space. "The new volunteer came early to help set up." She offered the information snippet in the habitual way that had come to be their limited exchanges. Bev hadn't warmed to Ash, no matter how charming she'd tried to be. The kids, on the other hand, had taken her into their space with open arms. Ash still didn't know why Bev had taken a dislike to her from the beginning, but now she suspected that her easy connection with the young people was the source of Bev's continued ire toward her.

As expected, Bev didn't answer. Ash retrieved the stuff she needed from the shelf and pulled a couple of pens from the pot on her desk. She took a breath and prepared to ask her next question, knowing that an explosion might be part of Bev's response. "Are you coming down today? We've got four volunteers, including the new guy, Matt. But he's helping me with the music session."

Bev looked up, the disdain in her expression clear. She placed her pen down slowly. "All of them are DBS checked, yes?"

Ash nodded.

"So you have enough staff for forty kids."

Bev picked up her pen and continued with her work, as if that were answer enough. Ash weighed up the pros and cons of challenging her. They weren't supposed to count a new volunteer in the ratio calculation of staff to kids, so technically, they could only have thirty-two kids, and that was if they were all a certain age. Add a few younger ones, and the ratio went down. Ash had done this session four weeks now, and the attendance ranged from thirty-five to forty-five. She was certain they'd need Bev down there at some point, though she was just a body rather than an interactive part of the session.

Ash picked up the two-way radio on Bev's desk and switched it on before replacing it in the charger. "I'll give you a shout if the numbers peak," she said and broke for the door before Bev could unleash another withering look.

When she got downstairs and went into the blue room, her other three volunteers had arrived and Matt had joined them. She greeted them and placed the folder and cash tin on the table by the door where the kids came in. They ran through a few pre-session checks, Ash allocated them to certain rooms, and she made sure everyone had the keys to lock off rooms if they emptied out as the kids moved around, depending on what they wanted to do. She double checked the ratios with everyone, and each of them checked their radios individually. They could have all done it at the same time, but Ash was feeling petty and irritated by Bev's behaviour and wanted the maximum noise impact in the office. It vaguely occurred to her that Bev could simply turn the radio off, but if there was an emergency, she needed to be reachable. Though it had become clear Bev wasn't particularly enamoured of her job, Ash didn't think she'd wilfully put the kids in danger.

Ash put Claire on register duty and had Matt shadow her. Moments later, the first wave of primary school children arrived direct from the school nearby. Ash stayed in the blue room and got the kids started on a jewellery beading project between short chats with the parents. That part wasn't Ash's favourite. It was like some of the mums hadn't spoken to anyone for days and mistook Ash's friendliness as a sign that they could bend her ear while others couldn't wait to drop their kids off for more precious alone time. Why those parents ever bothered to have children at all was a question that plagued her.

What kind of parent was Evie? *Here I go again.* Ash's thoughts had been veering off to Evie-land a lot since their second, and apparently last, date a few days ago. She'd been having a great time, and it looked like Evie had been enjoying herself too. The conversation had flowed, never stilted, and they'd swung from difficult topics to discussions of no consequence with no difficulty. Then came Evie's bombshell.

And Ash had been a complete prat about that. It had come from so far left field that it totally knocked Ash from her cosy little centre of the universe spot, and she didn't recover. Not even to say good-bye as Evie beat a hasty retreat out of the Snug. Ash couldn't blame her. It was hard to have a conversation with someone who'd stopped communicating. Even now, Ash had no idea why she'd been struck dumb. It was a shock, sure, but to not be able to speak? Maybe it was her past. She'd not considered settling down properly yet, let alone had any concrete thoughts about children and a family.

She knew that she wanted kids eventually, but she also wanted to be sure that her motives for it were pure. She didn't want them to be the result of any psychological damage from her own childhood experiences. And she'd certainly not considered stepping into a ready-made family. Evie's child was twelve. For all intents and purposes, he was a little adult who probably wouldn't take kindly to some stranger coming into his life and acting like another parent.

Ash cut short a conversation with a particularly unpleasant mother and went to the group of kids hanging around the table tennis. "Are we playing queeny-kingy-boss?"

A chorus of "yays" echoed around the room, and Ash chose the first two players around the same age to compete for the game's titular role then lined the rest of the players along the wall. Lou quickly scored two points against Josh.

"Boss," she cried out as she slammed the ball into the far right corner to claim her third and winning point.

Once in place, contenders had to score three past her, whereas she only had to score one to remain at the head of the table. Ash had found it was a great game to involve lots of young people at the same time and keep everyone moving and interested. On top of that, the older ones naturally eased up on the younger children to help them improve, but then were ferociously competitive with their peers. It was a great balance, and Ash loved it.

An hour flew by, and the secondary school kids began to arrive. With only regular-sized instruments, Ash had set up the music session aimed primarily at the older kids, though she had a few tambourines if the younger ones fancied joining.

"You haven't started without us, have you?"

Ash turned, recognising Izad's voice. "Never." She smiled. Ally and Katie stood either side of him grinning widely. Wherever Izad went, the girls weren't far behind. "You're already like a little band."

Ally nodded and shoulder-shoved Izad. "I told you. We should always walk around like this. You in the middle, and us either side. That way, no one can ever get us mixed up."

"That's good logic," Ash said and jingled her keys. "Are you ready to play?"

Ash announced the start of the music session, and word was put out over the radios. She ended up with another five young people. Perfect number. She checked back over the radio to make sure numbers were okay in every room, and when she was satisfied that they were, she opened up the green room with Matt, and they all rushed in.

All except Izad. He stood at the door watching everyone rush around the room, plucking and banging and knocking and shaking all the instruments. "What's up?"

"Nothing." He scanned the room. "I know what all of these instruments are and what they sound like…if you know how to play them."

"Impressive. Do you already know how to play any of them?"

Izad shook his head. "And I don't want to. I only want to learn to play the piano. Then I can sing and play, and I don't need anyone else to make music."

Ash inclined her head. His words would've sounded sad coming from anyone else, but Ash was fast learning that Izad wasn't like a lot of the other kids. He had a depth and maturity greater than his age, and she suspected he was neurodiverse in some way. "What about Ally and Katie? Don't you want to play with them?"

Izad nodded. "Yep. But mostly, I want to be able to play on my own." He leaned in and beckoned for Ash to come closer. "It's like my singing. It stops me from feeling alone," he whispered.

Ash's heart broke. What the hell was going on at home? She'd met his dad, and he seemed to dote on Izad. And Izad always hugged him when he left and when he came back to pick him up. She'd yet to meet his mum, but Izad had mentioned she was supportive of him when they first met. She had to tread carefully here and could do with going into the orange room, but that would leave Matt on his own in here, which she couldn't do. "What makes you feel lonely, buddy?"

"I want a sister. A brother would do too. But I *want* a sister."

Phew. The alarm bells stopped ringing, and Ash relaxed her shoulders. Disney was to blame for this little childhood drama.

"I've wanted one since I watched Frozen," he continued. "Anna and Elsa love each other so much. They keep each other company when there are no adults around."

Ash nodded. "They do, don't they? What other movies have got brothers and sisters in?" She saw Matt was trying to catch her eye. "Hang on, Izad." She motioned Matt over. "Have them rotating around the instruments and getting used to how they work. We'll play them something and have them provide rhythm with the drums, bongos, and tambourines." She inclined her head toward Izad. "I need a few minutes here."

"Okay. I can do that."

"You definitely can." Ash patted him on the shoulder as he turned. She'd had a good feeling about him since meeting at the half-term student volunteer fair, and his involvement in the table tennis game earlier compounded that instinct. It'd be good to have a guy around too because the rest of the staff team were female.

She turned back to Izad.

"Brave, with the bears and the bows and arrows. But she had brothers, and they were annoying. And Storks. Storks is like me. Except Nate wanted a brother and ended up with a sister. And his mum and dad lived together but mine don't." Izad looked up at her and shrugged. "Can we play some music now?"

Ash nodded and laughed gently. She enjoyed when the kids trusted her enough to open up and share some of their inner world with her. It reinforced her decision to work with kids instead of adults.

Working with them but not having one of my own. The difference was huge. This was a few hours, and then she went home with no responsibilities. What if, instead, she went home to a kid who asked her for a brother or sister? Would Izad go home tonight and ask his dad straight up for a sister? Or would he go guerrilla and play the movie, *Storks*, non-stop instead? The thought made her laugh. Interesting that his parents were no longer together, though. That was something Bev hadn't shared with her, not that she shared much about any of the kids or their parents. Maybe she didn't know enough about them to share. Izad certainly didn't seem affected by it. At least he had both his parents even if they were in separate houses. On the pros side, she supposed he must have two bedrooms too. She wanted to ask Bev if she knew anything more about the family but suspected her interest would be summarily shut down.

"Okay, we're going to play on the guitar and keyboard, but we want you guys to provide the rhythm for us. Sound good?" She began to play the keyboard and Matt followed her lead on the guitar.

As she played, she drifted back to her conversation with Izad. When she was a kid, Ash had a list of things she wished for. She wanted parents of course, but they were second to a brother. She was jealous of the siblings she saw at foster parent gatherings. It was as if they'd beaten the system that tried to hurt them. No matter how good or bad their foster parents were, they had each other. And even though a lot of the foster parents were good enough people, it was clear there was something special about having your own flesh and blood by your side every day, no matter what crap the rest of the world sent your way.

Inevitably, her focus returned to Evie and the end of their date. She'd suggested they become friends since a relationship was no longer on the cards after Ash had stuck her foot in her mouth without realising it. She hadn't thought about much else since. Plenty of people who were younger than her had kids. Evie had given birth when she was twenty-one. Her foster parent, Nat, had her son at twenty-four, and she was a wonderful mum. Ash decided she needed to take some time to think about where she was in life. Going to university had been her goal for so long, that's all she'd thought about. And when she'd finished university, deciding on a career and getting a job had become her primary focus. Now what? She hadn't stopped to think about it. What *was* her next goal? Maybe she'd give Nat a call tonight and organise to go over for a meal and a chat. It'd been a while since she'd seen them both, and they had another foster kid Ash hadn't met yet.

She looked around at the faces of the kids in the room, all fascinated by what she and Matt were doing, all engaged and happy. It was wonderful and heartening she was a big part of the reason for that…but what if she could do what Nat and Rich had done for her? There was a massive difference between youth worker and parent though. But what if she *could* be a positive influence, a mentor, and role model for a child *every* day rather than for just a few hours a couple of days a week? Could she be ready for that?

There were no quick answers for those questions, but she did know that she wanted the friendship that was on offer. She and Evie had made a connection, more than a sexual one, and Ash wanted to explore that. She'd spent so many years alone, floating in a sea of people but not attached to any one of them, always alone even when she was surrounded by others. Few people had come along in her life that were part of her soul group. Nat and Rich. Kirsty. Java. Maybe Evie was part of it in a different way than she might have hoped. Maybe they weren't destined to be lovers, but Ash didn't want to lose the possibility of a great friendship because of her inability to communicate properly.

Okay. She had a plan. Dinner with the fosters and a phone conversation with Evie. It wasn't exactly a step-by-step guide to the next stage of her life, but at least she'd recognised she no longer had a target or goal for her life. And she was always more settled when she was working toward something. Evie had come into her life for a reason. She was good people, and Ash hadn't had much experience of that. Enough, though, to know she had to grab hold. There was too much darkness in this world; she'd learned that in the most painful ways. But it had taught her to recognise true and pure light. Evie had that light. And Ash wasn't about to let that go.

Chapter Twenty-One

Can you forgive me for being an idiot? Any chance we can meet to chat? I promise not to go mute on you again!

Evie huffed when she read the message. It had been two days since she'd heard from Ash, and she'd been tempted to rescind her offer of friendship. What kind of friend left someone hanging for two days after such a huge discussion? But Ash had work and football, so perhaps this was the first chunk of time she'd had to open the line of communication again.

She opened the fridge and scanned the shelves, deciding whether or not to give Ash the benefit of the doubt, and not sure what she was looking for. Ash could've been angry too, she supposed, that Evie hadn't told her about having a child before she agreed to go on a date. Perhaps it had taken her a couple of days to calm down and think rationally about the situation.

She slammed the door shut. *The situation.* There wouldn't be a situation if she'd listened to her logical self in the first place and not swooned at the attention from the hot, sexy butch. No, she was being reactive, and that was never helpful. Of course she could forgive Ash for her reaction, and she did want to explore a friendship with her. She realised that she should be grateful for Ash's honesty. She could've played along and had more amazing sex for six months while Evie decided whether or not it was serious enough to introduce her to Izad.

She closed her eyes and images of Ash's naked body flooded her memory. God, the sex. Evie opened her eyes again and returned to the fridge, needing something to occupy her mouth. Ash was a great kisser too. The right amount of soft and hard. And then there was the unusual play, first with her in control, then Ash dictating the course. It was like they'd squeezed months of getting to know each other intimately into one marathon session.

The punnet of strawberries caught her eye. Mm, what she wouldn't give to be eating them from Ash's body again. *Stop it.* She was behaving like a sex-crazed uni student. She selected some leftovers, closed the fridge door again, and popped the plastic tub in the microwave.

Evie read the message again while she brewed some pecan decaf and finally pressed on the flashing cursor to respond.

I'm free tonight.

She sent the message and pushed the phone away, sure that Ash wouldn't be watching for her response and that by the time she did see it, it would probably be too late to go out anyway. Her phone pinged before the microwave.

I can be at the Snug in 45 mins. Unless I've ruined that place for you?

There was a smiley face on the end. Evie glanced at the time. She could easily match Ash's timing if she forwent dinner. They could chat for a couple of hours, and she'd still be home in time for a quick bath and a reasonably early night.

If you promise to speak, I can be there. And no, you couldn't ruin that place for me. It's too fabulous.

I promise x

Evie shook her head at the presence of the text equivalent of a kiss at the end of Ash's text. It used to be that the only person sending kisses would be loved ones, now it seemed common practice for everyone to use them. Even her plumber ended his messages to her with at least one. She stopped the microwave and put her coffee in her trusty Starbucks to-go flask, the one from Pike Place that Harriet had brought from a trip to Seattle. It had the original logo where you could actually see the mermaid's breasts, so it always made her smile. Perhaps one day, she could visit some of the places from which Harriet had brought her a souvenir. It wasn't likely, she supposed, while Izad was still young…but perhaps Tal might entertain a ten-day visit with Izad to allow her the opportunity to get Stateside. Perhaps Ash might accompany her. Friends went on trips together all the time.

Shoving the thought away to ruminate on another time, Evie ran upstairs and quickly changed into jeans, boots, and a sweater. She vaguely contemplated a five-minute shower but opted for another application of deodorant and a spray of Suede Orris. As soon as she put it on, she tried to rub it away. Ash had been particularly taken with the scent, and Evie didn't want her getting the wrong idea, as if she was trying to seduce her.

The question plagued her entire journey to the city. She was desperate to convince herself that yes, friends was better than nothing, and she could easily handle being in close proximity to Ash without constantly reliving their one night of outstanding sex. She was an adult in control of her sexual urges.

She managed to snag a spot directly outside the Snug, and the bouncer nodded at her and smiled.

"Nice car."

She returned the bouncer's smile and thanked her, happy in the knowledge that she'd probably make sure no one messed with Annie while she was inside. Evie was pleased to see Ash already there when she entered, and she'd got a private booth again.

Evie waved, and Ash smiled and stood. She sighed, loving and hating the gesture simultaneously. Loving it, because she always enjoyed such a chivalrous display, and hating it, because she'd be missing out on so much more of that action. *Stop it.* She reminded herself, as she didn't resist milking her approach for Ash's benefit, that she was a respectable psychiatrist in her thirties, not an over-sexed undergrad.

"We established a hugging precedent last time, but I'm not going to presume hugging rights tonight because I've been such a dick."

Evie shook her head and laughed. "I hug friends." She opened her arms, and Ash stepped into and pulled her close. She shuddered at Ash's warm breath on her neck as she held her there for a little longer than friend-hug protocol. Evie pulled away reluctantly. "Not for that long though."

Ash averted her eyes and retook her seat. "Sorry. Do friends only warrant a two second duration?"

"Two for beginner friends, yes. The length of the hug increases with the strength of the friendship." Evie placed her coat on the hook at the end of their booth and slid in. "I thought *everyone* knew that."

Ash grinned. "Duly noted."

How happy it made her to see Ash smile gave her some pause, but she ignored the thought and pointed to the four beverages lined up on the table. "Is one of those mine?"

"Yes. Any of them, in fact." She indicated to each one in turn as she spoke. "Rioja; Absolut and Coke; Seedlip Grove 42 and tonic; and non-alcoholic Bud. I didn't know if you'd be driving or taking a taxi, so I tried to cover all bases." Ash inclined her head. "Except coffee. I didn't cover coffee. Would you like a coffee?"

Evie shook her head and caught hold of one of Ash's flailing hands. "I don't want coffee. I want you to relax." Evie smiled at Ash's nervousness. It showed that she cared about what had happened between them.

Ash swallowed and nodded. "I'm sorry. I'm a little on edge.

I didn't know if you might show up just to tell me what a twat I was to you on Saturday *and* for the following two days of radio silence." She ran her free hand across the back of her head. "I'm sorry, Evie."

"Just take a breath." She released Ash's hand and gestured once again to the drinks selection, trying not to focus on missing the contact with her. "And talk me through the Seedy one so I can choose something to drink while we talk."

"Okay, so they've got a whole range of them. They're distilled non-alcoholic drinks they serve mostly with tonic. But I chose this one mainly because the bottle had a squirrel's head made from ginger root…and it's citrusy, which almost everyone loves, yeah? Oh, and I remembered that you said how much you liked Thai food, and this has lemongrass as well as ginger."

Evie laughed gently, more than a little impressed that Ash had remembered something she'd said in passing during their night together. "You're going to faint if you keep talking so fast without breathing."

"Sorry. Again. It's supposed to be the drink to drink when you can't drink…or something like that."

Evie drew the glass with the fancy orange peel garnish toward her. "It sounds perfect, thank you." She appreciated the effort Ash had gone to, but why hadn't she simply waited until Evie had arrived?

"I didn't want to waste time at the bar," Ash said. "If you were wondering why I bothered to order four drinks rather than wait to see what you wanted when you got here, that was the reason. It gets busy in here, and I imagine you've only got a couple of hours because of work tomorrow. I didn't want to be standing at the bar waiting for drinks when we could be talking and clearing the air."

Evie frowned. She thought she had a good poker face. How had Ash figured out what she was thinking? "Makes sense. I do only have two hours. I usually don't come out on a work night at all."

Ash bowed her head. "I'm honoured, thank you."

Evie couldn't tell if she was being facetious. "You're already on a timeout card, do you want to push it by being a smart arse?" She smiled to show she was only half-joking.

Ash held up her hands and shook her head. "I'm sorry. Too early for jokes. I understand." She picked up the Budweiser and took a long drink. She pulled a face, put the bottle down, and pushed it away from her. "You made a good choice not picking that."

Evie had sipped her own choice at the same time. "I'm happy with my choice, thanks." She waited for Ash to speak, but it was silent for a long moment. Too long. "You said you were going to speak this time?"

Ash looked serious and nodded.

"Yes… You want me to go ahead and dive right in?" Ash asked.

"Please do."

"Okay. I'm sorry for how our date finished on Saturday. The news that you had a son knocked me sideways. That's no excuse for going speechless and letting you walk out. I should've responded, and I should've walked you to your car." She reached across the table but pulled back before she touched Evie. "I'm truly sorry for that."

It took much of Evie's resolve not to grasp Ash's hands as she offered, and then withdrew, them. She bit down on her tongue to give her brain something else to think about and tried to remind herself she was here to get a friendship back on track.

"Also, I'm sorry for going dark for the past two days. I had a match yesterday, but again, that's no excuse either. I typed so many messages and deleted them all. I couldn't find the right words to say on Saturday, and I couldn't find anything that might make it better in a text." She took the vodka and Coke and sipped at it before she continued. "I don't think I'm going to find the right words now either, but I would like to take you up on your offer of friendship… I like you. I like you a lot, and I want us to be friends if…if we can't be anything else."

"I told you, my son comes first. He has to. And I'm looking for someone to share my life *and* my son with. I can't waste time on meaningless dalliances." However off-the-charts phenomenal the sex is. Ash looked wounded at Evie's words. "Not meaningless. I mean, relationships that aren't going anywhere."

"I understand. And I'm sorry I can't be that." Ash swallowed and glanced away. "I was abandoned when I was a kid, when I was a baby. I wouldn't want to be any part of doing that to another child…if we didn't work out."

Evie waited for more, but Ash took a long sip of her drink instead. She had questions, but she wasn't sure she had the right to ask them. Ash had made her position clear, and a friendship was all that either of them was offering. As stable as Ash presented, she clearly still had issues of abandonment and trust derived from her childhood, and it wasn't Evie's place to try to unpick that. Until she'd begun to address the issues she'd acknowledged, Ash probably wasn't ready for a relationship that involved a child. Evie wanted to believe she'd had a lucky escape, but there was something at the back of her mind telling her this wasn't one of her work cases; it wasn't that simple, and she shouldn't dismiss Ash so summarily. Despite her scientific background, it seemed Ash's romantic notion of soul groups had infiltrated Evie's usual rational and logical thinking. She sighed. "So we're going to be friends then?"

"Yeah." Ash smiled and raised her glass. "To friends."

Evie clinked her glass to Ash's. "Friends." They both drank to the toast, and Evie shrugged off the disappointment that's all they would be to each other. "Did you win?" Evie elaborated when Ash looked puzzled. "Your match on Sunday…did you win?"

"Ah, I get you. Yeah, we did. Fifteen nil."

Evie laughed loudly, then covered her mouth. "Fifteen nil? That sounds more like a netball score than a football score. Were half their team blindfolded? Or were their ankles bound together?"

Ash wrinkled her nose and narrowed her eyes. "Ha ha. None of the above. Our opponents are the whipping girls of this league, and everyone beats them by double figures. The pride is in which of the other teams can get the most goals in ninety minutes."

"Did you score?" Evie recalled Ash played left wing, and whilst she didn't watch that much football, she understood it and the positions. Although against an opposition like the one Ash described, it seemed that even their goalkeeper might have scored. Ash straightened up in her seat and looked rather pleased with herself.

"Yep, I got a hat-trick." She wiggled in her seat and smiled broadly. "It looked like I was going to finish the game with two, but we got a penalty in the last minute. The captain gave it to me so I could get my first hat-trick of the season."

Evie couldn't help but smile in return. Ash's enthusiasm was touching. "How did you celebrate?" Evie imagined Ash running to the corner flag and pulling off her shirt like she'd seen so many of the Premiership players do. Though if she had abs like Chichi Igbo, she'd do the same…and Ash was in damn fine shape. *For God's sake.*

"I ran back to the halfway line and clapped a few teammate's

hands on the way. It's not great form to celebrate manically when you're winning that easily. Maybe you could come and watch if you're free one Sunday?"

"I'm not a big fan of standing around in the cold and wet, which it almost always seems to be lately. Ask me again when it's warmer." It wasn't a complete lie. Evie didn't fancy freezing her buns off on the side lines. But she also didn't want the test of watching Ash running up and down, being all physical and sexy in a tight shirt and shorts, quite so early in the friendship. Once she'd managed to tamp down the attraction, she'd consider it.

This friend thing was going to take more effort than she'd bargained for.

Chapter Twenty-Two

Java barely touched the painted stick as he leapt over the hurdles, positioned on the fourth and final height, and Ash and Kirsty cheered. He grabbed the ball as it bounced back from the end of his run and hurtled back toward them.

"Good boy!" Ash rubbed his back and offered him a milk bone for his effort. He dropped the ball, gently took the treat, and curled up on her jacket to eat it.

"That's impressive." Kirsty sat beside Java and stroked him. "He's come a long way from that video you showed me of him dragging his back legs."

Ash joined them both on the floor and chuckled Java under the chin. "He has. It only took six weeks for him to progress from the bottom one." She pulled a hide stick from her pocket. "Watch this." She showed Java which hand the stick was in, put both her hands behind her back, made a show of moving the stick from hand to hand, and then brought both hands back out in front of her. Without any sniffing, Java placed his paw on her right hand. She opened it, and he claimed his prize.

Kirsty laughed. "That'd be an amazing trick if it weren't for the fact that dogs have a sense of smell a hundred thousand times better than us."

Ash huffed and patted Java on the head anyway. "Even the paw tap didn't astound you?"

Kirsty shrugged. "Okay, I'll give you points for that. Are you preparing him for a dog show or trying out for a new career already?"

Ash gave Kirsty a light shove. "No, and I'm happy with my job, thank you. It's given me something to do for the three hours of every visit, other than feed his ever-increasing appetite." As if on cue, Java looked up with the half-eaten chew sticking out from his mouth like a cigarette.

"Well, I can see why you couldn't leave him behind. He's cuter in the fur than in his videos and photos."

"Thanks again for being okay with me bringing him home." Ash had been so carried away with the rescue that it wasn't until she was leaving her resort that she'd called Kirsty to make sure it was okay to bring Java home. She didn't have a plan if Kirsty had responded negatively and she counted herself lucky she had such an amazingly huge-hearted friend.

"That was one of the easiest decisions I've ever had to make," Kirsty said. "We always had dogs in the house when I was growing up. I wanted my own, but with working all day all week, I didn't think I'd be able to have one…at least until I found a lovely wife to stay at home with the skin and fur babies."

Ash wrinkled her nose at the graphic description. "Skin babies? That's a gross way of thinking about children. And isn't wanting a stay-at-home wife a little misogynistic and anti-feminist?"

Kirsty shook her head. "Absolutely not. The role of homemaker is much maligned and misunderstood. It's an unpaid career."

"So you've already thought about having children?" Family hadn't been something she and Kirsty discussed, and they'd never talked about their future relationship plans other than their mutual wish to meet and marry the two most amazing women in the world, who would probably be twin sisters since their tastes tended to run the same way. Ash hadn't thought about that happening for a while. She was settled as Kirsty's roommate, and she hoped it would stay that way for a while.

"Of course. The sooner the better for me. I want to have plenty of energy to run around playing silly games and chasing my kids around the house. I don't want to be out of touch and like, fifty, when my kids are discovering their sexuality and need my advice. And I don't want to be in a wheelchair when they graduate from Oxford. You know?"

Ash shook her head. "Nope. I hadn't thought that far ahead. I had the goal of going to uni. Then I had the goal of getting a job. Java jumped into the picture, and I hadn't planned him or beyond him. But you're already thinking about what university your kids are going to? And about how many kids you're having?"

Kirsty grinned. "Yep. I want two kids. And no, I don't want a boy and a girl for symmetry because I'm an architect, before you make that joke. And I don't think in binary or box terms to put kids into. I want two kids close in age so they can grow up together and support each other, like me and my brother did."

Kirsty's sentiments echoed the wishes Izad had expressed to her a few weeks ago. "That makes a lot of sense. I was always jealous of other foster kids with siblings when I was growing up." *Completely alone.* Ash had been thinking a lot about her childhood recently. She'd come to the realisation it was because of her new friendship with Evie, and Ash's instant dismissal of the notion of being involved in a child's life as a parent figure rather than a mentor. She'd also concluded that she was circling back to the same feelings of loneliness she'd had as a child. But they were issues she'd truly believed she'd assimilated and moved beyond. It was good to be reminded that her psychology degree had personal applications. That, coupled with her recent dinner with Nat and Rich had reinforced her growing awareness that she had to deal with them before they spiralled out of control. After much discussion with Nat, Ash had resolved to reconnect with her old therapist and get back on track.

"Exactly. I've met a few women who were the only child at home, and they had sharing and control issues."

Ash shook her head. "I don't think you can tar an entire subset of people with your questionable data from a few interactions."

Kirsty waved her away. "Don't go all psychobabble on me. I'm just telling you what I've experienced."

Ash plucked another hide chew from her pocket and gave it to Java, who had been waiting expectantly but patiently on his back. His appetite seemed to be lessened by the copious amount of tickles he was getting from both her and Kirsty. "I know. I'd say that you should remember that I'm an only child, but I don't know if I am." Her joking tone belied the stab of pain in her heart at the admission. Yep, she was looking forward to her therapy session at the end of this week.

Kirsty inclined her head. "You okay, buddy?"

Ash nodded. "Yeah, don't worry. I'm dealing with it. I've got a session with a psychobabbler on Friday." She shoulder-shoved Kirsty and grinned, glad that she was able to share her shit with her best friend.

"I'm here. You know that, don't you? Always."

Ash squeezed Kirsty's shoulder. "I do. And I'm grateful for that."

"Anyway, speaking of Friday. How's it going with your new best friend?" Kirsty clutched at her heart and looked as though she'd been mortally wounded.

Ash smiled at the change of subject. "You're a dick. You can't be replaced…at least, not in three weeks."

"Now you're being a dick," Kirsty said and punched Ash's upper arm. "I'm irreplaceable."

"You definitely are." Ash thought about the past few weeks. Despite Evie's protestations that she didn't go out on work nights, they'd met for drinks and pool five times on her two weeks without her son. And they'd gone ten pin bowling and to the movies on the middle weekend.

"So how goes it? Are you managing to control yourself in the presence of the hot mind doctor?"

Ash inclined her head as Java climbed onto her lap, put his head on her chest, and closed his eyes. She cuddled him tight and stroked his silk-like ear, which she'd found helped him sleep. "Well, I've not accosted her in a dark alley and ravished her, if that's what you're asking." Though the thought had crossed her mind more than a few times, and definitely more than was acceptable for someone professing to be a friend.

"But you want to, don't you?" Kirsty wagged her finger. "I can see it all over your face. You're desperate for a re-run of your one night together, aren't you?"

Ash batted Kirsty's finger away, only slightly irritated that her friend was able to see the truth. She hoped she was doing a better job of keeping it from Evie. "As would you be if you'd slept with her."

"Except you didn't do much sleeping, did you? Although you're absolutely right. I saw that cute picture of you at the bowling alley. You look good together, I have to say. And I can imagine her trailing those long tresses over my body, along with some hot kisses."

Ash narrowed her eyes. "Stop imagining it."

"But why? Maybe she's my ready-made family?"

Kirsty was joking, of course. They had a pact and would never make a move on ex-lovers or would-be girlfriends, and Evie fit into both of those categories. "She's not the stay-at-home type of woman. Too busy being a stunningly successful doctor at a prison hospital to play wifey to you."

"You're right. She's impressive though, holding down a career like that *and* raising a child."

"Absolutely." Ash nodded. She loved when women proved doubters wrong by being successful in their work and personal life. "But she gets a lot of help. She says that the dad is wonderful, and they co-parent equally."

"Did she get pregnant by him…naturally? Is she bi?"

"She had sex with him once." Ash remembered Evie telling her, but she'd have preferred not to know. It seemed like an invasion of her privacy. She shouldn't have told Kirsty, but she trusted her not to say anything untoward if they ever met. "And I don't care whether or not she's bi. And that's not just because it's a friendship. Even if I hadn't blown it and we *were* in a romantic relationship, I wouldn't care if she were bi or whatever other label she might give herself." Ash disliked the human tendency to categorise and put everyone in neat boxes, but she did understand the desire to be seen for who they were, who they knew themselves to be. "We don't talk much about her son. I don't even know his name, and I don't know the name of the dad. We don't talk about her work either. I think when she's out with me, she wants to be Evie, not Doctor Evie and not Mum Evie."

Kirsty frowned. "Don't you think that's strange? That's two huge parts of her life she's not sharing with you—as a friend, obviously."

Ash shrugged. "I haven't questioned it or given it much thought. It's not like she asked me not to talk about either of those things. Our conversation goes naturally in other directions."

"And you manage *not* to talk about your incredible sex marathon?"

Ash sighed and shook her head. "You're more obsessed with that night than I am." Which was a complete lie. Ash had spent many nights playing that night over in her head while she played with herself, especially when she got home from being with Evie and her expensive perfume lingered on Ash's clothes, transferred from their hugs, which had lengthened with each meeting. Ash glanced at her watch when she heard the gate open and close at the bottom of the path. "Time's up. Thanks for coming today. It was nice to have some company."

"No problem. I wanted to meet the little tyke who's going to be sharing our house in a couple of months." Kirsty gave Java one last cutch before she stood.

Ash smiled at Kirsty's reference to it being *their* house, and she sighed deeply, letting the soft embrace of simple belonging settle around her. Their conversation had given her lots to think about. Kirsty was a year younger than Ash, but she had her whole life planned and couldn't wait to start building her own family. If Kirsty was ready for it, why wasn't Ash? Maybe raising a child wasn't such a scary prospect after all.

Chapter Twenty-Three

Evie clinked her glass to Harriet's. "I can't believe this is the second time I've seen you in less than a month, *and* we're getting to go out dancing. We haven't been out on the scene together for years."

Harriet raised her eyebrow. "There's a good reason for that, Evie." She gestured onto the dance floor below. "It seems our time has passed. Everyone down there looks about thirteen."

Evie laughed. "You're exaggerating, and speak for yourself. *They* don't look that young, and *we* don't look that old."

Harriet fake-preened. "I didn't say we looked old, darling, just that they look pre-pubescent. Do you think they even bother to check ID these days?"

Evie shrugged, her pride only slightly jarred that they hadn't been carded. "What about those four over there?" She pointed to a group of women who looked about their age. "And those…and them…and her," she said as she continued to identify potential dancing partners.

"Fine. I'm being dour." Harriet caught hold of Evie's wrist and began to pull her toward the stairs. "Let's shake our asses and see what happens."

Evie used her other hand to pull the phone from her pocket. The lack of an envelope at the top of her phone screen dampened her spirit some.

Harriet turned around and shook her head. "Aw, what's the problem? No message from your new bestie?"

Evie pulled away from Harriet's grasp and swatted her shoulder lightly. "Bog off. She's not my new bestie."

Harriet didn't answer until she got to the bottom of the stairs. "You've been spending an awful lot of time with her. If she's not your new bestie, what is she?"

Evie narrowed her eyes. Harriet was teasing her, but her questions hit their intended target. She knew well enough that Evie was struggling with the friendship. "If you were around more, I wouldn't have to spend so much time with another friend, would I?"

Harriet grinned then tutted. "That might hurt if it weren't for the fact that you were trying to cover up *your* actual feelings by attacking mine." She caught hold of Evie's wrist again and pulled her onto the dance floor. "It also might hurt *if* I had feelings to hurt and I wasn't a cold and emotionless ice queen."

Evie ran her hand through her hair and tried to shake her tension off. "Indeed. Exactly how do you manage to remain so distant from the possibility of a relationship?"

Harriet began to dance, and Evie joined her, careful to keep enough distance between them so that anyone watching wouldn't mistake them for lovers, given that Evie was in the market tonight.

"Look at my life," she half-shouted into Evie's ear. "I'm always travelling. I barely have time for you. I don't have time to keep another woman happy. And I'm truly happy on my own. I've got you for sharing what little emotional stuff I do have, and I have plenty of other transient company for the other stuff… I don't do lonely. It's not in my genes."

Evie nodded, and they carried on dancing. It was too loud to have any kind of real conversation anyway. Hearing Harriet talk about her life reminded her how she'd planned on being the same. Busy career. Busy love life. Izad had changed all that. From the moment she'd first held him in her arms, he'd shown her a different and special kind of love that, for a long time, meant she hadn't needed the other kind. And she'd satisfied her sexual needs with similar short-lived dalliances to those Harriet frequently enjoyed. Now that she'd recognised that need again and opened up the possibility of meeting someone, she'd become rather taken with Ash, the one person she couldn't have. Not fully, anyway.

But that hadn't stopped her gleaning as much time as possible with her, even forgoing her previous dictum of not going out on work nights. If she hadn't sacrificed that, she'd only ever see Ash on the weekends every two weeks. *And why isn't that enough?* Because she was enjoying herself immensely. They laughed and talked for hours, discussing everything from serious topics like climate change to the nonsense of why it was called Krispy Kreme and not Crispy Cream. It was all so easy. She didn't have to be anyone else around Ash. She didn't have to be the sensible, grown-up doctor, and she wasn't the thirty-something mum of a young adult. They didn't talk about her work or home life at all, yet they never struggled for conversation. And the silences, when they arose, were comfortable. Evie didn't feel the need to speak to fill the empty space. There was great freedom in that, and Evie treasured those moments almost as much as their chats.

God damn it. Why couldn't Ash just want kids? She was mature and kind, generous and loving. She'd make a wonderful mother, and Evie was certain Izad would like her. She squeezed her eyes shut and tried to concentrate on the music instead. She loved dancing, and she hadn't been out like this in an age. *Feel the beat. And stop thinking about why she hasn't text me yet.* The bass throbbed along the floor, up through her heels, and right into her head, but it didn't stop her wanting to know where Ash was…and who she was with.

This was stupid. Perhaps she should consider not seeing Ash anymore. If she couldn't enjoy the friendship they had instead of constantly thinking about the relationship they weren't having, what was the point? The point was that she relished their time together, and she didn't want to let that go. She'd get a handle on the attraction part eventually. Ash certainly seemed to have it under control.

Evie touched Harriet's arm and nodded toward the bar. She needed a drink to quiet all the questions.

"Is she still joining us tonight?"

Evie shrugged. "She said she'd meet us here, but she didn't say when."

They ordered drinks, and Harriet added them to her tab. Evie sipped her vodka and Coke and scanned the dance floor. Perhaps if she could find someone else more appropriate to focus on, Ash wouldn't be so alluring.

"Are you actually looking, or are you pretending to look? Because if you're seriously looking, the brunette over there in a sea of blond guys keeps checking you out."

"I'm looking." Evie couldn't convincingly confirm that she was doing it in earnest, but she was trying. She caught the eye of the woman Harriet was referring to and returned her smile. It was good to know she'd still got it, though she also found it strange that she'd already seemed to have lost her confidence around women. It hadn't been that long ago when she was as predatory as Harriet. Von had a lot to answer for. At least she wasn't— *Crap.*

Von skipped onto the dance floor with the next dupe in tow. At the same time, someone tapped on her shoulder. She tore herself from Von to look straight into Ash's beautiful eyes. "Oh my God," she whispered and immediately hoped no one had heard.

"I haven't heard that from you for a few weeks." Ash wiggled her eyebrows and grinned, before she partially turned away and pulled another woman into view. "This is my best bud, Kirsty. Kirsty, this is Evie."

Evie opened her mouth but no words came. Between seeing Von again and Ash's reference to their night together, she was somewhat flummoxed. Kirsty extended her hand, and Evie took it. "I'm sorry…I was—"

"Miles away?"

Ash smiled again, and Evie could feel the confidence almost vibrating from her. Was it alcohol-fuelled or was it the presence of her wing-woman? However it was coming about, Evie needed Ash to tone it down, or she'd be pushing her up against the bar and sticking her tongue down her throat. *Is that the alcohol talking? Get a grip…and not of her.* She arched her eyebrow and tried hard to look unaffected. "Hi, Kirsty. It's lovely to meet you. Ash has told me so much about you."

Kirsty squeezed Evie's hand gently and placed her other hand on top. "And everything she's told me about you was far from the exaggeration I took it be."

Heat crept up Evie's neck at the compliment, and she pulled her hand away as politely but as quickly as possible. Kirsty was a slightly shorter and marginally less attractive version of Ash. Evie might have mistaken them for sisters if she didn't know Ash's story.

"And I'm Harriet."

Harriet draped one arm over Evie's shoulders and reached out with her other to shake Kirsty's hand and then Ash's. Evie didn't miss the way Ash's eyes darted toward Harriet's arm on Evie, and the way her jaw clenched almost imperceptibly. Perhaps she hadn't got control of her attraction after all. The possibility warmed her considerably.

"What the fuck is this?"

Evie closed her eyes. She knew that voice and slowly turned in the general direction of the grating sound. "Hi, Von."

Von snarled. "Don't you 'Hi, Von' me like there isn't unfinished shit between us. Your bed's barely cold, and you're already warming it with a dirty little foursome? Classy."

Ash stepped into the small space between Evie and Von. "You've got the wrong idea, friend."

Von craned her neck to get in Ash's face. "I'm not your friend. Get out of my face."

Evie gasped as she saw Von draw back her fist, but Harriet was already pulling her to the side and out of the fray. Ash weaved to her left, grabbed Von's outstretched arm, and used her own velocity to smash her into the bar. She pulled her arm up behind her back and kept Von's pressed face down on the bar with her forearm.

"Would you fetch a bouncer, please?" Ash asked calmly, as if she were simply asking for a top-up of ice in her drink.

Evie swooned a little. Whether it was the alcohol, the heat of the hundreds of bodies in the club, or the sight of Ash in action, she wouldn't say out loud. The barkeep nodded, and Evie suspected she'd seen and heard the whole exchange. Von struggled under Ash's pressure, but her rangy body was clearly no match for Ash's strength. Two bouncers swiftly arrived, and Ash handed Von over to them with a quick explanation that must have matched the barkeep's story. They thanked her and pulled a cursing Von away and out of sight.

Kirsty patted Ash on the back and turned to the bar to order drinks as if what had just happened was a regular occurrence.

"Can I get you ladies anything?" Kirsty asked.

Harriet raised her glass and nodded toward Evie's. "We're all good, thanks. But let me buy your drinks."

Kirsty protested, but Harriet would have none of it and indicated for their order to be added to the card she'd given the bar staff when they'd got there.

"If that was who I think it was, I can see why you're mistrusting your judgement," Harriet whispered.

Evie shook her head slowly and laughed. If she hadn't, she might have simply begged off for the evening and gone home to cry into her pillow. She couldn't believe they'd run into Von. She'd said she was leaving the city for good, and Evie had no idea why she'd think they had unfinished business. Evie had been clear they were over the night she found her shooting up in the club toilet.

Ash placed her hand on Evie's shoulder. "Are you okay?"

Evie sighed and swooned a little more. Ash's gallantry made her heart race and had her feeling rather giddy. She nodded and took Ash's hand. "Thank you… You were amazing."

Ash looked away briefly and smiled, her adorably shy side pushing through the confident bravado once more. Evie couldn't decide which she liked most.

"It was nothing."

"No, it was definitely something. Where did you learn to do that?" Evie didn't know what exactly "that" was, whether it was self-defence or some sort of martial art, but it was damn impressive.

"I trained in capoeira and aikido for a while. It's the usual cliché; bullied at school and wanted to be able to protect myself. You know the story."

Evie wanted to pull Ash closer, tell her that she didn't know her story but wanted to. She wanted to know it all. And she especially wanted to comfort her and thank her in all manner of ways for protecting them from Von. But she couldn't do any of that, because they were just friends, weren't they?

Chapter Twenty-Four

Ash watched Evie and Harriet make their way to the dance floor. Evie looked stunning in a deep plum dress that hugged and stretched in all the right places, but how she walked in those four-inch heels on this wet, scuzzy floor and remained not only upright but sexy as all hell was something to behold.

Kirsty slapped her on the back hard enough to make her drink spill. "You couldn't have paid that woman to make you look any better."

Ash smiled and jutted her chin. "You think it impressed Evie?"

Kirsty laughed. "Are you kidding? She practically creamed her knickers when you put that mean bitch down."

Ash swatted Kirsty with her free hand. "Christ, you can be crude."

"Crude but truthful." She shrugged. "Such a shame you two aren't an item, because she wants to take you home and fuck your brains out."

Ash grinned at the thought before the bitter reality seeped in. Her lack of maturity and fear of commitment had ensured they were not, and never would be, an item. "If only…" Ash took a long pull on her beer. She'd been rather tipsy when they arrived at the club, but the incident with Evie's stalker/crazy ex-girlfriend had sobered her up instantly. Now she needed her senses dulling once more, and she needed to stop thinking about what she'd lost with Evie and concentrate on gaining her as a friend. A crazy hot, unbelievably sexy friend.

She turned away from the dance floor and back to the bar where the barwoman she'd spoken to earlier smiled and gave her *the look*. Ash returned her intentions with interest. Maybe a distraction would be good to get her lascivious thoughts focused elsewhere. "I'm going to the toilet. Won't be long."

Kirsty acknowledged with a tip of her beer bottle, but her attention was on the dance floor, no doubt looking for her next forever. Ash gave the barwoman another glance before heading up the stairs to the restroom. As she turned to go up the next flight, she saw the woman lift the counter and begin to follow her. Ash's pulse quickened. It was probably just a coincidence. She wasn't actually following her. She probably needed something from the upstairs office.

Ash concentrated on the steps and made her way past the few people on the upper floor. It was still early so everyone congregated on the ground floor. In a couple of hours, this area would be impossible to navigate without pushing and shoving to make a path. She opened the door and went to a sink to splash some cold water on her face. The thought of having her brains fucked out by Evie had done all sorts of good and bad things to her body and mind. She turned and was about to enter one of the four empty cubicles when the barwoman entered.

"Hey, cutie," she said. The door had barely closed before she'd walked across to Ash and pressed her body against her. "I'm Meg."

Ash backed up slightly against the marble counter top, a little stunned by Meg's brash approach. This kind of thing only happened in porn movies and her dreams. "Uh, hi, Meg. I'm Ash."

"Now that we know each other's names," she nodded toward a cubicle and ran her hands over Ash's chest, "do you want to finish what you started? I only have a ten-minute break."

Ash smiled, then frowned. "What did I start?"

"Don't be shy," Meg whispered. She leaned closer and kissed Ash's neck. "I've only ever seen moves like that in action films."

Meg's hot breath caressed Ash's neck like the touch of a familiar lover.

"You're all…strong and hot." She ran her finger along Ash's collarbone and down the line of her chest to the opening of her shirt. "The way you handled that druggie woman turned me on… so…it seems only fair that you should deal with what you've done to me now." She took Ash's hand and placed it on her breast. "Please…"

"Fuck…" Ash swallowed and ran her tongue over her dry lower lip.

"Yes, please." Meg nodded. She took Ash's hand and pressed it against the crotch of her jeans. "See how hot you've made me?"

Yeah, Ash could feel it all right. Meg was running hot enough to melt a polar ice cap. She closed her eyes…and saw Evie etched on her eyelids. Her eyes sprang open. Where was the harm? They were just friends. Evie had come here tonight looking for someone to do this with. She wouldn't begrudge the same for Ash, would she? They couldn't have each other, so why would they deny someone else?

Ash ran her hand through Meg's hair. She only got an inch or so before the fingers were tangled up in too much hairspray. It wasn't soft and bouncy like… *For fuck's sake.* This couldn't be her future, seeing Evie every time she tried to get hot for another woman. *Trying to get hot?* She shouldn't be *trying* to get horny. She should already be there. Meg was beautiful, young, sexy. The heat should be "pooling between her thighs" like in all those erotica anthologies Ash had read to pick up tips and get better in bed. She wrapped her other hand around Meg's neck and tipped her head to look into her eyes. "I'm sorry. You're beautiful…but I—"

The bathroom door opened and Harriet came in, closely followed by Evie. Ash jerked to stand and pushed Meg away as she and Evie locked eyes for the briefest of moments before Evie looked away. She took her hand from Harriet's shoulder, pulled her back, and they were gone, the door banging shut behind them.

"What the hell?" Meg straightened her blouse and looked mighty pissed.

Ash held up her hands. "I'm sorry… I'm so sorry." She pushed away from the counter to follow Evie. Once in the corridor, she saw they were on the mezzanine above the dance floor. "Evie," she shouted to be heard over the booming music.

Evie glanced over her shoulder and her mouth turned up in the briefest of smiles, but her eyes showed a different emotion. "Yeah?"

Her voice faltered a little, as if she were trying to keep her tone light. Harriet smiled in a way that looked sympathetic. *What the hell was going on?* Why had she left a potentially perfect night of entertainment stranded in the bathroom and chased out of there after Evie, her *friend*? She knew the answer. It was a stupid question.

Harriet took a step away from the balcony. "I'm going to fetch some drinks."

"I'll come with you."

Evie reached out for Harriet, but she shook her head and motioned toward Ash. "You should stay here."

Two steps forward, fifty-five steps back. She'd impressed Evie with the incident downstairs, and now she'd disappointed her with Meg. "Evie." She walked toward her, hesitant that Evie would bolt and follow Harriet despite her tacit instruction to talk to Ash. Evie didn't move, and Ash stood beside her, close enough to touch, but she couldn't.

"Yes?" Evie asked again, this time without looking at Ash.

"Nothing was happening there." She hoped the simple statement might be enough, but deep down, she knew it wouldn't. There was no need for an explanation. They didn't owe each other anything. They could touch, kiss, and have sex with whoever they wanted, couldn't they? If that were the case, why did she feel like she'd been caught *almost* cheating on her lover?

"It doesn't matter if it was, Ash." Evie glanced at her but didn't hold eye contact. "You can do whatever you want with whoever you like, can't you?"

Ash nodded. "Just like you can."

Evie turned toward her, and Ash could clearly see the pain in her eyes. Evie's jaw clenched and unclenched repeatedly as if she were angry or biting back the words desperate to escape and be heard. She looked upward and blinked as if she were holding back tears. Ash's chest tightened and constricted around her heart. The last thing she wanted was to cause Evie pain. Ash stuffed her hands in her pockets to keep from reaching out, from shifting the strands of hair that had fallen across Evie's face, from cupping her chin and telling her…telling her what? That she couldn't stand this arrangement? That she wanted to be more to Evie? That being friends with her, being this close to her and not being able to touch her, was unbearable torture, mentally and physically? Would Evie take her seriously?

"What if I don't want to? Be with someone else, I mean." Ash asked, her mouth engaging before her brain had the chance to stop her.

Evie shook her head. "Don't do this, Ash…I can't…I *can't* do this."

"Do what?" Ash needed to know what Evie was feeling, what she was talking about. And she couldn't let her leave without having this conversation now she'd started it.

"You know what I'm talking about, Ash. Don't make me spell it out." She shrugged and looked exasperated and forlorn at the same time. "There's no point."

Ash reached out and closed her hand over Evie's on the balcony railing. "Yes, there is. I need to hear it."

Evie pulled her hand from under Ash's. "You need to hear what? That I feel like I'm being torn into pieces every time we're together but not together? That I'm so desperate to spend time with you that I'm fooling myself into believing we can be friends?" Her voice rose, and she poked her finger at Ash's chest. "Is that what you need to hear? That the older woman you fucked senseless for one night is falling for you? Is that what your ego needs to hear?"

Ash took Evie's hand and pulled her close. Evie tried to push away, slapped her hands against Ash's chest, but Ash held her there until she stilled. "This isn't about my ego, Evie. It's about you and me. It's about what we could be to each other. It's about your call to me, and how I can't ignore it, as much as I've tried."

Evie frowned. She pulled her hands from Ash's grip and rubbed the heels of her hands against her forehead before she dropped her hands to her side. For a moment, Ash saw what she thought might be a glimmer of acceptance and resignation that whatever was between them was more than either of them had been willing to acknowledge or accept.

"No, Ash, please. Please don't do this." She shook her head and wrapped her arms around herself. "Let's forget the last ten minutes and go back to normal, go back to being friends. Wasn't that working? Wasn't that better than nothing at all?"

Ash took a step closer, but Evie simply took a step back.

"You're killing me, Evie. Being around you is like torture and the sweetest salve at the same time."

"Well then, if it's that bad…perhaps we should stop seeing each other altogether." Evie glanced to the floor, and her whole body appeared to sag.

"No." Panic rose like a spectre and pulled at threads that were already beginning to unravel. "That's not what you want, I can see that. And it's not what I want. Doesn't that matter? Doesn't how we feel count for something?"

Evie laughed gently, but there was no humour in the sound. "Would that it were that simple, Ash. But this can't be just about what you and I want. I have a child, and he has to come first. And you said you weren't ready for children in your life." She shrugged. "So no, what I want doesn't count for anything, does it?" Evie moved closer and took Ash's hands. "Perhaps this is too hard for both of us. Perhaps you are the right woman for me. But this is the wrong time, and I can't do anything about that." She shook her head slowly, brought Ash's hands to her lips, and kissed her knuckles gently. "I'm going to leave." She nodded toward the bathroom. "You should go and enjoy yourself. I can't do this anymore."

Ash swallowed. Everything had gone wrong. She opened her

mouth to speak and again, her words failed her. The soft burn of tears began to rise, and she struggled to pull in a breath. "I don't want to." When she finally spoke, she sounded childish and immature, like she wasn't being allowed to play with her favourite toy. She didn't want Meg back in the toilet cubicle. She didn't want any woman other than Evie. "I want you."

Evie released Ash's hand, reached up, and caressed her cheek. "That's the problem, sweetheart. It's not only me you get. I'm a package deal."

Evie gave her a last, lingering look before she turned and walked toward the stairs. Ash's legs were leaden, her feet like concrete blocks chained to the floor. *Don't let her leave.* An internal scream ripped through her, fierce and sharp, shredding her heart. Was this what it felt like to let go of part of her soul group? But she couldn't give Evie what she wanted, what she needed…unless she *was* ready to be a parent.

Chapter Twenty-Five

Evie let the phone ring four times before she finally rejected it. She'd spent most of the night alternating between crying and cursing, between punching her pillow and cradling it as if it were Ash. Last night had been a disaster. Ash had revealed yet another appealing side to her nature in the non-aggressive but cool and confident way she'd handled Von. Why did Evie even go to the upstairs bathroom? She could've waited in the downstairs line for the loo, and she would never have been any the wiser. Ash could've had her quick fumble, or whatever it was going to be, and Evie could have continued enjoying her night, covertly coveting Ash from the dance floor.

She shouldn't have reacted as she had either. Why hadn't she simply smiled and acknowledged them and gone into a cubicle quietly? If she had, Ash wouldn't have known how conflicted she was about her feelings for her. That would have had quite the opposite effect, and Ash would have assumed that Evie had moved on and was happy with their friendship as it stood.

But no, the sight of some other woman's hands on Ash was like a sword running straight through her. She'd been unprepared for her reaction, hence her swift and unwieldy exit. She recognised the woman from the bar. She'd been the one Ash had asked to get the bouncers. And no doubt, the woman had been just as impressed as Evie when she'd witnessed Ash in action. It was sexy beyond anything she'd ever seen before, and knowing Ash could take care of not only herself, but everyone around her, was swoon-worthiness at the highest level. She couldn't blame the woman at all. In different circumstances, Evie would have pinned Ash against the bar as soon as Von was dragged out of the picture.

But they hadn't been different circumstances. And whilst she'd spent some of her little sleeping time dreaming about how different the night could have turned out, it wasn't to be...nor would it ever be.

Her phone began to ring again. Clearly Ash wasn't one to give up easily. Evie had been ignoring her intermittent calls all morning and willed the afternoon to come in the hope that Ash would have a football match and thus Evie would have a short reprieve from the temptation. Initially Evie had considered answering, almost had. But then she thought about Ash's voice and the things it did to her, and she couldn't do it. Instead she was ghosting her and moping around the house with no distractions and nothing to do but think about what she could be doing with Ash if only they were at a similar point in their lives.

"Is that going to be your strategy then, not facing the problem? You're just going to hope it goes away?"

Evie jumped, startled at the intrusion before she remembered that Harriet had stayed the night. "That's the plan, yes. You find fault with that course of action?"

Harriet dumped her overnight bag by the kitchen door, helped herself to a cup of fresh coffee, and sat at the breakfast bar. "I'd have no problem at all with it…if you were fifteen."

She arched her eyebrow and stared accusingly at Evie, who glanced away and topped up her own coffee. "You don't understand, Harriet. This isn't just about me and Ash. If it were that simple, there'd be no problem. We like each other a lot. But I have a son, and Ash doesn't want a family yet. She wants me, but she doesn't want my child."

"Has she ever actually said those words to you?" Harriet picked up a croissant and began to pull it apart.

Evie shook her head. "She doesn't have to. She said she wasn't ready for a family yet, and I'm already a family unit. That's why we agreed to be friends."

"Ghosting her isn't how you treat your friends."

"But now we can't be friends, Harriet. It's too hard for both of us." Evie pushed her phone away when it pinged with yet another message. "What's the point of us talking when there's no solution?"

"So, that's it? You're just cutting her off?"

Evie ran her hand through her hair and sighed. "I don't see what other choice I have. I said all that was left to say last night." She slid her phone back across the counter and read the new message.

"What's it say?" Harriet asked.

"She wants me to answer the phone. She wants to meet to talk." Evie shoved her phone away again. "I should never have opened the door to friendship, then it wouldn't have escalated to this…this," she threw her hands in the air, "ridiculous situation. Now everybody's hurt."

Harriet took Evie's phone and pushed it back across the

counter top. "Tell her that. Don't have her calling and texting you all day. That'll make her feel even worse, and there's definitely no need for that."

Evie shook her head. "I can't call her. I can't speak to her. I'll cave, and I'll go meet her… If I meet her—"

"Don't call her then, but you're a classy lady, Evie. Text her and tell her what's happening. She seemed like a nice woman, and she doesn't deserve to be kept hanging."

"You're right." Evie picked up her phone and thumbed a message to say that she couldn't see Ash anymore and that she was sorry, but she had to protect them both from further pain. It was mere seconds before she received a response.

Please don't let it end like this. Meet me so we can talk about it properly. Please x

"She wants to meet up." Evie leaned her elbows on the counter top and covered her face with her hands. "I can't meet her, Harriet."

Harriet pulled Evie's hands away from her face gently. "You don't have to. Repeat what you've just said and say you won't be answering her calls and texts. And ask her to please respect your wishes. If she's half the person I think she is, she'll do it."

Evie closed her eyes, wishing it would all go away. She hadn't been in pain like this since…since never. She didn't get this attached. Von had been a bad judgement call, and that had hurt in a way far removed from the sharp and crushing feeling around her heart right now. But if it all went away, she wouldn't remember their night together, or the conversations they'd had, or the fun. Which was worse? The knowing and the loss, or the lack of feeling in the first instance? Better to have loved and lost than never to have loved at all…but it couldn't have been love. Evie couldn't believe that it was possible for her to have fallen for Ash so quickly. It wasn't something she believed in, and it had certainly never happened before.

Evie put Harriet's instructions in her own words. She hesitated for the briefest of moments before she hit send. If Harriet was right and Ash did respect her wishes, there would be no more texts, no more calls, no more contact. Was that what she truly wanted?

"Only do it if you're absolutely sure, Evie."

She wasn't sure. How could she be? But she couldn't face Ash, and she couldn't keep her hanging on. No, she wasn't sure she never wanted to hear from Ash again, but she couldn't see any other options.

She pressed send and left the message app open. She saw that Ash read her message and then… no more bubbles. Evie waited. She couldn't name the rising surge of emotion and did her best to push it away. Still no bubbles. So that was it. All that promise rejected with a simple message.

"How do you feel?" Harriet asked after a few moments of silence.

"Like shit, actually. How am I supposed to feel?" Evie shook her head. "Ignore that. I'm sorry." She closed her eyes, tilted her head back, and sighed deeply. "Caring for people stinks, Harriet. Perhaps you have the right idea, after all."

Harriet smiled. "I keep it simple because I like my own company, Evie, not because I'm frightened of caring for anyone."

Evie opened her eyes and looked at Harriet. "I'm not frightened of caring for someone. I just want to make sure I'm caring for the right person. You know, someone like Ash instead of someone like Von."

"Speaking of her, what the hell was that about?"

Evie shrugged. "I have no clue." She didn't want to think or speak about Von. She thought she'd managed to put that short but painful part of her life behind her.

"I know you don't want to talk about how amazing Ash was, but the way she controlled the situation was impressive. You've got to give her that."

"I'm not denying her that at all." It was Ash's actions that had made Evie crazy. Von had managed to mess with her life again without even realising it. "I'm glad she was there. Von was crazy."

"Had she been violent with you before?"

"No, not really. It wasn't a particularly friendly parting, but I don't know why she acted the way she did last night." Evie picked up her coffee mug and wandered out of the kitchen. The house always felt empty without Izad, but today it was lonely too, even with Harriet there. And she wished…yes, she wished that Ash was here. She'd like to hear her laughter fill these rooms. She looked at the huge sofa where she and Izad sat to watch his Disney movies on the giant flat screen above the fireplace. She pictured Izad in the centre with herself on one side and Ash on the other, a huge bowl of popcorn on his lap that all three of them were dipping into.

"Shall I order some food?"

Evie registered Harriet's voice distantly and shook her head. "I'm not hungry." She'd baked fresh croissants but hadn't touched them. She certainly didn't fancy anything more substantial. "I think I'd like to be alone." It had been wonderful seeing Harriet for the past few days, a rare treat, but Evie no longer wanted company and was sure she'd be a poor companion. The only person who might have been able to make her feel better was her mum, and her absence gave Evie even more to sob about. Right now, all she wanted to do was wallow in the infuriating desperation of the situation and to see if she could cry Ash out of her head.

"Are you sure? We could sit and watch inane TV and movies all day. I promise I won't talk unless you want to."

Evie turned to see Harriet in the archway between the kitchen and lounge. She went to her and took her hands. "It's a lovely offer, but no. I've got some new patient files to look over for next week." She had no such work, but she didn't want to hurt Harriet's feelings by refusing her company outright.

Harriet inclined her head as if to divine Evie's true intentions.

"You have plenty of ice cream in the freezer for the inevitable rom-com double screening this evening?"

Evie laughed. No matter what, Harriet could always make her smile, even if only for a moment. "I have ice cream, but I have no idea what you're talking about. Is that some sort of sad, lonely woman tradition?"

Harriet nodded. "That's exactly what it is. A sad, lonely woman tradition that always follows an epic and heart-breaking parting of star-crossed lovers."

Evie pondered Harriet's choice of words, however flippant; was that what this was? A heartbreak? "Okay. Well, now I know, I'll be sure to honour the tradition as soon as I've finished my paperwork." She released Harriet's hands and smiled as genuinely as she could manage given that all she wanted to do was sob. Harriet took the hint, turned around, and grabbed another croissant from the counter.

"Seems a shame to waste these," she said and grinned. Her expression turned serious. "Call me anytime, Evie. I'm heading out again on Tuesday, but I'm always on the end of the phone. You know that, don't you?"

Evie nodded. "Thanks, Harriet. I'll call you if I need you."

Harriet retrieved her bag and headed toward the front door. Evie waited for the metal click of the lock to confirm Harriet had left before she collapsed onto the sofa and curled up into a ball.

She thought of the Persian adage, *this too shall pass*.

As heaving sobs overtook her body, she hoped it would do so quickly.

Chapter Twenty-Six

Evie wasn't there?" Kirsty asked as she pulled two beers from the fridge, opened them, and handed one to Ash.

"Nope." Ash took a long pull on the bottle and wished the ice cold liquid would douse the fire in her heart and head. "Sarah said she wasn't going to be in for a few weeks because of a crisis at the hospital… I'm sure she was lying. She could barely look at me when she spoke."

"What did you say?"

Kirsty headed out of the kitchen and into the lounge, and Ash followed. They flopped onto the sofa and Ash kicked off her boots and put her feet up. "I said, 'I suppose she'll be back as soon as Java leaves and I'm not coming every Friday?' but Sarah assured me that wasn't the case. 'She's a busy woman,' she said, then asked why I would even think such a thing. It was fucking obvious she knew exactly what's happened between us."

Five days of complete silence. Ash had respected Evie's request, and she hadn't called or text her. She had hoped that she would see her today though. And that if they saw each other again, Evie might falter and give their friendship a second chance. Because having Evie's friendship meant more to her than any relationship she'd ever had in the past. So what if they wanted to sleep with each other? So what if they both wanted more and couldn't have it? Wasn't something better than nothing at all?

"Do you think she might be out on the scene tonight?"

"I don't think so. She's got that crazy bitch *and* me to avoid now. It's probably enough to turn her to online dating." Ash laughed but it wasn't funny.

"And remind me again why you can't be with her?"

"Because I don't have my shit together. Because I opened my mouth without thinking. Because I was coasting, and I'd forgotten I work better when I set goals. Take your pick." Ash drank her beer and hoped they had more in the house. Maybe a little obliteration and temporary memory loss would ease the hurt for a while. It wasn't a long-term solution, but right now it hurt too much to not want some transient relief.

"And how's your goal setting going? You've been seeing your therapist for a month now."

"Boy, do I know that." Her bank account was crying with the weekly expense. With that, Java's kennel fees, *and* a couple of weeks out most nights with Evie, she'd annihilated what little savings cushion she'd built. She needed a couple of months in to keep her outgoings to a minimum. "It's going well. I'm looking for another part time job to supplement my income short term."

Kirsty shook her head. "That's not what I'm talking about, and you know it." Kirsty finished her beer and got up from the sofa. "Another one?"

Ash raised her bottle for inspection. "I'm still good with this one, thanks." Her previous plan to get hammered and fall unconscious had faded as quickly as it had occurred.

"Get it down you so it loosens your tongue. I'm going to get some nibbles too. But I want a real answer when I get back."

When Kirsty left, Ash leaned her head back against the couch and closed her eyes. She'd been making good progress with her therapist, and maybe better than that, she was opening her eyes at work too. She'd always known that she wanted to work with kids, especially ones in less than favourable home and economic situations, and most of the kids at her centre fitted that bill. There were a couple of kids from the slightly nicer area that sat within the centre's catchment zone, but they still attended the local school, and they weren't posh kids roughing it. More often than not, their parents were locals who'd managed to make a successful career for themselves but wanted to stay attached to their roots and didn't want to move. Ash admired that, coveted it even. What she would give for roots somewhere, anywhere really.

But what her work was teaching her was that she *did* want to make a difference to a child's life in a more substantive way than seeing them for a few hours a week. The long and surprisingly deep conversations she'd been having with quite a few of the kids she worked with was making her long for a stronger connection with a child. She'd had no idea this job would make her feel this way. On the way home after every shift, she thought about what it might be like to have a child, to be responsible for their happiness and health, to be the one they had conversations with about their homework, their first love, and what they wanted to be when they grew up. She wanted to be someone *she'd* never had.

Kirsty bounced onto the sofa and nearly made Ash drop her bottle.

"Did you drop off?"

"No, I was thinking about work. I might be learning more about myself there than I am in my therapy sessions."

"How so?" Kirsty crossed her legs and sat sideways on the couch, facing Ash. "I'm in my serious listening pose. Lay it on me."

Ash laughed and was once again reminded how lucky she was to have such a great friend. "I told Evie that I wasn't ready to have a kid before I knew she had one."

"Big mistake."

"Obviously. If she'd told me first that she had a kid, I wouldn't have said anything. Not because I would have wanted to lie to her—I'd never lie to her—but it would have given me the thinking time I needed to wrap my head around the idea. I mean, she was never going to introduce me to her son and move me straight into the house to play happy families. I think she planned to date me for a while to be sure I was a good fit for her and her son. That would have given me the time to grow into the role. It's something I've always wanted to be a part of, a real family, and Evie is an amazing woman."

"And what's all that got to do with your job?"

"I'm around a whole group of wonderful kids. Some are in loving homes, some are in desperate situations with neglectful grandparents, and some have got parents who can't cope. But spending time with them is making me realise how much I want to be a bigger part of a child's life."

"Why don't you tell her that?"

"She's not going to take a chance with me now, not where her son is concerned. And I've got to be sure I'm ready, and that this isn't some honeymoon period with my new role."

"You don't know for sure that she wouldn't take a chance. Maybe she's already missing you and wishing she hadn't blown you off."

"She didn't 'blow me off.' She just didn't want to get hurt, and I can't blame her for that."

"So what are you going to do?"

Ash took another sip of her beer. "Keep up the therapy. Work my ass off. And keep analysing myself. It's good that Evie isn't around while I'm doing that anyway, so maybe what happened last week was for the best."

Kirsty frowned and narrowed her eyes. "That's some twisted logic. Wouldn't it be better if you were still spending time together to make sure all of this is even worth it? What if she's not your forever femme anyway?"

Ash laughed. "I have no idea whether or not she's my forever. I can't know that after a few weeks together—"

"And one awesome night of mind-bending sex." Kirsty raised her bottle, and Ash clinked hers to it.

"That too, yes." Ash nodded, and memories of that night flashed through her mind. It *was* the best night of sex—of something more than sex—she'd ever had. "There's definitely something there, something powerful calling to me, that's for sure. But I'm not a besotted kid who thinks one night together could be the basis for *all* our nights together. And I've got no intention of letting Evie go, but I'll respect her wish for radio silence until the time's right."

"And what if the time's never right?"

Ash was silent for a moment. It was a notion she hadn't entertained. Somewhere, beneath all the doubt and confusion, a certainty had settled deep within. She wasn't sure of forever, no. But she was sure that at some time in the future, she'd get another chance with Evie.

And when that call came, she'd be ready.

Chapter Twenty-Seven

Three weeks, two days, and fourteen hours. Plenty of time had passed since Evie had held Ash's hands to her lips and kissed her knuckles, but if she concentrated hard enough, she could still imagine the way Ash tasted. And that was the problem; why was she remembering? Why couldn't she simply forget and move on? Why was it that she'd tucked Izad up and then jumped into bed with her iPad to stalk Ash on Facebook? She was surprised Ash hadn't unfriended or even blocked her given that Evie had demanded no contact. And Evie's Facebook wasn't exactly interesting reading. She never posted anything personal, never interacted fully with the few friends she did have, and she had no photos of Izad on there because she believed he had the right to his privacy. It wasn't fair play. Ash couldn't stalk her back.

She laughed and chided herself for entertaining the notion that Ash might still be interested after the way Evie had treated her. No doubt she'd moved on already and probably started with that easy, attractive bartender at the club. Evie flicked through to Ash's photos and videos. There were a few over the past couple of weeks, mostly of her with Java at the kennels. Evie was glad to see Java's back legs had strengthened, and he was tackling the top rung of Ash's homemade hurdles easily now. There was only one week to go before Java would be allowed to go home with her, and Evie could resume her Friday afternoon volunteering. It was rather childish cancelling on Sarah. But she truly couldn't face Ash, sure that one look of her sad, blue eyes or a flash of her cocky grin, and Evie would be rolling back her blanket ban on their friendship. And after that, it would only be a matter of time before they fell back into bed.

She closed her eyes and tried to picture their night together. It had been quite the revelation. They'd explored so many aspects of a potential sexual relationship in a relatively short space of time, and Evie had enjoyed every second of it. Ash was so open to everything they'd done, and all of it had been so natural… and so fantastically filthy. There were so many deeply buried and unexplored fantasies Evie would have loved to have shared and realised with her.

Evie opened the top drawer of her bedside cabinet and retrieved the wooden box that held her small but powerful chrome bullet vibrator. She flicked the clasp, took out the sex toy, and checked the battery. All was well. She placed the box on the cabinet surface and picked up her iPad. Evie opened the gallery app and then the album of particularly sexy photos of Ash that she'd curated. She tapped on slideshow and slid her hand beneath the duvet. She turned the bullet on and gently offered it to the tip of her clit. She gasped at the instant stimulation and pressed her head back into her pillow. She drew the machine over her clit in lazy circles as she enjoyed photos of Ash in tank tops, shirts, tight T-shirts, and leather jackets. She'd only chosen the ones where Ash was giving that cocky, sexy smile with her come to bed eyes. After a few moments, she closed her eyes and reran their night together like a movie in her head. She got to the part when Ash put her hot mouth on her, and she lost herself in a quick, powerful orgasm.

She switched her trusty little machine off and relaxed into the strong pulsing between her legs, still imagining Ash there. When she finally settled, she took a deep breath and went back to a little light stalking. She switched over to Ash's friend, Kirsty, and found plenty of photos of football matches. Ash looked cute in her black and white striped kit, though all of it looked too big for her and most of the other players. She clicked on a link to a local newspaper's coverage of a recent match and discovered the name of the team. A few more investigative clicks, and she had the rest of the season's match locations and times, home and away. They were in the premier league and attracted quite the fanbase… maybe she would go and watch as Ash had invited her to. She could easily be lost in a crowd that size and be all but certain that Ash wouldn't see her. Izad was going back to his dad's tomorrow, and Ash had a home match on Sunday. She checked the weather app. It looked like it was going to be a nice weekend. There were worse ways to spend her time than watching Ash tear up and down the left wing, scoring goals, and celebrating with her shirt off.

There were more useful ways of spending her Sunday too, of course. Like forgetting about the woman she couldn't have and trying to find one more suitable. Though now she had no friend to navigate the local scene with, she was at a loss as to how she was supposed to do that. Harriet had left the country on another mysterious contract and wouldn't be back for a couple of months. That left Sarah. They hadn't been out together for a while, but Evie felt guilty about backing out of her volunteering responsibility for the past few weeks. She hoped it wouldn't make their friendship awkward.

She wiped the bullet with a tissue, popped it back in its case and then back in the drawer. She decided to call Sarah now. Maybe she had a friend Evie hadn't met and they could go on a double date. She was open to anything right now…anything to get her mind off Ash and silly thoughts of hiding in football crowds to catch covert glimpses of her.

"Hey, Evie. I'm glad you called. I've been missing you."

Sarah's voice was as genuine as it always was, and Evie relaxed her shoulders, aware that she must've tensed as she made the call, perhaps expecting a different response. "You're not mad at me?"

Sarah laughed. "Of course not. Why would I be mad at you?"

"Oh, I don't know. How about leaving you in the lurch with no notice for the past three weeks?"

"You're a volunteer, Evie. I don't get to have unrealistic expectations of volunteers. I'm grateful that you spend any time with us, but I don't take it for granted."

Evie prided herself on her professionalism, and volunteer or not, she still took her responsibilities to Sarah's work seriously. "I hated letting you down, Sare…but I…I couldn't…"

"It's okay, Evie, honestly. I understand. How have you been?"

Evie didn't want to talk about how she'd been. Her first instinct was to ask if Ash had said anything about her. "I'm okay. Busy at work as usual. How have all your pups been? Has Kirby been picked up yet?"

"Ah, can you believe that he has? It was a little over a week ago when his owner turned up at the kennels unannounced, wanting to collect him."

A pang of melancholy kicked at her tummy. She hadn't been able to say good-bye to the big, lolloping pooch and that bothered her more than she thought it would. Seems she was getting easily attached to people *and* dogs nowadays. "Was Kirby happy to see him? I imagine he'd all but forgotten what the guy looked and smelled like."

"Strangely enough, he was all over him. I went to get Kirby from the kennel myself while Harry chatted to the owner. He pulled me all the way back to reception. It was all I could do to stop him from running. And when I opened the door, I had to let his lead go before he yanked me to the floor in his rush to get to his owner." She laughed. "Mind you, he almost knocked him over when he jumped at him. The chap is quite small, and when Kirby stood up on his hind legs, his paws were on the chap's shoulders. Made for quite a sight, it did."

"And he settled his bill?" Whether or not he had was none of Evie's business, and as such, she wasn't sure why she'd asked… other than to keep from inquiring about Ash, of course.

"Absolutely. I don't like to hold the dogs to ransom, but our policy is that the outstanding balance has to be paid before pick up. And he paid in cash. A big stack of those nice, new plastic twenty-pound notes. Harry had lots of fun counting them. He said he'd never had so many English notes in sequential order before. I would've been concerned they were fake, but since they've only just been released, Harry assures me they're coming out of the cashpoint like that. Still, I took them straight to the bank in case."

"And they were okay?" Evie had visions of the mysterious stranger hoarding steel briefcases of cash he'd exchanged for sub-machine guns.

"Yep."

There was a small pause. Evie was still preoccupied with Ash. "Are you going to ask, or do you not want to know?"

Sarah clearly knew that Evie had no interest in Kirby's owner's ability to pay his bill. The jig was up. "Fine. Did Ash say anything about my not being there on Fridays?" There was a huff on the other end of the line, and Evie could imagine the expression that went with it.

"Why do you want to know?"

Evie sighed. Ash's smiling face looked up at her from her iPad so she pushed it a little further away from her. *Why* do *I want to know?* "Don't you want to tell me?" Evie knew Sarah loved to talk about all things relationship related, and she'd been thrilled to hear that Evie and Ash had hooked up and then gone backward to dating…and then even further backward to just friends…and then to nothing at all.

"Ha. Of course I want to tell you. But I'm interested in why you want to know when you're trying to distance yourself from Ash and get over her."

"There's nothing to get over. We were friends who had an extraordinary night together." She wasn't convincing herself and doubted Sarah would be fall for it either.

"I hate to say it, but you know you're contradicting yourself, don't you? I feel like, as a psychiatrist, you probably should know that."

Evie smiled at Sarah's teasing tone. Her mind tumbled with a minefield of contradictions. She should probably stay silent until she had actually got over Ash, because there was no denying that's what had to happen. "In the spirit of getting over the woman I *didn't* have a relationship with, I was calling to see if you had any viable single friends that you could force out on a double date with you and Harry?"

"Ooh, really? Are you that desperate?"

"Wow. Thank you for being so subtle in your acknowledgement of my hopelessness. I'm truly grateful for your compassion." Evie laughed, then glanced at her iPad and a stab of disappointment settled, seeing the screen had gone black. She should probably delete that album…tomorrow.

"Subtlety and compassion aren't my strong suits, Evie. You've called the wrong friend if that's what you need."

Sarah's laughter seemed to fill the room without even being on speaker phone. Evie turned the volume down a little. "But have I called the right friend to help me get back on the proverbial horse?"

"Oh yes, I'm definitely the correct choice for that particular job. Are you looking for something fun or something serious?"

"I can't have both?" Evie pouted. *Ash* was both.

"Eventually, probably. But for now, I need to know if you're looking for a quick hook up or a potential relationship… Which is it?"

Evie blew out a long breath. She'd thought Ash was just going to be a bit of fun, at most. She was supposed to be a bridge to get her into the serious dating game. She'd decided she was looking for something serious, someone to introduce to Izad, someone to share their life. Getting straight back into that seemed like the best course of action. "I'd like potential relationship material, please. And I'll be super impressed and forever grateful if you could organise that for tomorrow night."

Sarah laughed. "You'd be surprised what I can organise in a short time; play parties, orgies, swing—"

"No, no, that's okay. A double date with you and Harry would be lovely, thank you."

"Consider it organised. Let's say seven, and I'll text you the restaurant tomorrow once I've made a reservation. Sound good?"

"Sounds perfect." Evie fiddled with her hair and pulled a face at the black screen of her iPad. *Do I want to know?*

"And the other thing?" Sarah asked as if reading Evie's mind. "Did she seem angry or upset?"

"A little of both. She looked…lost. I think I made her angry by telling her there was a crisis at the hospital. She said something along the lines of expecting the crisis would end when she picked up Java and didn't come back… Mm, maybe angry is too strong a word. Bereft might be a better description."

The thought of Ash being upset was like a slap across the face. The thought that Evie was the cause of that pain was like taking a beating from an MMA fighter. But there was no way to make it right. Time had to be the healer, not Evie. Just like time would have to make her feel better too.

Time might have too big a job on its hands.

Chapter Twenty-Eight

Do you have brothers and sisters?"

Here we go again. Over the past couple of weeks, if Izad wasn't learning piano, dancing, or creating bead bracelets with Ally and Katie, it was a fair bet he'd be with Ash talking about anything and everything. Today he was back on family, not Ash's favourite topic in the past, but she wanted to understand what a *real* family felt like. And Izad definitely fit into that category, though not into the traditional family setting Ash had always coveted. He waxed lyrical about his wonderful mum and dad, and he seemed happy and settled despite them living apart.

Ash sank back into the bean bag and studied Izad's latest move. "Not that I know of, buddy. Remember I told you that I don't know my parents?"

Izad nodded. "I remember," he said and frowned as if perturbed that Ash had thought otherwise. "But that doesn't mean you can't have brothers and sisters."

Ash moved her knight and took one of Izad's pawns. "I guess it doesn't. But as far as I know, I don't have any. I was just a baby, so if I had older brothers and sisters, I don't remember them. I don't remember a home at all. I think I was abandoned pretty much as soon as I was born." Ash figured it was okay to share her story; it was no worse than the plots of the Disney movies Izad loved so much. Bev had said he didn't usually speak to anyone other than his two girlfriends, but maybe this was why Izad had taken to her so easily. Ash's early life wasn't dissimilar to a Disney plot.

He was silent for over a minute, contemplating his next move. She'd left her knight exposed to attack from his bishop on purpose, and she could see he was working out whether or not it was a trap.

"In all the houses you said you had to live in, were there other children who *could've* been brothers and sisters?" Izad advanced a pawn instead and left Ash's knight in place.

Ash quickly ran through the ten-plus families she'd spent time with, and as she struggled to recall the detail Izad had requested, she realised she'd begun to bury memories of her past. That was something to talk to her therapist about in her next session, particularly as Ash was running out of things to talk about and the counselling seemed to be coming to a natural ending. She searched harder, and the answer finally came. "Some of them already had their own children. Others had more foster kids like me. I don't remember liking any of them enough to want them to be my brother or sister." Ash took another of Izad's pawns with one of her own.

"Mm…"

Ash scanned the room and checked numbers. *Fourteen.* It was a busy night, and Bev was actually working. She'd been pissy when Ash called her down on the radio, and Ash was glad to be in here with Matt rather than with her. It had been about fifteen minutes since Ash had heard her on the radio, but if everyone was happy in their rooms, radio silence wasn't unusual. Matt chatted with a few of the older boys and played cards. He caught her glance and grinned. She'd been right about him. He was a great guy and fast becoming the kids' favourite. She returned his smile and continued to check everyone was okay. Ally and Katie were beside them, playing Connect Four and chatting about their latest history assignment. The rest of the kids were playing other board games.

"If you weren't so old, would you have liked me enough to be your brother?"

Ash had been taking a drink from her bottle of water and nearly spat it out all over the chess board. "You think I'm old?"

He nodded, said nothing else, and simply waited for a response.

She laughed gently, put aside the unintended insult, and focused on the reason behind Izad's question. He was seeking assurance that she liked him, which made sense. He had two female friends, and Ash had never seen him converse with anyone else unless he was forced to. And in situations where it would have been expected of him, he often didn't bother speaking. The other kids generally gave him a wide berth, and she'd reprimanded a few of them on several occasions for teasing him. He was different to most of the kids here, and he chose his friends carefully. "I would have loved to have you as my brother in any of those families. You're an amazing kid."

A corner of his mouth rose, and Ash smiled widely as warmth spread in her chest.

"I want a sister. Do you think my mum or dad can get me one?"

Ash laughed harder as the intense emotion in the moment

disappeared. "I don't think it's quite that easy, Izad. You don't get them off the shelves at Tesco."

Izad shook his head. "I *know* that… I'm still going to ask."

Ash inclined her head. "Good luck." *That* would be an interesting conversation when he got home. How would she handle it if her son came home with the same request? She didn't know, but she had a growing feeling that she wanted to.

Izad gestured toward the chess board. "I know you're letting me win. But I don't know why… Why are you letting me win?"

Ash shook her head, not surprised by the sudden change in subject as Izad was wont to do. "I'm not letting you win…but I'm not trying to win."

Izad narrowed his eyes. "Why?"

Ash laughed. Was this going to be one of those kid to adult conversations where "Why?" would be the answer to anything she said? "So that you don't give up. Losing can be hard on anyone's motivation to continue."

"My dad says that I can learn more from my defeats than my successes," Izad said. "I don't mind losing to you. Eventually I'll learn to beat you."

Ash smiled at his confident logic. It was probably true. She was no chess genius, and with his intelligence, he'd soon figure out Ash didn't think more than one move ahead, let alone try to anticipate her opponent's strategy. Gambits, openings, countergambits—she couldn't even name a chess strategy, let alone apply it.

"We're going to play in the green room, Izad. Are you coming?" Ally pulled the safety bar from beneath her game and the red and yellow discs tumbled out onto the table. "I'm bored."

She and Katie got up, went to the door, and waited.

Izad glanced at his friends and nodded, then turned back to Ash. "When I come back, can we carry on with this game?"

"Of course."

"But I want you to try to win," he said and looked serious. "I want to win because I'm that good, not because you let me."

Ash nodded. "If that's what you want?"

"I do."

As Izad joined his friends, the three young guys that had been playing cards with Matt also rose.

"Let's go and play kingy. Are you coming, Matt?"

Matt looked across at Ash. "Is that okay?"

With Izad and his friends leaving plus the three guys, there was only a need for one member of staff in the room. "Of course. Switch out with Gabby if you need to, and keep an eye on numbers."

"Will do, boss."

After they'd left, Nawal got up from her laptop and came across to sit opposite Ash.

"Will you teach me to play?" she asked.

"Of course." Ash pulled her phone from her pocket. "Let me take a photo of this game so I can set it back up to finish later." She quickly did so, then reset all the pieces. "Have you played before?"

Nawal shook her head. "No. Is that bad?"

"Not at all. Let's start with what all the pieces are called, yeah?" Ash settled back on her bean bag and began tutoring Nawal with the basics.

***

Ally burst into the room, breathless and pale. "Smithy, there's been an accident. Come quick."

Ash jumped up and went to the door. There were two volunteers and eight children on various tables painting and crafting in the blue room. "Chloe, would you cover the red room for me? There's some sort of emergency."

"What's happened?" she asked as she got up and headed toward Ash.

"I don't know yet. Keep everyone calm." They exchanged places, and Ash rushed into the blue room, with Ally following close behind. There was no one in the room, but she could hear the kids' agitated voices outside the emergency exit. She followed the sound and went out onto the concrete steps to find a group of kids and Matt on the ground, surrounding a child prone on the floor.

She saw the growing pool of blood and recognised the trainers that she'd commented on earlier. *Izad.* "What happened?" she asked as she took the steps three at a time.

Matt looked up, complete panic clear in his expression. He shook his head. "Izad, Ally, and Katie were out here like they often are, sitting on the edge. I'd told them they were okay if all they were doing was sitting. I was inside with everyone else. Then I heard a scream."

"Step back, please, guys," Ash said, parting the sea of kids to get to Izad. He was conscious and bleeding profusely from a cut above his eye. She pulled her phone from her pocket, unlocked it, and handed it to Matt. "Call for an ambulance."

After Matt had taken her phone, she knelt down to Izad. "Hey, buddy, are you okay?"

He looked up at her, and she was glad to see he could focus and was still lucid. But his bottom lip quivered, and he began to cry.

"Everything's going to be fine, Izad, I promise." She took his hand and squeezed it gently. He felt cold. Izad closed his other hand around hers. She glanced over her shoulder and located Ally. "What happened, Ally?"

She pointed to the metal bannister that ran alongside the steps. "Me and Katie were doing somersaults over the bar. Izad tried to do one and fell."

Ash knew what she meant. She'd even done them herself one day before a session started. As a kid, she used to do things like that all the time. Monkey bars, climbing frames, anything she could swing and twist on. It was one of the reasons she was strong as an adult. "Jesus," she whispered. She tried to fend off the rising panic at the thought of any of the kids getting injured on her watch, let alone Izad. He'd fallen seven feet, but he must have managed to shield his head with his arms before his head made contact with the ground. "Has he been unconscious at all?"

Ally shook her head. "I don't think so."

"Ambulance is on its way," Matt said and placed Ash's phone on the ground beside her.

Ash could hear the fear and distress in his voice, so she kept hers even and calm. "Go and get me a first aid kit, please, and take the rest of these kids upstairs out of the way into the blue room. And where's Bev?" Ash had scanned the scene as she emerged at the top of the steps. There were eleven kids. Matt should never have been on his own.

"Come on, guys, back inside," Matt said. He looked at Ash and shrugged. "She said she was nipping upstairs for two minutes."

"How long ago was that?"

Matt was clearly struggling with the situation and what his next words might implicate. "Ten, maybe fifteen minutes."

Ash clenched her jaw and flared her nostrils. Her fury took flight, and she struggled to rein it in and stay visibly composed. Everything inside her raged, and she wanted to smash Bev's head into the same ground that was now covered in Izad's blood.

"Ally, go with Matt, and bring the first aid kit back for me, quick as you can. Matt, keep everyone together in the blue room."

He acknowledged her repeated request with a nod. "No problem."

Ash turned her attention back to Izad as Matt herded the kids back inside. "How are you doing, Izad?" She smiled, but her fear for his health and her wrath toward Bev warred for dominance over her outer poise.

"I'm cold," he whispered weakly.

Ash unzipped her hoody and wrapped it around him, careful not to move him in case he had any broken bones. "Does anywhere hurt?"

"Everywhere," he managed to say between sobs.

She pulled the radio from her belt. "Matt, call Izad's parents and let them know what's happened, please. Make sure they have my number so they can keep in touch. I'll ride in the ambulance with him."

"Will do," Matt said.

"Ambulance? What's happened to Izad? Ashlyn?"

Ash clenched her fist so tightly that her forearm ached. She didn't answer Bev's questions, because she couldn't be sure of what she might say and who might hear it. She'd wait until she got back from the hospital before she confronted Bev. She pushed away those thoughts and concentrated on Izad. His eyes were fluttering, and his skin was beginning to pale.

"I feel sick, Smithy."

Ash barely heard his words they were so quiet. She rubbed his back gently and tucked her hoody around him. In the background, she could still hear Bev's grating voice and Matt responding. "It's going to be all right, Izad, I promise."

She had no right to promise anything. *Please God let it be all right.*

Chapter Twenty-Nine

I'm here to see Izad Sayed. I'm his mother." Evie tapped her phone on the desk when the nurse didn't respond as swiftly as she would've liked. She'd barely managed to get the words out without breaking down. From the moment she'd received the call from some guy called Matt from Izad's youth group, her energy flushed away, leaving her body an empty shell somehow managing to walk around. How come she could handle myriad crises at work, but one accident involving her son all but incapacitated her? She took a deep breath and tried to compose herself.

The nurse looked up and checked his paperwork. "He's in cubicle three. The doctor is with him."

Evie smiled though she thought it probably ended up looking like some sort of weird grimace. She didn't care. She thanked him and headed along the corridor to her son. Her stomach rolled and churned with worst-case scenarios. The guy from the youth group said Izad had fallen seven feet onto a concrete floor. *Seven feet*. Concussion was the least of it, brain damage the worst. Murderous notions invaded her head. She'd like to get her hands on whoever had let this happen.

She straightened her shoulders and sucked in a breath as she pulled open the cubicle curtain. A vice gripped her chest and tightened, making it hard to breathe. Her legs buckled beneath her, but she managed to grab onto the end of the bed to stay upright. Her beautiful, handsome, wonderful son looked…awful. One side of his face was swollen, and his eye was closed. A large bandage encircled his head, and he looked so pale, he was almost her skin colour.

"Mrs Sayed?" the doctor asked as she stepped toward Evie.

Evie shook her head. "No. I'm Izad's mother." When the doctor squinted and looked somewhat confused, she held her hand up. "His father and I aren't together."

"Ah, I see. I'm Dr Stirling." She pointed her pen to the chart in her other hand. "Izad is not quite stable yet. He's got some swelling of the brain so we've heavily sedated him while we monitor that. He has a large cut above his eye which we've stitched up. As you can see, his right eye is currently very swollen so we can't assess the possible damage to his sight until that calms down. I've sent the nurse to get another ice pack."

Evie faltered, unable to decide whether she found the matter of fact way Dr Stirling had delivered her prognosis on her son was welcome or callous. What she also couldn't seem to do was speak.

Stirling stepped closer and put her hand on Evie's forearm. "Are you okay?"

Evie pulled her arm away. "Am I okay? You've just told me my son is in a coma, and you don't know if he'll be blind in one eye. I don't feel like I should be okay." She saw Stirling's face harden and Evie shook her head, realising she was out of line. "I'm sorry. I just…"

Stirling reached out again and squeezed Evie's forearm gently. "I understand. I'm sorry, too. I was blunt. To be clear though, Izad is heavily sedated. That's not a coma." She gestured to the chair beside Izad's bed. "Would you like to sit down?"

Evie nodded and allowed Stirling to guide her to the chair. She sat, then reached out and held onto Izad's hand. His skin was cold, making Evie shiver. "Is he going to be all right?"

Stirling consulted her chart again before she looked up at Evie. "We'll need to monitor Izad over the next twenty-four hours. We'll do an MRI in the morning, and that'll tell us if we can bring him out of sedation. Once he's conscious, we'll be able to do some more tests and give you a clearer picture of how he's doing." She put her hand on Evie's shoulder. "I'm sorry I can't give you better news yet, but he's healthy in every other way. He's got a strong chance of a good recovery."

"Is that different to a full recovery?"

Stirling shook her head. "Forgive me. A full recovery is possible, but," she said and smiled pensively, "I can't give you any more details until we've run more tests." She replaced the chart on the end of Izad's bed. "I have to see other patients. The nurses will keep an eye on him, and he'll be moved to a different ward soon. You're welcome to stay beyond visiting hours this evening."

Evie nodded. She had no more words that weren't angry or unanswerable questions. Where was Tal? He said he'd be there before her. How had this even happened? What kind of a place let a child fall seven feet onto their head? Why was that hazard even there in the first place? Stirling opened the curtain and left quietly.

Evie touched the side of Izad's face that wasn't damaged and stroked his cheek gently. "Everything's going to be okay, baby boy," she said, trying to convince herself more than her unconscious son. Stirling had been clear that Izad was heavily sedated, but it looked too much like a coma to her. Someone was going to pay for this. And if Izad *didn't* make a full recovery… She put the brakes on that train of thought, not wanting to entertain anything other than Izad recovering completely. Like the doctor had said, he was a strong and healthy young man. He was going to be fine.

He had to be fine.

Through the haze of her own thoughts, the sound of Tal shouting filtered in. She tuned in to hear him tearing someone a new arsehole and realised he was probably having a go at a youth centre staff member. She rose from her chair, threw open the curtain, and headed in the direction of his voice. She wanted a piece of whoever Tal was chewing out, and she wanted answers.

"This is outrageous. How could you let something like this happen? Have you seen him? Have you seen his face? My boy is practically in a coma, and you think an apology is going to appease me?"

Evie was certain Tal was close given the volume of his voice. Sure enough, she came around the corner to face Tal as he pointed his finger at someone with their back to Evie.

"No, Mr Sayed, I don't think—"

"You don't think? You obviously weren't thinking when you allowed my son to fall *seven feet* onto his head, were you?"

Evie came to an abrupt stop. She recognised that voice, even though Tal had cut her off mid-sentence. Height, hair, build…it couldn't be. "Ash?" The person turned, and Evie put her hand to her mouth.

"Evie?" Ash said, her expression one of utter surprise. She glanced over her shoulder at Tal, and then turned back to Evie. "I'm sorry, Evie. I can't talk right now."

"You know her?" Tal's voice raised an octave.

"I don't understand…" Evie's legs threatened to give way again, and she placed her hand on the wall for support. "What are you doing here?"

Ash wrinkled her nose and shook her head as if Evie's presence was an irritating mosquito dive-bombing her. "Seriously, Evie, I can't talk right now." She turned back to Tal.

"How do you know Evie?" Tal narrowed his eyes.

Ash glanced back and forth between the two of them, and her mouth fell open. "You're…Izad's mum?"

Evie nodded slowly. "Why are you here?"

Tal prodded Ash in the shoulder. "She's the reason our son is here."

Evie shook her head. "I don't understand…"

"Evie…" Ash reached out and hooked her arm under Evie's. "Are you okay?"

"What does he mean? What have you got to do with Izad being here?"

"I work at the youth centre Izad comes to. I came with him in the ambulance—"

Evie pulled her arm from Ash's grasp and pushed her away. "You. You let my son…" She put the heels of her hands against her forehead and pushed hard. This couldn't be happening. She pulled her hands down to cover her face. If she couldn't see Ash, perhaps none of this was real.

"Evie…"

God, no.

"You should leave," Tal said.

Evie parted her fingers slightly to see Tal grasp Ash by her shoulder and pull her back.

"You've told the doctor what happened. Now, go. We don't want you here."

Ash stumbled with the force of Tal's movement and steadied herself against the wall. Evie moved her hands from her face in time to see two security guards coming toward them, no doubt alerted by Tal's raised voice.

"Evie, please. Let me—"

"Get out." Evie held up her hand to stop Ash speaking. "Get out now. You shouldn't be here."

"What's happening here?" one of the guards asked.

"This woman's harassing us. She's nearly killed our son, and now she won't leave us alone." Tal gestured toward Ash.

"What?" Ash asked, panic audible in her voice.

She looked to Evie, but she shook her head and glanced at the security guard. "Please make her leave."

The guard took hold of Ash's forearm. "If you could follow me, please, miss."

Evie saw Ash move almost imperceptibly to jerk her arm away from the man's grasp, but she seemed to stop herself. No doubt she could easily escape if she wanted to, given the skills she

displayed at the club with Von, but Ash was in enough trouble. Evie wanted to know what she had to say. She had to know how this had happened, but right now she couldn't face her at all. Really, she'd had a lucky escape; if Ash was this reckless with the young people she worked with, she was clearly not parent material. Ash's proclamation that she was still a kid herself wouldn't get her out of this mess. This was negligence at the least and wilful abuse at worst.

And again, Evie hadn't seen it. She'd been blinded by Ash's sparkling personality, much as she'd been blinded by Von's. She shook her head. She couldn't trust her heart anymore.

Chapter Thirty

Contempt. Disappointment. Surprise. Even hatred. Evie had conveyed all of those emotions and more in one withering look that had made Ash want to shrink away. She caught an Uber back to the centre. The club had finished over an hour ago, but she hoped Bev would still be there. Ash had some serious questions for that woman. She saw Ally and Katie waiting at the gate and took her time to pay the driver, not wanting to face them. Nausea tumbled around her stomach, and she was on the verge of vomiting at any moment. She thanked the driver and climbed out of the car slowly as both of them rushed toward her.

"How is he?" "Is he okay?" "Is he going to be all right?"

The girls fired those and other questions at spitfire rate, and Ash held up her hands. "Woah, slow down." She waited until they were quiet before she spoke. "Izad is stable. I'm afraid I can't tell you any more than that. His mum and dad are with him. Do you know them?"

Ally shook her head. "We know his dad, but we've never met his mum."

That seemed strange. Izad's records showed a home address a few streets up from the centre in the slightly more affluent area of the city. Maybe Evie lived somewhere else. She supposed that made sense, and she'd never seen his mum either…at least, she hadn't known she'd seen his mum. And she'd done a lot more than *see* her. God, this was a mess.

"I've got a number for his dad from when Izad came for my birthday sleepover. I'll get my mum to call him," Katie said.

Ash shook her head. "Wait until tomorrow at least. They're likely to be at the hospital all night, and I don't think they'll want bothering." She didn't *think* that; she *knew* that. She hadn't spent long "speaking" to Tal, but she was certain he wouldn't appreciate non-familial intrusions this evening. And Evie…Ash swallowed and nausea burned at the back of her throat…Evie looked destroyed.

Ally pointed inside. "Bev went wappy and sent everyone home early. Matt left here in tears. I heard her shouting at him."

None of this was Matt's fault. Bev had left the room, leaving poor Matt with more young people than he should've had. Ash clenched her jaw. She couldn't say anything to Ally and Katie, but she hoped they knew whose fault this all was. "I'll call him. You peeps better go home. It's getting late."

Ally smiled. "She probably hasn't even realised I haven't come home yet."

Her words wrapped around Ash's heart and squeezed. She ached for all these kids without the quality of home life every child deserved. If she could win the lottery, she'd…she'd what? She'd been concerned she wasn't ready for one child, and now she was thinking of looking after a houseful of them? *People change.* Though it wasn't so much of a change as a simple realisation that she *was* ready for that responsibility after all. "See you Wednesday?"

They both nodded and came in for a hug. "Bye, Smithy."

"Bye, peeps."

They turned to leave, and Ash watched them for a while before she took a deep breath and entered the building. The receptionist raised her eyebrow and acknowledged Ash with a nod but didn't say anything. Christ, what tale had Bev been spinning while Ash was at the hospital? She walked through and did a quick check of the rooms, but everything had already been cleared up. She opened the fire exit door in the green room and stepped out onto the concrete steps. She pulled her phone from her pocket, turned the torch on, and shone it onto the spot where Izad had fallen. A large patch of bright concrete stood out where Izad's blood had obviously been cleaned up. She bet that Bev had made Matt do that since they didn't have a cleaner, even though he was only a volunteer. He probably wouldn't come back to work again. She typed a memo into her phone to remind her to call him on her way home.

First, she had to deal with Bev.

Ash closed the door and made her way upstairs to their office. She could hear raised voices, but she didn't knock. Their chief executive, Michael, was sat at her desk, and though Bev looked suitably distressed, she still managed to shoot Ash a look of utter scorn.

"Ashlyn. We've been waiting for you," Michael said but made no move to vacate Ash's chair.

She pushed some paperwork back and sat on a nearby two-drawer filing cabinet. "I've been at the hospital." Ash glared at Bev and clenched her jaw. What she *wanted* to do was grab her by the hair and smash her smug face into her desk. Repeatedly.

"Can you explain what happened, please?" Michael asked.

"Sure." Ash recounted what she knew from the moment Ally had ran into the red room to tell her there was an emergency. Michael held up his hand when she got to the part where she'd asked Matt where Bev was. Bev shifted in her seat and narrowed her eyes.

"You left Matt in the green room with eleven children?" Michael inclined his head and looked directly at Bev.

"There were only eight children in the room when I left. I told Matt to radio if more young people came into the room, and he never did." Bev sat back in her chair and steepled her fingers.

Ash again quelled an aggressive instinct to break those fingers. She had no idea where these thoughts were coming from. She was usually so controlled. Was it because she cared so much for Izad? Would she be this violent of mind if it had been any of the other young people?

Michael nodded and turned his attention back to Ash. "What did Matt say to you when you asked where Bev was?"

"He said that Bev had told him she was nipping upstairs for two minutes. When the accident happened, she hadn't returned and Matt thought she'd been gone between ten and fifteen minutes." Ash could feel Bev's stare burning into the side of her face, but she ignored it. There was no way she was covering for her. Even if she'd been a half-decent boss instead of a complete bitch, Ash wouldn't have obscured the truth after she'd put a child's life at risk.

"That's not true," Bev said. "He's lying."

"Is there any way of verifying the number of young people in the room when Bev left?" Michael asked.

"Robbie was in that room. He's OCD, and he's always counting everything. He has a habit of counting the numbers for us in any of the rooms. I'm sure he could tell us how many children were in there before, during, and after Bev left the room."

Bev tutted. "You can't rely on what Robbie or any of that group say. They'd say anything to protect Matt. He's their hero."

"So, it's a child's word against a member of staff?"

Michael's question seemed rhetorical. Ash stayed silent for a moment but couldn't hold her tongue for long. "We had over forty young people at the club tonight. Whichever room they were in, it was all hands on deck. Every member of staff, paid or unpaid, should have been on the floor."

"What are you saying, Ashlyn?" Michael asked.

"I'm saying that Bev should never have come up to the office, especially not for quarter of an hour. We needed everyone downstairs with the kids."

"You're just saying that to protect Matt." Bev looked at Michael. "The two of them are thick as thieves."

Ash would've laughed at Bev's clichéd phrasing if the situation weren't so serious. "I wouldn't lie to protect anyone who had put a child's life at risk…including you."

Michael held his hands up. "Okay, okay. That's not going to get us anywhere. Tell me the rest of the story."

Ash wasn't telling a "story," but she didn't correct him and continued recounting the events, including the first aid she'd administered whilst waiting for the ambulance, the doctor's prognosis, Izad's state when she left, and his parents' reaction. A bowling ball settled in the pit of her stomach when she told of Tal and Evie's response. God, what Evie must be going through now. She must feel so helpless. Ash had wanted to pull her into her arms and say everything was going to be all right, but not only could she not promise that, Evie made it clear she wanted Ash as far away from her as possible.

"Do you think they're inclined to sue?" Michael asked.

His question stumped her. *That* was what he was most worried about right now? She shook her head. "I have no idea. I would think that their main concern is whether or not Izad will wake up with brain damage or…" Ash didn't want to contemplate the alternative, but it had to be said, "whether he wakes up at all. I don't imagine that their current priority is to call a claims lawyer to see if they can make any money out of us." Ash pointed at Michael. "And you should be concerned about Izad, *not* the money, for Christ's sake."

"Be careful what you're saying, Ashlyn." Michael wagged his finger. "Remember who you're speaking to."

In her peripheral vision, she could see Bev's smug smile, and Ash gripped the edge of the filing cabinet until her fingertips ached and she had to release them. "Shouldn't you be writing all this down? Did you get Matt's account of what happened? Did you speak to any of the young people who were in the room?"

"I won't tell you again, Ashlyn. Calm down." He pointed to his phone on her desk. "I'm recording this conversation."

That would've been nice to know, but it wouldn't have changed her story. The way Bev's eyes widened indicated she hadn't known what Michael had been doing either. Slightly comforted by that fact, Ash held up her hands. "I'm sorry. I'm upset. There was a lot of blood…and Izad's father pushed me around a little. I'm rattled."

"He assaulted you?" Michael asked.

No way was she allowing that to be used against them. "No, not at all."

Michael frowned. "But you said he pushed you around."

"It wasn't assault. He has nothing to answer for. I would've behaved far worse than he did if the same thing had happened to my child." And there it was. Parental instinct. She did have it…just too late for it to matter to Evie. Ash had to tell her what had happened. She couldn't have Evie believing that she was to blame. Ash would never have let anything happen to Izad. He was special. And though she knew she shouldn't have favourites, she couldn't help but be drawn to him more than any of the other kids.

Michael pushed back in the chair and put his feet on her desk. "I think you should go home, Ashlyn. And don't talk to anyone about this, especially anyone connected to the Sayed family. Do you understand?"

"Yes."

"Come in as usual on Wednesday. My secretary will have transcribed this meeting, and you can sign it. You can be assured I'll get Matt to come in to talk to me—Bev, get me his number, please—and I'll speak to the young people who were in the green room at the time of the accident… We must stick together though, Ashlyn. Do you understand?"

Ash bit the inside of her cheek to stop words coming out that she might regret. She nodded instead of speaking. "I need my stuff." She pointed toward her messenger bag and jacket on the wall hook beside her desk.

"Of course." Michael pushed back from her desk so she could retrieve her gear. "I'll be in touch. But remember, say nothing to anyone, please. We don't want this blowing out of proportion."

Ash closed her eyes as she faced the wall and put on her coat. What proportion was it, exactly? A child was in a coma. That seemed like a matter of epic proportions already. Michael's talk of sticking together and not speaking to anyone smacked of a cover-up and made Ash nauseous. There was no way she'd let Bev get away with this, and she wouldn't allow Matt to take the fall either…even if that did mean losing a job she loved.

Chapter Thirty-One

Evie was grateful that Doctor Stirling had arranged for a small cot to be installed in Izad's room so she could be there throughout the night. She'd drifted in and out of light sleep and checked her watch almost every half hour. The night dragged and the morning eventually arrived, but she wouldn't have been anywhere else. It was afternoon now, and the lack of sleep had her grabbing quick naps between visits from the nurse.

Evie jerked upright when she heard Izad murmur. She blinked a few times to clear her blurry eyes and focus. "Izad?" She'd said his name too many times to count during the night, and every time a stab of pain seared through her body when he didn't answer. The morning's MRI had shown Izad's swelling had gone down, so they'd reduced the sedation considerably, enough so that he would be able to come around…if his body was ready to let him.

"Momma?"

Evie swallowed hard. Had she heard correctly? She lunged toward the bedside light and turned it on.

Izad turned his head away from the harsh illumination. "Too bright."

She switched the light off and pulled him into a hug.

"Too tight," he said, sounding a little breathless.

She released him and drew back but grasped his hands in hers. "I'm sorry, sweetheart. How are you feeling?"

There was a moment of silence, and Evie held her breath. The doctor had said brain damage was a possibility.

"My head and face hurt."

She laughed gently. "Kissing the concrete has that effect." She loosed one of her hands and pressed the call button. She wanted Izad checked over as soon as possible.

"Where am I? This bed's scratchy."

"You're in hospital, sweetheart. Do you remember what happened?" Evie squeezed her eyes shut then opened them wide in an effort to focus. *Please God, let him remember.* It was a good sign that he'd woken so soon after the doctor had reduced his sedation, but there could still be all sorts of complications, including memory loss.

"I fell at the club."

He glanced up at Evie, then looked away, a little sheepish. She was about to press for more details, when the cubicle curtain opened and Dr Stirling entered.

"You're awake," she said and smiled at both of them. "Let's have a look at you."

Evie watched Stirling work for a moment before she pulled her phone out and text Tal, who was resting in an empty bed a few cubicles along. He joined them moments later, and she saw her own relief reflected in Tal's expression. He came in beside her and slipped his hand in hers. She squeezed it gently, united with him in their love for Izad.

"At least now I don't have to kill anyone in revenge for our son."

She heard the humour in his voice, but it was tinged with genuine rage. Tal wasn't the murderous type but losing a child could drive even the most stable of individuals to actions beyond their usual scope. "It's good that Izad won't have to grow up with his father in prison." Thoughts of Ash pushed, unwelcome, into her mind. Tal's anger had been directed at her. She'd been the one to bring Izad in and was of the one the club's youth workers. Izad had often enthused about *Smithy*, telling Evie all about how she was teaching him the piano and how they played chess together. If she were honest, she was jealous of their relationship. How was she to know Smithy was Ash when she'd never asked her surname?

Evie looked at the time and then her phone. Should she text Ash and tell her that Izad had come around and seemed to be okay? She shook her head and pressed the heel of her palm to her throbbing right eye, a migraine pulsing behind it ready to explode. She put her phone away and stowed the urge to contact Ash. She'd been the one to let this happen to Izad; she didn't deserve to know how he was doing.

She turned her attention back to Stirling and watched her run through a raft of tests with Izad. When she turned to face Evie and Tal, she smiled widely.

"I'm pleased to give Izad a clean bill of health. I'm sending him for a final scan, but everything is looking good."

"Thank you, doctor." Evie slumped after Stirling left, as if the bones in her body turned to soft rubber, but Tal caught her.

"Are you okay?"

She nodded. "I'm just… I don't know what I'd do if…" The

sentences didn't need finishing. Tal would surely know and share her feelings.

"Momma… Daddy…"

Evie recognised the guilt in Izad's voice. He clearly had a confession to make. Having a child that couldn't lie had been useful more than a few times before tonight. "Yes, sweetheart."

"If I tell you something, will you promise that you won't stop me going back to my clubs?"

Evie raised her eyebrow, and she felt Tal bristling beside her.

"I don't think it's a good idea you go back to that place at all, Izad. They shouldn't have let this happen," Tal said.

Izad's face creased into sadness, and he stuck out his bottom lip. "But, Daddy, it wasn't Matt's fault."

"Who's Matt?" Evie sank onto the edge of Izad's bed and pulled his hand into hers again. She pushed down the tears of relief that swelled against her eyes when Izad gripped her gently.

"He was in the green room when I was doing somersaults on the bar. Ally and Katie were doing them, and I wanted to be able to do them too…"

"Somersaults on what bar?" Since the club was close to Tal's house, Evie had never been there and had no idea what Izad was talking about.

"Do you mean on the fire exit?" Tal asked, and Izad nodded. "You've been told not to play on that before, haven't you?" After Izad nodded again, Tal turned to Evie. "There's a pyramid of concrete steps leading down from the fire exit, and there's a metal, circular barrier along the edge of them. When I used to go to that club, I did the same—except I never fell. It's about seven feet from the top of the stairs to the ground." He shook his head and shivered. "They should've put upright struts on that thing years ago."

"Has anyone ever fallen from it before?"

"Not to my knowledge. Someone died when they fell through the glass roof two floors up, but they *were* trying to rob the place, so…"

Izad coughed. "If you did it too, Daddy, you can't be mad at me for doing the same."

Evie sucked in her lips to supress a laugh. Izad's logic was absolutely spot on.

"It's not—"

"The same?" Izad pushed himself up on the bed. "Why not?"

Evie shook her head. This wasn't a discussion Tal would win.

"Daddy's not mad at you, sweetheart. He's worried about you. We both are."

"I promise I won't do it again. Please don't stop me from going back." Izad began to cry. "I need to see Smithy. She's teaching me to play the piano, and I really like her…" He looked up and gave them both his best sad face. "I don't like many people, but she's special."

Evie glanced at the floor, unable to hold Izad's serious gaze. Evie shared Izad's appraisal of Ash, and if he thought she was special, she must be someone extraordinary. "Where was Ash—I mean, Smithy—when you fell?"

Izad tilted his head and looked puzzled. "Why?"

"Because she was the one who rode in the ambulance with you and brought you in. We thought she was in the room with you."

Izad wrinkled his nose and shook his head. "Smithy was in the red room. We'd been playing chess, but Ally and Katie wanted to play in the green room for a while. I went with them."

"Why do you care whose fault it was? If they work there, they were responsible. Full stop." Tal put his hand on Evie's shoulder. "You never did answer how you knew that Smithy girl."

"She's not a girl. She's in her mid-twenties."

Tal jutted his chin toward her. "And how do you know that?"

"Let's talk about this later." She turned back to Izad, tucked his arms under the duvet, and pulled it up under his chin. "You better get some sleep."

Izad yawned and nodded. "Okay, Momma."

She leaned in and kissed him goodnight before moving out of the cubicle while Tal said goodnight. He closed the cubicle curtain behind him and gestured with his thumb that they head down the corridor to the café.

Evie took a seat in a booth while Tal got two teas.

"So what's the story with this Ash Smithy then?" he asked as he placed the tray on the table.

"We were involved for a little while, and then we were friends, and now…we're not even that." She didn't want to say they were nothing. That seemed so final. But Evie *had* asked Ash not to contact her again, and Ash had respected her request. Seeing her again in the hospital earlier reinforced that the tug of attraction was still strong in spite of the circumstances.

"And you didn't know she worked at Izad's clubs?"

"No. I never told her Izad's name."

"How could you be involved with her and not talk about your son?"

The judgement in Tal's voice rang clear, and Evie didn't appreciate it. "We were getting to that, but it got a little complicated. We tried to be friends, but it was too hard. Look, I don't have to explain any of this to you, Tal. I was seeing if she might be a good fit for me and Izad and…" She couldn't say Ash wasn't a good fit, especially not after took into account Izad's glowing reports of "Smithy.". Izad was incredibly choosy about giving his affection to anyone, but he'd clearly made a connection with her. And Ash's concern was bleeding out of her yesterday, that much was clear.

"Too hard to be friends?"

Evie clenched her jaw and ran her hand through her hair. "Yeah, kind of the opposite of us. You know, no attraction so it was easy to be friends for us. A situation diametrically opposed to that." She sighed. "Look, I don't want to talk about it anymore. And it's none of your business."

Tal inclined his head. "That's not strictly true, is it?" His voice softened. "We agreed that we'd give each other the opportunity to vet people that could be in Izad's life on a permanent basis."

Evie nodded slowly. "I know. But it didn't look like that situation was going to present itself."

Tal put his hand on Evie's shoulder, then pulled her into a hug. "But you wanted it to, didn't you?"

She allowed herself to be manoeuvred into his arms and sank into the softness of his cashmere sweater. Yes. Yes, she did want to see if Ash could be part of her life permanently, part of Izad's life, and part of their life together. But nothing had changed. As far as Evie knew, Ash still thought herself too young to be involved in parenting a child. Her tears pushed again for release, and this time she let them fall. Whether they were tears of relief or sadness, Evie wasn't certain. Being close to Ash again, seeing her concern for Izad, had brought all her feelings dangerously close to the surface. And Izad being so vulnerable, his life in such danger, had taken her by the throat and squeezed mercilessly, choking her.

As she continued to sob against Tal's chest and give her emotions free rein, she resolved to text Ash later to put her mind at rest. She cared for Izad, and she deserved to know he was okay. Beyond that, it was in the hands of destiny.

Chapter Thirty-Two

A sh hooked her iPhone up to the monitor on her desk and glanced at Matt. He looked nervous, and she couldn't blame him, but what she was about to show them all would clear him of any wrongdoing or negligence. She hit play and stepped to the side so everyone could get a clear view of the video—one of the kid's videos.

"What are we watching, Ashlyn?" Michael asked.

Ash noted the impatience in his voice, but she didn't care. She'd been deliberately dramatic and wanted this to play out perfectly. It was time to see Bev crash and burn. "Ronnie and Tianna were practising their dance moves for the Bright Stars club last night. They used Ronnie's phone to video their performances so they could watch them back and perfect their moves."

"And?"

Ash held up her finger to pause Michael's line of query. "From the position of Ronnie's phone, you can see almost all of the green room, yes?" She looked to all three of them, and they each nodded in turn. Bev shifted in her seat. *You're going to get a whole lot more uncomfortable.* She scrolled forward. "You can see from the digital wall clock that it's 6:41 p.m." The bright red digits showed the time perfectly, so that there was no question. Ash pointed to Bev in the centre of the frame as she spoke to Matt and then began to walk toward the main exit. "There's Bev leaving the room." Ash glanced across at Bev and supressed a grin. The woman was practically squirming. She knew damn well what the video was about to reveal. "There are eleven young people in the room." She flicked through the video again. "There's Izad, Ally, and Katie going out of the fire exit, and you can see Matt says something to them—he asked them not to play on the rail. The time on the wall clock is 6:51 p.m." Ash focused on Matt and smiled as she scrolled forward again. "That's Ally running back into the building, screaming to Matt, and running out of the room to get me."

She let the rest of the video run in real time and saw everyone in the room empty out of the fire exit, with Matt at the front of them all. Seconds later, everyone could see that Ash ran into the room and toward the melee outside.

She paused the video and pointed to the time. "That's 6:58 p.m. Bev had been gone for seventeen minutes, and there were eleven young people in the room." She unplugged her iPhone and sat on the edge of her desk. "I think that clears up who's telling the truth and who isn't, Michael."

Michael took a deep breath and nodded. "Ashlyn. Matthew. Would you leave us, please? If you could go and wait in the orange room, and I'll be along shortly."

Ash half-smiled in Bev's direction. She didn't have a smug smile on her face now, and there was no way she could talk herself out of what the video clearly showed. "Of course. No problem." She got up and headed toward the office door. She patted Matt on the back as they left and went downstairs to the orange room as requested.

"Jesus Christ, I don't think I've ever been so nervous," he said, flopping down into one of the few comfy chairs around the room.

"It's Bev who should've been nervous, not you. You weren't the one lying about what happened."

He nodded but frowned. "I know, but I was still the one in the room. I shouldn't have let them go out there when there was just me. Izad got hurt because I wasn't paying attention."

"Hey, no, don't do that. You had a lot of kids in there, and there was a *lot* going on. Music, dancing, table tennis…it's a big room, and there should always be at least two adults in there even when there are less young people. Bev knew that, but she left you in there alone anyway."

"I know…but still."

"Ally and Katie had been told repeatedly not to do somersaults on that bar. The centre should have put some wooden slats across so the kids couldn't even do somersaults. Lots of things could've been different, but they weren't. And I got a text from Izad's mum half an hour ago. She said he's going to be okay." *Izad's mum…Evie.* She hadn't known whether to open it or not when she'd received it. Ash had looked at the unopened message for ten minutes, trying to hold back the pessimistic voice in her head telling her Izad had gone downhill overnight…or worse. In the end, she asked Kirsty to read it.

"Oh my God, that's great news." Matt jumped up, bent down to Ash, and enveloped her in a bear hug. After a few seconds too many, he pulled back and retook his seat. "Have you told anyone else?"

206

Ash shook her head. "No. They can stew. They can wait until Izad's parents tell them…if they decide to. They may not want to speak to them."

Matt narrowed his eyes. "So how come the mum contacted you? She never comes here, does she? I've only ever seen the dad. And he's huge. I wouldn't want to be on the end of his anger."

Ash blew out a breath. She *had* been on the end of it, and Matt was right to want to avoid the experience. "It's a long story," she said and avoided eye contact. It wasn't one she wanted to share with a straight male colleague.

"What do you think is going to happen to Bev?"

She shrugged, glad he'd taken the hint and switched back to what was happening upstairs. "I honestly don't know. I haven't worked here long enough to know if they're a 'sweep-it-under-the-carpet' kind of organisation or whether they'll admit to their wrongdoing. Everyone knows the ratio rules though, and Ronnie's parents could show the video to anyone; local news, other parents, Izad's parents. There's not much chance of them keeping all of this secret."

"Do you think the parents will sue?"

"Who knows? We're becoming more like America, a more litigious society. Why wouldn't they sue? Even if it's not for the money, it could serve the purpose of making the company ensure the fire exit is safer, make them tighten up their procedures. Suing us could save other kids from getting hurt."

Michael entered the room and saved Ash from not having the answers to any more of Matt's questions.

"Thank you for coming in and telling your side of the story, Matt. Can I count on you to keep volunteering with us?"

Matt stood up and nodded slowly. "Of course…if you still want me?"

Michael strode over to Matt and slapped him firmly on the shoulder. "Absolutely. Ashlyn tells me you're a great worker, and I'd hate to lose you over this. We need to keep hold of all the good staff that we have."

Ash felt a little awkward as the only one to be seated, so she also rose. "You are great, Matt."

"Super. Well, that's all for today then, Matt. You'll be here for the club on Wednesday as usual?" Michael held the door open, clearly indicating for Matt to leave.

Ash shook her head at the high and mighty treatment. Michael had no idea how to treat his staff properly. "See you tomorrow,

Matt." She smiled as he left, and he returned her smile along with a frown as if to say, what the fuck? He was barely out of the door before Michael closed it behind him and stayed in the room. Ash hovered awkwardly for a moment before dropping back into her chair. Michael took the seat opposite with practiced efficiency.

"How would you feel about a promotion to club manager?"

Ash raised her eyebrows, not quite able to process what Michael had just said, and what it meant… for her *and* for Bev. But she wasn't too blown away to ask for more details. "On what terms, permanent or temporary?"

"Permanent. We'd advertise the position internally, as we're entitled to do, and I expect you'd be the only candidate."

The way he said it made it clear that even if anyone else did apply, Ash would still be the successful applicant. "The same terms and pay as the previous incumbent?"

He shook his head. "Ten percent increase on salary."

Ash tried to hide an audible gulp. Bev worked thirty-five hours compared to Ash's sixteen. She had no idea what Bev's rate was, but it had to be more than she was on, given the difference in responsibility, *and* he was offering a pay rise. Although Ash had been doing Bev's job for the past few months anyway, so the responsibility didn't faze her. It'd mean she wouldn't have to get that second job.

"It's the least we can offer you. By all accounts, you've been doing the job of club manager more or less since you started work here. I knew you'd be a good appointment, but I had no idea that Bev was such a bad one…" He rolled his neck and sucked in a breath before he stood again. "Have a think about it. If I could have a decision in the morning, that would be lovely. I've fired Bev so I need a replacement as quickly as possible." He headed for the door, opened it, and turned. "Thank you for your part in uncovering the truth about last night's incident. I'm hopeful we'll be able to learn from the mistakes that were made and be a better provider of children's service because of them."

He let the door close behind him and his inane, emotionless words, and Ash watched him leave before she punched the air with both fists. She'd hoped to progress but hadn't counted on it happening so fast. She pulled her phone from her jacket pocket and unlocked it. A stab of sadness marred her jubilance. Most people her age should have a loved one to call and share the news with. Ash scrolled to Kirsty's number and pressed it, trying to ignore the thought. Kirsty *was* a loved one, not in the sense

Ash was thinking of, but she *was* her best friend and the closest person she had to family after her foster parents.

Kirsty's phone rang until it went to answer phone so Ash hung up. She checked the time and figured Kirsty was busy at work. She flicked through and hovered over Nat and Rich's number but couldn't get past the notion that she wanted to share the news with Evie. Which of course, would be totally inappropriate. What would she say? *Hey, great news. Your son's accident got me a promotion!*

She went to her messages instead and reread Evie's morning message yet again. It read as her messages always did: grammatically correct. Had Ash expected more? XOXO, maybe? The dull ache in her heart indicated that *she* definitely wanted more. It had been their first communication since Evie had asked her not to text again. And Ash still hadn't responded to this one. Did Evie want her to? Or was it a courtesy text, and the embargo on any exchanges was still in force?

Ash took a deep breath and thumbed a message, remembering Evie's motto, *no rocking chair regrets*. Ash didn't want any of those either.

That's brilliant news. Please give him a huge hug from me, and tell him we have a game of chess to finish when he's up for it. The boss has been sacked for letting this happen. I have a video of what happened if you'd like to see it? I'm thinking of you…as always x

She lingered over pressing send for the briefest of moments, before she drew courage from somewhere and went through with it. She locked the phone and slipped it back into her pocket, not wanting to see how quickly it was read…or ignored. She'd said a little of what she wanted to say and that would have to be good enough until such time as Evie allowed her the opportunity to say more.

And every fibre of her being longed for Evie to give her that opportunity.

Chapter Thirty-Three

Evie's phone vibrated against her thigh but she tried to ignore it. Every time it had kicked into action since she'd sent the text to Ash, she'd rushed to check it, hoping for a response. Instead all she'd received were well-meaning messages for Izad. She appreciated them, of course she did, but she only wanted to hear from Ash.

Perhaps she had no right to hope for a response since she'd been the one to cut off communication, but surely this situation overrode that previous instruction. Perhaps she should've made it clear that she was open to a reply. A quick check of the time revealed it hadn't been that long since she'd sent her message to Ash, and most likely, she was busy. But still…she waited.

Curiosity and hope got the better of her, and she pulled her phone from the deep pocket of her sweatpants. Her pulse raced when she saw Ash's name, and she grinned.

"What's made you smile?"

Evie fumbled her phone, almost dropping it at the sound of Tal's voice. He'd been so quiet, she'd forgotten he was there. "Nothing."

"Right. Nice shower?"

She nodded and ignored his disbelieving tone as she towel dried her hair. "Lovely, thanks. You're welcome to take one."

"That's okay." He gestured toward his crumpled clothing. "I need to get home, change, and get to work, if you're okay with Izad for the day?"

"Yep, no problem. I've put in emergency leave for the rest of the week." Her phone buzzed again to indicate she hadn't read the message, but she wanted to open it alone. Her initial excitement had given way to the possibility that it might be a courteous "thanks for letting me know" text, and she didn't want to share that disappointment with anyone. "You might want to have a quick shave too."

Tal ran his hand across his stubbly chin. "Nah, I haven't got the time. I've got an important client coming in at two. Beards are all the rage right now, aren't they?"

Evie laughed. "I think you're about a year too late for that trend, but a little growth does suit you, actually."

He pointed to the ceiling. "I'm going to do one last check on our boy before I go."

"Don't wake him. Dr Stirling said he should rest as much as possible."

"I won't, but I want to see him one more time before I leave."

Evie didn't miss the choke as Tal finished his sentence but said nothing. They didn't need to share what they'd both been thinking last night, especially since none of it had come to fruition and Izad had been declared fit and healthy. She waited, her patience practically anorexic, while Tal nipped upstairs and said a quiet good-bye to Izad. He jogged downstairs, kissed her on the forehead, and left. Evie locked the door behind him and moved swiftly to the lounge. She dropped onto the sofa, opened her messages, and read the new one from Ash.

The video sounded interesting, and she did want to see it, but the thing that caught her attention were Ash's last words, *I'm thinking of you…as always.* She rested the phone on her leg and leaned back, not wanting to rush her reply. Ever since she'd asked Ash not to message her, she'd hoped for one to come through anyway. She'd spent nights scouring Ash's Facebook and plenty of those had ended with Evie attending to her growing sexual frustration with her trusty bullet.

But this was about more than an off-the-charts sexual chemistry. It was something deeper, a connection she couldn't explain, and one that had come quickly and hit her off guard. And with this new knowledge of how much Ash meant to Izad, she'd shown herself to be the complete package. Was Evie kidding herself into believing this changed anything? Was she pinning her hopes on Izad being such a great kid that Ash couldn't help but want to be more involved in his life? It was a giant leap from weekly youth worker to regular co-parent.

But Evie couldn't help but let that hope, however miniscule and distant, infuse her heart. Her usual analytical self had seemingly melted away, leaving her in an unfamiliar limbo territory. She was stuck between where she wanted to be emotionally and where she'd put herself in reality. She looked at Ash's last sentence again. Weren't the words like putting her foot in the door? All Evie had to do was pull it wide open. *If it's that simple, do it.* She thumbed the return message box and took a deep breath. *What to say?* She didn't want to come on too strong or too desperate, but if she were honest, she was both of those things and more. She'd never been one to play games, nor did she think Ash was a player.

And what would be the point of holding back now, anyway? They'd shared their most intimate selves with each other. The door to a potential future together was ajar and being timid with the truth would only serve to pull it closed, perhaps for good.

I want to know what happened, definitely. Would you email me the video? I'll give Izad that hug when he wakes, but maybe you could finish that game of chess with him at our house? Evie took a breath and reread her words. How had she written an invitation to their home so freely? She began to delete it but stopped herself. It would be good for Izad to see Ash this week, and it would probably cheer him up especially since Tal was still ruminating on whether or not he would be allowed to attend his clubs again. She stretched out her fingers over the phone screen and then pressed send before she pulled away like it might self-destruct. She immediately wished she'd used a messenger service where you could delete the words before the person read them. She shook her head and dropped the phone onto the cushion beside her. No, that wasn't what she wanted. One way or another, this had to be done, and she had to know. If circumstances had changed, Evie wanted Ash in her life, in Izad's life. She wouldn't deny him that, and she was done denying herself that. She pressed her head against the sofa and closed her eyes, not wanting to see when the message changed from *delivered* to *read*.

Leaden weights tugged her eyelids and she realised how tired she was, having barely slept last night. Sleep pulled at her consciousness, lulling her into its warm and comforting arms, and she succumbed to the desire to recharge.

She jerked awake when headlights shone through the front window momentarily and was scarcely conscious when her doorbell sounded. She rolled her neck and ran her tongue across her teeth to get some moisture in her mouth, before she pushed herself up from the sofa and headed toward the door.

She opened it to a pizza delivery woman holding a familiar XXL sized box with a tub of ice cream sitting atop, and the smell emanating from it was divine. She hadn't thought about takeout but now she wished she had. "I'm sorry, but there must be some mistake. I didn't order a pizza."

The woman frowned and looked at the side of the box. "Evie Jackson? Is that not you?" She held the box label up for inspection. "That's this address, isn't it?"

"That is me…" Evie rubbed her eyes to focus. "And that is my address. But I still didn't make any order."

The woman pulled out her phone and scrolled her screen for a moment. "It was ordered and paid for by an Ashlyn Smith. Ring any bells?" She sighed and looked at her watch. "Do you want it or not?"

Evie smiled despite the woman's impatience. "No, it's fine. I'll take it, thank you." Evie glanced back in the house, trying to locate her handbag to give the woman a tip, but she was already turning and going back to her car. Evie closed the door and took the tasty treasures to the kitchen. She put the ice cream in the freezer but not before noticing that it was Izad's favourite flavour. She turned back to the breakfast bar and inspected the label on the box to find that it was halal BBQ chicken, Izad's favourite again. Evie couldn't have chosen a better pick-me-up meal for him. She opened the box, popped a few slices on an oven tray, and stuck it in the oven to keep warm.

She checked the time and couldn't quite believe that she'd napped for almost an hour. Her heart raced, and she quickly headed upstairs, needing to check on Izad. She pushed his door open to find him sleeping soundly, the slow rise and fall of his chest provided an instant comfort, and her own breathing evened out. Evie sat softly on the edge of his bed, placed her hand on his shoulder, and gently rocked him awake. His eyes flickered open, though his right eye was still badly swollen, and she stiffened at the combined sight of that and the stitches above the same eye.

Izad smiled then sniffed the air like a bloodhound. "Is that BBQ chicken pizza?"

"And hello to you too, sleepy head." Evie stroked his hair, but he batted her hand away.

"Not my hair, Momma."

"You've already got bed head, sweetheart. I don't think I could do any more damage."

Izad sat up, grabbed his phone, and examined himself with the camera function, shifting strands of hair this way and that. "I need to shower and wash my hair."

She laughed at his youthful vanity. "Do you want to do that before or after your pizza and ice cream?"

His eyes lit up, and he grinned widely. "Ice cream too? What flavour?"

"Your favourite, of course. Smithy sent them."

He wrinkled his nose, as he did when deep in thought. "I want to shower first." He got out of bed slowly.

"Are you feeling okay? Not dizzy or faint?" Evie helped him

to his feet.

"I'm fine, Momma. Did you put the pizza in the oven?"

"Yes, and I even put the ice cream in the freezer too."

"Good. I hate melted ice cream."

Evie watched him walk to his en-suite shower room, happy that he looked steady on his feet. "How does your head and face feel?" she asked before he closed the door.

"It hurts."

She nodded. "You can have some pain killers with your food, sweetheart. They should make you feel better."

"Yes, please," he said and closed the door.

His visible pain made her heart ache, and she wanted to draw it from him and take it on herself. It was always the same whenever he was ill, but this time the feeling was stronger still. That made sense, of course, but Evie didn't want to dwell on the seriousness of Izad's experience. She wanted to hold him tight and thank someone or something for making everything all right.

As she wandered back into the lounge, she yawned so hard she thought her jaw might dislocate. She picked up her phone, wanting to check her messages and say thank you o Ash before Izad came down. Evie smiled when she saw there were four from Ash, three received while she'd been napping:

Send me your email address? I'd love to come to your home. Name the day and time, and I'll be there x

Are you guys hungry? I bet you don't fancy cooking x

I ordered pizza and ice cream for you. It'll be there in thirty minutes x

Did I overstep with the pizza? I know it was naughty getting your address from Izad's file at work. Forgive me…again x

She clicked through to respond.

Sorry, I fell asleep. And you are completely forgiven. The pizza and ice cream were a stroke of genius, thank you so much. Izad is showering before he comes down to eat. I'm impressed that you got his favourites. He normally doesn't tell anyone much about himself. He must think you're special too.

She stopped short of sending kisses and hugs, then reconsidered and added both. She hit send and immediately began a second message.

Can I call you tonight after Izad has gone to bed? x

Evie headed back to the kitchen and put her phone on the breakfast bar while she grabbed some plates and poured them both some sparkling peach water. She was getting some kitchen roll when her phone buzzed, and she smiled in anticipation.

Izad is a wonderful kid. Don't tell any of the other parents, but he's my fave. Please call me, no matter how late tonight. Can't wait to talk to you x Enjoy your dinner x

Evie's smile widened. Cracking the door open hadn't been that hard. Now she had to open it completely.

Chapter Thirty-Four

Ash slowed the car as she approached number fifty-nine. The neighbourhood was beautiful; all big houses and groomed gardens, and her car had two decades on the oldest car she'd seen in any of the driveways. She felt out of place, like she should be here as a tradesperson rather than a visitor.

There were no cars on Evie's driveway, and she assumed the Audi would be tucked up in the garage with a duvet over the bonnet to keep it warm. Ash didn't want to assume anything *or* risk doing the wrong thing before she'd even got past Evie's threshold, so she pulled alongside the front of the house. She checked herself one last time in the rear-view mirror, decided she was presentable, and blew out a long breath. This wasn't just progress, it was an "Advance to Go" Monopoly card, and Ash had skipped the dangerous "Go to Jail" obstacle.

When Ash had started her new job, she'd hoped it would be a spring board to a whole new life, but she hadn't expected her world to change this much. In just three months, she'd got a dog she never knew she wanted, a promotion, and now the possibility of a relationship with the perfect woman…and her wonderful son. Java came from the back seat onto the passenger seat and then thudded onto her thighs in a series of seamless leaps. She ruffled the fur on his head and laughed. "Impatient much?"

Ash clipped Java's lead on and let him out of the car. She grabbed her bag, tugged at the front of her shirt to straighten it, and headed up to Evie's front door. Izad opened it before she got there and greeted her with a wide smile.

"Hi, Smithy."

"Hey, buddy." Ash winced at the purple-blue bruising surrounding his eye. "That looks sore."

He nodded. "It's the most pain I've ever been in." He inclined his head and focused on Java. "Your dog is house trained, isn't he?"

Ash laughed and nodded. "I'm working on it." She swung her backpack around to the front and patted it. "I've got special pee pads so he won't do anything on your carpets."

Izad opened the door further. "He is cute for a dog."

Ash remembered showing him photos and videos of Java

and Izad saying he liked cats more than dogs. "That's quite the compliment coming from you." Java made a sound like a buff rather than a bark, something Ash had discovered he did when impatient. "He says thank you."

Izad shook his head. "Dogs can't speak, Smithy. I didn't believe that Doolittle film for a minute."

Ash laughed at Izad's honest dismissal of the recent kids' movie. "So you're okay with magic and princesses who can freeze the world, but you're drawing the line at talking animals?"

"I am."

"Why didn't you park on the driveway?" Evie asked as she came up behind Izad and put her hands on his shoulders.

Ash's breath hitched at the sight of Evie in a loose sweater and lounge pants, her hair free and wild over her shoulders, and her eyes sparkling with happiness. *Izad.* That right there. That could be a problem. Controlling her desire for his mother when Izad was around…but the anticipation would drive her crazy and that was a good thing. She shrugged. "I didn't want to presume." She motioned to Java, who was growing more impatient by the second to be let into the house to discover new and exciting territory. Ash shared the sentiment for different reasons. Seeing Evie for the first time in these circumstances was thrilling and terrifying in equal measure. "Thanks for letting me bring Java."

"It's no problem. He's spent too much time in kennels on his own." Evie knelt down and rubbed his ears. "And it's best that you don't leave him at home alone longer than four hours anyway."

Ash swallowed as Evie's movement gave her an uninterrupted view of the tops of her breasts as the deep V in her sweater billowed forward. "You've already decided I'm staying longer than four hours?"

Evie rose and winked. "If you behave as well as your dog, yes. Come in."

Ash's body flushed with arousal. How was she supposed to keep her hands off Evie around Izad if she was going to tease her that way?

Java didn't need a second invitation and jumped over the front step into the house, tugging Ash behind. "I've got some training pads for him. Do you mind if I put one down here and at the back door?"

"Of course. Is he still chewing anything and everything he can get his paws on?"

Ash shook her head. "He grew out of that bad habit in the kennels, thankfully."

"Then feel free to let him off the lead." Evie motioned towards the stairs. "I've blocked entry up there, but he can have free run of the rest of the house."

Ash opened her backpack and laid a pee pad on the front door mat, before she knelt to draw Java's attention to it. "You need pee pee, you go here, okay?" Java licked her nose.

Evie began to walk down the corridor. "I'll show you to the back door."

Izad tugged on Ash's shirt. "When you've done that, can we finish our game of chess?"

"Absolutely. I brought a portable board with me in case you didn't have one."

Izad wrinkled his nose. "Of course we have one…although Momma doesn't play me much because she hates losing."

"I heard that," Evie called as she continued down the corridor.

Ash followed her while Izad took a left into the lounge. "And is it true?"

Evie turned and placed her hand on Ash's chest. She glanced over Ash's shoulder, probably to see where Izad was.

"I hated losing you." Evie pulled away quickly, turned, and opened the fridge. "Would you like a drink?"

Ash missed the heat and pressure of Evie's hand as fleeting as her presence had been, but the weight and meaning of Evie's words left an even deeper impression.

"We have Coke Zero, flavoured water, tea, coffee…"

Ash recovered herself enough to ask for a Coke Zero, then pulled another pad from her bag and placed it at the back door. She stood, and Evie pressed an ice-cold glass into her hand.

"You better go through to Izad before he explodes. Patience isn't a virtue he's particularly familiar with."

Ash bit her lip and shook her head. "It's not my friend either…" She stared into Evie's eyes, wanting to do just that for hours. Ash's soul reflected back in their depths, and she could see, almost feel, everything she'd been searching for since she was conscious of the human need for partnership. The time they'd spent apart had only reinforced the notion that Evie was part of her soul group, and somehow, they had to be together. "But I'll wait for you."

Evie gave her a wicked grin. "Off you go then, handsome. I'll be right behind you."

Ash sighed, smiled, and headed off to find Izad. "Come on, Java." In the bay window of the lounge, Izad sat at a small table with the most exquisite, hard-carved chess board and pieces Ash had ever seen. Theatrically, he swept his hand towards the seat opposite.

She sat and did a double take of the board since it looked to be set up exactly as it had been when he'd left to play in the green room two nights ago. "You remembered where we left the game?" Ash pulled out her phone and brought up the photo she'd taken. The position of every piece was perfect.

"Of course."

Evie was already halfway into the room, and she placed a glass of what Ash assumed to be water on the table beside Izad.

"We're almost certain that he has an eidetic memory." She leaned down and kissed the top of his head. "It's one more thing that makes him unique."

Izad moved his head away and frowned. "Momma, my hair."

"Sorry, sweetheart." Evie moved away, sat on a circular cuddling armchair close by, and Java jumped up on her knee. "He hates anyone touching his hair."

Ash nodded. "He told me."

Evie smiled. "He's told you a lot of things he never tells anyone."

Izad moved his bishop to take Ash's knight then rolled his eyes at Evie. "That's because I love Smithy, and I only share important stuff with the people I love."

Evie had been taking a sip of her glass and lurched forwards as if she was about to spit it back out, and Ash coughed. She'd definitely not expected that, nor the surge of emotion that followed. She looked up at the ceiling and blinked away the resulting swell of tears. Ash looked across at Evie, who looked similarly blown away, while Izad continued to study the chess board as if he'd merely commented on the weather. Ash hesitated. She wanted more than anything to reciprocate. She had a connection with him that she didn't share with the other kids at the club, though she'd done her best to ignore it. But once she'd found out that he was Evie's son, the connection made perfect sense. Izad was part of her soul group too.

But what would Evie make of her declaration? She'd only just allowed Ash back into her life, and she didn't want to blow it before they'd had the chance to talk about a potential future together. As usual, Ash's instincts won out. "I love you too,

buddy."

Izad glanced back up at her and grinned widely. "I know you do."

Ash looked across at Evie in an effort to measure her response and was rewarded with a sparkling smile that lit a fire in her heart. "Okay, buddy. Let's play."

She and Izad played three games before Evie suggested they have something to eat at around five. Ash followed Izad and Evie into the kitchen and took a seat at the breakfast bar to watch them prepare dinner. Seeing Evie in full on Mum mode shifted something in Ash, and if it were possible, her attraction deepened. Mother and son moved around the kitchen with such ease—Izad helping wherever Evie gave him instruction to do so—that Ash was sucked into a fantasy where this domestic dance was her daily routine and commonplace. By the time dinner was served, Ash's jaw ached from smiling so much. They ate at the breakfast bar with Izad between her and Evie, which was definitely a good thing. The urge to draw Evie into her arms and show her how much she'd missed her grew stronger with each passing moment.

"Right, little guy. It's time for bed," Evie said.

Izad looked at the wall clock. "It's not my bedtime for nearly two hours."

"That's your usual bedtime. The doctor said you needed more rest to make sure you recovered fully from your fall. Okay?" Evie raised her eyebrows and inclined her head. "Okay?"

Izad wrinkled his nose and blew out a short breath of resistance. "*Okay.*"

He got down from the bar stool and gave Ash a hug. She responded but squeezed him gently, conscious of his recent ordeal.

"Will you be here in the morning?" he asked, looking from Ash to his mum and then back again.

Ash drew in a deep breath and said nothing. She eased off her own stool and patted her leg. "Come on, Java. Let's take you outside." This wasn't a conversation she should be part of, and she didn't want her presence to be a pressure on Evie in any way. She didn't think for one second that she'd be staying over—though she did always carry an emergency overnight kit in the car—but that didn't mean she didn't desperately want to. Every fibre of her being ached to touch and be touched, but she didn't want to rush this. She didn't want to mess it up. She wanted to be part of Evie's life just as badly. Now they'd got this far and found their way to back to each other, she'd leave it to Evie to decide how that came about.

Java stood at the back door and yipped at her to go back in. When she entered, Izad patted his leg in the same way she'd done.

"Come on, Java. You can come to bed with me for a while."

Ash looked to Evie to confirm that was okay, and she nodded, but Java was already dutifully following behind Izad as he left the kitchen, clearly not waiting for approval from either of them.

Evie shrugged and smiled. "It's a good thing. We've got a lot to talk about, and I'm going to need all of your attention."

Ash rolled her neck and closed the door softly. "You've got me as long as you want me, and you *definitely* have all of my attention."

Chapter Thirty-Five

Evie couldn't believe how the fast the afternoon had disappeared into the evening. Watching Izad play chess and be so natural and open with Ash had been quite the revelation. She'd never seen him so relaxed with anyone other than her and Tal, not even close family. Any fears she'd had about Izad getting close to a new partner or him not liking someone she chose to spend time with, were blown out of the water. All the plans she'd had to vet her potential lover over six months to make sure she was a good fit for their little family may as well have been wishes in a whirlpool. It was clear Ash had already stolen Izad's heart much as she had her own. She couldn't pinpoint when it had happened exactly, when Ash had slipped under her skin and nestled into her chest, and she could no longer deny it.

Right now though, she needed to understand where Ash was coming from and if she'd had a change of heart about being part of a family. Last night's conversation had been brief, cut short by Izad calling out for Evie, his sleep interrupted by a nightmare. He'd crawled into bed with her and spent the rest of the night cradled in her arms just as he had when he was much younger. His unplanned cuddle time meant that she and Ash hadn't been able to continue their conversation, and Ash had agreed to come over today to talk.

And now here she was, in the corner of Evie's couch sipping on a bottle of light beer, dressed in Evie's favourite combination of tight T-shirt and faded jeans, looking slightly tired and expectant. She sighed deeply. There was much to discuss before she could even think about unwrapping *that* gift. Evie sat on the opposite corner of the sofa so that she could face Ash and took a long drink of her wine before she set the glass down on the wooden table beside her.

"Izad is quite taken by you," she said, deciding to begin with a soft approach. "I can't impress upon you enough how unusual that is."

Ash smiled, and the genuine care obvious in her expression melted what little ice she had left around Evie's heart. Resisting would be impossible if Ash made any attempt to seduce her before they sorted anything out. *No.* She had to stay strong, for

Izad's sake if not her own.

"I've said it before," Ash said. "He's an amazing kid. He has your eyes. Maybe that's what called to me." Ash lifted her beer and took a sip. She spread her legs open a little further and leaned forward, resting her forearms on her thighs. "You can ask me anything you want to, Evie. I promise to answer honestly, however uncomfortable that might make you…or me."

Evie didn't know quite how to take that. Was Ash about to break her heart and tell her that she wasn't ready to take on a ready-made family? That she thought Evie was a wonderful woman, but she wasn't prepared to risk hurting Izad? Evie simultaneously loved and hated that Ash felt so strongly for her son.

"You should stop overthinking everything, Evie. There's steam coming out of your ears from your brain working so hard. You wanted to talk. I'm here, as desperate to talk to you as I have been since you cut me out of your life."

Evie didn't miss the hurt in Ash's words or the sadness that flickered across her eyes. Both things instilled hope that she wasn't about to make another huge mistake. "I'm sorry about that. You probably disagree, but I didn't feel I had a choice. You said you weren't ready for a family, and there's no getting away from the fact that I have one." Evie shuddered at the memory of the night at the club when she burst in on Ash in the toilet. "And when I saw you with that bartender, I knew that us just being friends couldn't possibly work. I wanted you too much…and it hurt." Evie shrugged. "I couldn't take it, so I asked you to leave me alone."

Ash leaned back on the sofa and ran her hand through her hair. "I don't disagree, and that's why I respected your decision and left you alone. But I couldn't do anything with that bartender because all I could think about was you." She smiled ruefully and shook her head. "You're all I've thought about since. I thought we could do the friends thing too, but I was wrong. And you're absolutely right; it was too painful." Ash fiddled with the label on her bottle. "But it's also painful not being in your life at all." She edged forward on the sofa, looking as if she wanted to cross the carpet between them. "Talk to me, Evie. You said you wanted me…do you still want me?"

Evie resisted the almost overwhelming urge to fall into Ash's arms. She wanted to press her head against Ash's chest, feel her strong arms wrapped around her. She wanted Ash to tell her none of this mattered, and together, they could go through anything. She pushed her bum into the sofa to will herself motionless. "What do *you* want, Ash?" The road was open before them, but Evie wasn't in the driver's seat, Ash was. *She* was holding all the cards. *She* was the one holding back. "My end is non-negotiable. I'm a single mum with a boy about to become a teenager. Whether or not I want you… it's largely irrelevant." Evie paused, recognising that while she'd attempted to start off lightly, their conversation had changed direction pretty quick. But she'd wasted enough time already, and she needed to know one way or the other. "Look, you've been working with Izad for a few months now, and you've become an important part of his life. I can't jeopardise that, regardless of how I feel about you. So I ask again, what do *you* want?"

Ash sighed deeply before she placed her beer on the table beside her, as if she were about to stand and leave. Evie looked down at her lap and closed her eyes. *So much for talking.*

"Evie, I've hated every minute of these past few weeks without you. And the pain isn't just emotional…it's physical. I can't breathe properly. When we were talking that afternoon, I didn't know you had a kid when I blurted out that I wasn't ready for a family. I didn't know what I was or wasn't ready for. I'd never thought about it, and you'd done a damn fine job of not giving any hint of having a son." She wiped the heel of her hand across her forehead and shook her head. "None of this is coming out right…"

Evie didn't fill the silence. Whatever Ash had to say, Evie didn't want to force it or prompt her or put words in her mouth. Whatever was coming had to come from Ash's heart, not be steered by what Evie wanted to hear.

"I've been…I've been *working* on myself. My psychology degree has come in pretty handy recently." She laughed gently. "I realised I was coasting and hadn't thought about my future since I started uni. I landed a job I wanted, and I was living with my best friend. Everything was looking good for me for the first time in my life, and it was all my doing. I suppose I was feeling quite impressed with myself, and I wasn't thinking about what came next." She looked across at Evie and smiled. "And then you came along. And I definitely wasn't ready for you."

Ash retrieved her beer and took a long drink. Evie nibbled at her lower lip. She was desperate to speak *and* desperate to hear what Ash had to say. The competing feelings churned her insides like nothing before. Not knowing where Ash was going with her train of thought was torturous, but still she remained quiet.

"I started to analyse what was going on at work, and what I enjoyed about it. That turned out to be me being part of these kid's lives in a way that made a difference. And that got me thinking about how wonderful it would be to be involved in a young person's life every day, not just for a few hours a week." Ash tugged at her T-shirt and looked across at the chess board she and Izad had been playing on. "And *that* got me thinking about how amazing it would be to be involved with you and your son…though if I'd have known your son was Izad, I would've been knocking on your door weeks ago."

Evie laughed, though the relief and joy that ran through her pushed its way up to her eyes and she had to blink away the tears. Caution hooked around her heart and tugged her back a little. "That's quite the epiphany in a relatively short space of time,' Evie said

Ash shrugged. "It wasn't quick enough for me. I've wasted too much time already."

Evie saw the subtle clenching of Ash's jaw and that her eyes glistened, hinting at her pain. Evie remembered Ash's background. Had she been reluctant to think about family because of her lack of one? "Are you sure?" This wasn't the time to hold anything back.

Ash nodded. "I can't predict the future, Evie. I don't know how any of this might play out. But I know how I feel, and I know that I want a family." She swallowed hard. "I want that to be with you and Izad. And I can only imagine how protective you're feeling about allowing me into both of your lives this way, but I promise I won't let you down."

Evie smiled slowly and shook her head. "You can't make that promise, Ash. No one can."

"But—"

"It's too big a promise." Evie moved closer. She took Ash's hands and squeezed them gently. "You can promise to work hard at being the best parent you can be. You can promise to try to be the best partner I could ever want. You can even promise to make love to me every day." Evie winked and grinned to break the almost unbearable tension. "But there are no guarantees and as you said, none of us can predict the future."

"So where does that leave us? *Is* there an 'us'?"

Evie considered the question. It seemed that from the moment they'd met, there was destined to be the "us" Ash asked of, and after her initial hesitation at Ash's age, the only thing that stood in the way of them had been Evie's reluctance to expose Izad to potential pain and loss. But as she sat here now, beside the woman who'd landed in her life without warning, had she been protecting *herself* just as much? Ash had gotten into Evie's heart so easily that she feared it could break twice as fast.

"If you're worried that this is about my past, you don't need to be," Ash said. "I'll never be able to say that I don't think about why my parents dumped me sometimes, but I won't let it define me. I won't let it dictate who and what I become…and who I can be to others." She pulled Evie's hands to her lips and kissed them. "I won't let it spoil who I can be to you…and Izad. If you'll let me."

The warmth of Ash's lips on her skin flooded heat through Evie's body. She slipped her hands from Ash's grip and put her hand around the back of Ash's neck to draw her closer. "I want there to be an us. I want that more than anything. That hasn't changed from the moment I started to fall for you." She kissed Ash gently, inviting the memory of their one night together back into her consciousness, as explosively as one of the many orgasms Ash had given her that evening. "Are you sure you're ready to take on a single mum and her son?" Evie asked the question she only half wanted the answer to, in case Ash gave her a response she didn't want.

Ash nodded and carefully moved a strand of Evie's hair that had fallen across her eye. "I'm ready."

Evie almost sank to the floor, the weight of Ash's words heavy with emotion and commitment.

"What now? Should I go home?" Ash asked.

Evie flashed her a wicked smile and motioned to the ceiling. "Your dog's staying over. It doesn't look like *you* have a choice."

Chapter Thirty-Six

Ash turned around as Evie closed her bedroom door quietly. As they'd come up the stairs, giggling like two drunk school kids trying not to wake their parents, Ash was relieved to find Evie's room was at the opposite end of the corridor to Izad's. His door, covered with glowing stars and a chalk board declaring that none should enter unless explicitly invited, made her smile, and she could only imagine how flamboyant it was on the other side. What she wouldn't have given to have had a room like that, freedom like Izad had, and a mum who loved her.

But she was here for a different kind of love, and one that she thought she'd lost her chance at having. Standing in Evie's tastefully decorated bedroom felt a little off kilter and strangely self-conscious. Their tryst in the hotel room had been wild and exciting, and Ash hadn't held back. Their sex had been loud and unrestrained, and they'd thought nothing of the noise they'd created. But here, in Evie's family house, Izad was asleep at the end of the corridor and only last night, he'd wandered to Evie's room and stayed with her all night. What if he came in while she was…while they were…the thought dampened the heat Evie had conjured downstairs.

Evie leaned against her bedroom door and smiled. "I'll lock the door if that's what you're worried about."

Ash frowned, simultaneously puzzled and pleased that Evie could see beyond the veil of her eyes. "How did you know that's what I was thinking about?"

Evie laughed. "How could you not be thinking about it?" She slid a bolt across the door and slowly walked toward Ash. "Especially after all the commotion we made last time we were together like this." She hooked her fingers over Ash's belt and pulled her closer. "You don't need to worry. He has soft music on all night to help him sleep." She pressed her lips against Ash's neck and nipped her flesh lightly. "I can always gag you if you think you're going to be that loud when you come for me."

Ash's body thrummed in response to Evie's touch, her proximity, her words.

"Speaking of that night, where did all that come from?" Evie asked.

Ash ran her hand through Evie's hair and came to rest on the back of her neck. "I could ask you the same question." She pulled her into a kiss and sighed against the softness of Evie's lips against her own. God, she'd missed that. It was as if Evie's kiss that night had ruined her for anyone else. Evie's tongue probed between Ash's lips, and Ash licked at it with her own. She broke off. "You were the one giving the orders."

"Mm," Evie sighed and captured Ash's mouth again. "And you were the one letting me lead." She pushed against Ash's chest, and they tumbled onto her bed.

Ash cushioned Evie's landing and let herself enjoy the weight of Evie's breasts against her chest. "You'll laugh."

"What's wrong with laughing?" Evie pushed up and manoeuvred herself to sit on Ash. "Laughter's supposed to be the best medicine."

"You're the doc, Doc." Ash trailed her hand along Evie's arms until she reached her hands. She took Evie's hands in her own, entwining their fingers slowly, almost to convince herself this was happening and Evie *was* straddling her.

"I'd never done anything like that before…" Evie glanced away and nibbled her bottom lip. "But it was the hottest sex I've ever had."

Ash grinned. She assumed Evie would have had plenty of sex—how could a woman as hot as she was *not* have had—and topping that list would always have been her goal. To know she'd already achieved it relieved the pressure she hadn't been aware she was carrying. "You really want to know?"

Evie nodded. "Of course." She brought Ash's hands to her lips, drew one of her fingers into her mouth and sucked on it, her eyes never leaving Ash's.

Ash pushed her hips upward against Evie, and she responded by pushing down. Evie was making her crazy in the best way. "I'd just read an erotica anthology that was full of stories on the edge. It gave me some ideas and I wanted to experiment." Ash struggled to concentrate on her words as Evie gave each of her fingers the same delectable treatment with her lips and teeth. "I want to experience everything and anything I can. If I'm reading anything other than memoir, it'll be a sex book." She tried to pull Evie toward her, but Evie resisted and continued her tongue teasing. "I want to be the best lover I can be." Ash thought about how sexy and powerful Evie had been that night, a woman who knew exactly what she wanted and liked. It was surprising to find she wasn't a pro at playing those kinds of games.

Evie released Ash's fingers from her mouth, pressed her arms above her head, and let go of her hands. "*I* want you to be the best lover you can be. How about we work on that now?"

She unbuttoned her blouse, shrugged it from her shoulders, and tossed it onto the floor. Ash licked her lips and swallowed at the sight of Evie's breasts encased in a white lace bra. Evie wasted no time in stripping that away too, and Ash palmed them gently, almost reverently, loving the way Evie's nipples tickled her hand. "Thank you for not laughing," Ash murmured, her breath ragged from arousal. The total truth was that Ash didn't want to let Evie down, though she'd never believed that they would've ended up in bed that night…*and* she'd been reading while getting herself off so she could handle being close to Evie. But it was a little too early to be *that* kind of honest.

Evie placed her hands on Ash's chest and squeezed hard. "I'm all for self-improvement, especially when it has such beneficial effects for me."

Evie leaned closer and kissed her, flicking her tongue playfully at Ash's. Ash softened beneath Evie's touch, her whole body light and alive to every part of her that connected with Evie. She explored Evie slowly, stroking her back gently and pulling her closer, deeper, further into her arms. Evie moved her hips against Ash's crotch, and the pressure of her jeans against her swelling sex made her gasp into Evie's mouth. She wrapped her hands around Evie's wrists and flipped her onto her back in one fluid move. She crawled onto her, not wanting to lose their physical connection, needing to be as close as possible. Evie's eyes flashed, her desire evident, and she moaned when Ash pressed her weight over her.

"I need your skin on mine," Evie whispered.

Ash pushed up and straddled Evie as she pulled her T-shirt off. Evie jutted her chin. "And the jeans. I want you naked."

Ash raised her eyebrow and climbed off the bed. She unbuckled her belt and drew it from the loops slowly, milking it as she enjoyed Evie watching her. She had a knack of making Ash feel like she wanted to devour her, as if she was the only woman she'd ever craved. She opened her jeans, pushed them to her ankles, and stepped out of them. Ash put her thumbs in the waistband of her briefs and tugged them. "*Naked*-naked?"

Evie ran her tongue over her top lip and sighed. "Naked-naked. Yes, please."

Ash discarded her underwear and socks in short order and stood before Evie. Her bravado drained away, and she became self-conscious of all her physical flaws; her chunky thighs, the scars on her shins from numerous bad tackles over the years, her rounded stomach that, for the love of God, never flattened out regardless of how many crunches she did. Ash wanted to dive under the covers and turn off the lights.

"You're so beautiful," Evie said, shaking her head as if she couldn't believe it.

Ash shook her head for a different reason. "No, I'm not."

"You are to me." Evie got up from the bed and joined Ash.

She pressed her body against Ash's, and her warmth eased the chill that had descended over Ash's ardour. But her fears rooted her to the spot. Nothing like this had ever happened to her before, and she struggled to make sense of it, to move past it.

Evie cupped Ash's chin and looked at her searchingly. "Are you okay?"

Ash swallowed and scrunched her nose, casting around in her head for the words. She'd spent the last few weeks not able to speak to Evie, but she was here now and she didn't want to be struck dumb by her insecurities. "I'm scared." She looked down after the admission and tried to find the carpet weave interesting.

Evie gently brought Ash's face up so they were eye to eye. "What's scaring you, sweet baby?"

Ash sighed and nibbled at the inside of her cheek. *Sweet baby.* She'd been called a few pet names in the past but none resonated like that one did coming from Evie. She glanced across at Evie's bed. "Can we get into bed to talk?" As well as her ebbing self-esteem, the bedroom wasn't exactly summer hot.

"Of course."

Evie stepped aside and Ash climbed under the covers. Ash watched as Evie shed the rest of her clothes, stirring her arousal, but Evie's expression was of clear concern as she joined Ash.

Evie puffed up her pillow and leaned against it to face Ash. "Talk to me. What's bothering you?"

Ash pointed her finger between them. "This. Us. It's what I've been hoping for, what I've been waiting for, but now I'm here…" She squeezed her eyes shut, concentrating, trying to find the words. "I've got stage fright. Our first night together was amazing, something straight out of a romance novel. It's a lot to live up to…but it's not just that. It's everything. What if I can't be what you need me to be?" Ash paused as she processed what was happening. Just saying the words out loud, just sharing them with Evie seemed to remove their power over her. And the soft acceptance and complete lack of judgment in Evie's eyes dissipated her apprehension. The realisation hit her with the force of a knockout punch. She was safe here. Wanted. Needed. Loved? Evie's heart was the home she'd been blindly searching for her whole life. "I want to be everything you need and everything you've ever wanted. I love you, Evie." The three little words she'd never said to another soul before tonight tumbled from her mouth. They hung in the air as if in a comic bubble, and Evie pressed her lips to Ash's, her kiss deep and hungry yet soft and careful.

"I love you too, sweet baby."

Ash's heart raced, pounded against her chest, fuelled by Evie's reciprocation of her declaration. The words had been said to her twice before, but she'd known even then that they held no meaning, so significance, no longevity. They'd just been words, said to prolong a mere moment of connection. But hearing Evie say them, Ash shook her head. It was all she'd wanted to hear from Evie's lips for weeks. Her call to her, their connection, was beyond explanation. Evie was part of her soul group, and now that she had her, Ash was never letting go.

"Let me show you how much I love you, Ash."

Evie moved closer, placed her hand on Ash's shoulder and slowly traced it along the length of her arm. She pushed beneath the covers until she came to Ash's hip. Ash jumped slightly when Evie moved down the sensitive curve of her hip to between her legs. She opened her legs and gasped as Evie slid her fingers over her clit and between her lips, still slick from earlier.

"You're wet for me," Evie whispered, closing her mouth over Ash's, searching for her tongue.

Ash murmured an affirmative, falling into Evie's kiss, every part of her coming alive to Evie's touch. "You make me so hot for you, I can't control it," she said between the deepening kisses.

"Don't try to control it." Evie slipped her fingers inside Ash and pressed her palm over her pussy. "Let it be." Another kiss. "Let yourself go."

Ash pushed her face against Evie's shoulder to muffle her cry as Evie began a steady rhythm inside her, her fingers filling Ash and igniting her fire beyond lust and sending her toward an inevitable headlong crash into all that lay beyond it, the power and prize of an unfathomable love. Evie's kisses edged

Ash to an almost senseless state where she couldn't quite grasp where she ended and Evie began. It was as if her body became insubstantial, almost intangible to everything other than Evie's caress. Arousal, love, lust, and connection all rose and meshed together in a flaming mass of sensation within her core. The heat of the sun blazed within every cell in her body and set them on fire. Ash lost all perception of herself and her body. She let herself go as Evie had demanded and gave into the perfection of Evie's pacing, released herself to Evie's will.

Awareness of the rest of her body disappeared as Ash crested the peak of her pleasure, and her tears fell along with her walls as her orgasm crashed over her, leaving her breathless but full of life, full of love. Evie held her tight as Ash shook in her arms, her cries becoming soft sobs. Evie kissed the top of her head and murmured sweet, soothing words. Ash looked up to see Evie's eyes, her tears welling in their corners, barely held back. "Love me forever?"

"Forever's a long time." Evie smiled and ran her hand along Ash's cheek and over her lips. "You'd better be sure that's what you want before you ask for it."

"I'm sure. I'm sure I want my forever with you." Saying the words out loud solidified their sentiment in steel, encasing them for eternity with the strength and potency of Ash's overwhelming emotion. They held a fervour so passionate and forceful, it was as if they might literally explode within, her body incapable of withstanding their intensity.

Peace settled deep within her soul, a peace she'd never had before. Every dancing nerve, every unstable emotion, every negative thought pushed back by a force so exceptional that the darkness of solitude was powerless against it. Evie's love called to the deepest places within Ash's heart and promised her everything she'd ever dreamed of.

Ash snuggled into Evie's warm embrace and vowed to answer that call for the rest of her life.

What's Your Story?

Global Wordsmiths, CIC, provides an all-encompassing service for all writers, ranging from basic proofreading and cover design to development editing, typesetting, and eBook services. A major part of our work is charity and community focused, delivering writing projects to under-served and under-represented groups across Nottinghamshire, giving voice to the voiceless and visibility to the unseen.

To learn more about what we offer, visit: www.globalwords.co.uk

A selection of books by Global Words Press:
Desire, Love, Identity: with the National Justice Museum
Aventuras en México: Farmilo Primary School
Life's Whispers: Journeys to the Hospice
Times Past: with The Workhouse, National Trust
World At War: Farmilo Primary School
Times Past: Young at Heart with AGE UK
In Different Shoes: Stories of Trans Lives
Patriotic Voices: Stories of Service
From Surviving to Thriving: Reclaiming Our Voices
Don't Look Back, You're Not Going That Way

Self-published authors working with Global Wordsmiths:
John Parsons
Emma Nichols
Dee Griffiths and Ali Holah
Helena Harte
Karen Klyne
Ray Martin
Valden Bush
Simon Smalley

Other Great Books
by Independent Authors

Addie Mae by Addison M. Conley
At the beginning of a bitter divorce, Maddy meets mysterious Jessie Stevens. They bond over scuba diving, and as their friendship grows, so does the attraction.
Release scheduled for October 2020 (ISBN 9780998029641)

Sliding Doors by Karen Klyne
Sometimes your best life is someone else's.
Available from Amazon (ISBN 9781916444386)

Cosa Nostra by Emma Nichols
Will Maria choose loyalty to the Cosa Nostra or will she risk it all for love?
Available from Amazon (ISBN 9788636877899)

Nights of Lily Ann: Redemption of Carly by L L Shelton
Lily Ann makes women's desires come true as a lesbian escort, but can she help Carly, who is in search of a normal life after becoming blind.
Available from Amazon (ISBN 9798652694906)

The Women and The Storm by Kitty McIntosh
Being the only witch in a small Scottish town is not easy.
Available from Amazon (ISBN 9798654945983)

Isabel's Healing by Maggie McIntyre
A devastating car accident leaves Bel broken, but when a young assistant steps into her life, could Bel learn to live again?
Available from Amazon KDP & Smashwords (ISBN 9798650898733)

Stealing a Thief's Heart by C L Cattano
Two women, a great escape, and a quest for a soulmate.
Available from Amazon (ASIN B085DW2MZ7)

Maddie Meets Kara: Remember Me by D R Coghlan
Who is her enemy? Who is her friend? And what really happened that night?
Available from Amazon (ASIN B085WP5CDF)

Printed in Great Britain
by Amazon

42363396R00138